喚醒你的英文語感 ！

Get a Feel for English !

喚醒你的英文語感！

Get a Feel for English !

New TOEIC 新制多益
奇蹟筆記書

急速征服多益
第一眼就與眾不同

立基於全方位的分析與研究

以考古題資料分析為依據，完全聚焦於真正會考的黃金內容。

針對多益實際試題之詳細題型分類、可視為線索的語句，以及出題頻率高的詞彙等進行深度分析，
並充分展現於本文當中，本書以幫助各位應試者掌握並學習多益最新出題趨勢為己任，依此進行編纂。

多益試題分析
17,600
題

最近一年的多益考古題概念分析
↓
題型：40 種
↓

詞彙分析：11,000 個　　出現次數：210,245 次

*以過去一年內的多益考古題分析為基準

謹慎作答與專注力是在極短期間內提升分數之鑰

採用考古題高出題率地圖排出出題頻率的高低順序，
並整理出須小心慎選及集中注意力的部分。

本書果斷放棄出題頻率低的高難度領域及題型，
內容以出題頻率最高的題型和詞彙為主，以期讓應試者在短期間內獲得最大的成效。

濃縮文法概念
及命題共費時
148,926
小時

出題頻率

以出題頻率
高低
縮小題目範圍

出題最頻繁的詞彙及次數

company	631
work	610
meeting	566
business	536

概念

*以過去年度多益考古題為基準

無論是哪一種測驗，想要拿高分都必須投注許多時間和心力。

不過，即便是同樣的測驗，每個不同應試者的「必備等級」都不同，依據每個人讀書方式的不同，要達到「必備等級」所須花費的時間也大不相同。

不求拿下機率渺茫的高分，完全只把焦點放在讓讀者考取自己的必備等級上，以長時間的研究結果與考古題資料科學分析為基礎，再加上一線明星講師的洞察力，僅收錄最核心的祕技，才使這本能夠讓讀者急速征服多益的《奇蹟筆記書》得以呈現在各位的眼前。

考場上立即應用的大師級實戰技巧全收錄！

有許多試題只要聽到疑問詞，或只要看到空格前後的單字，就能馬上選出正確答案。為了確保讀者絕對能夠答對這些可以用技巧破解的試題，本書集結了有助於在短期間提升英語能力的多益 A 咖代表講師群所驗證過的關鍵祕技。

奇蹟
筆記書

由人氣名師精選的 163 個多益祕技

一本濃縮，精準掌握，囊括**短期提升英語力的多益祕技。**

儘管過去只有厚重的
多益基本參考書籍……

LC	1,890 PAGE
RC	8.2cm
VOCA	

*以커넥츠영단기出版品為基準

90% DOWN ↓
199 PAGE
1.0cm

VS

如今，已截然不同！

1 高出題率地圖

完美分析多益考古題，註明各類型試題在過去一年間出現過幾次。透過這樣的註記讓該試題的重要度及出題頻率一目瞭然，使讀者能夠充分掌握。出題次數較多的試題，請集中火力攻讀！

2 文法用語解說

用淺顯易懂的方式來說明對應試者而言可能難度較高或較為生疏的文法用語。

3 大師級名師的多益祕技

本書大量收錄了經一線明星講師驗證的多益祕技。為了讓應試者習得技巧，此處標註的是必備的詳解筆記、依各種不同類型區分的出題次數，以及務必要背起來的記憶重點。補充說明以套色為標記，該詞彙在一年間的多益測驗出題次數則以灰色顯示，方便讀者區分。

Unit **10** **動名詞**
相關考題在 Part 5 出現了 7 次，在 Part 6 出現了 5 次。 溫習紀錄

高出題率地圖
技巧 46. 動名詞若放在主詞的位置，其後應接單數動詞。1次
技巧 47. suggest 後方不能接 to 不定詞，動名詞才是正解。1次
技巧 48. 空格後方如果有補語或受詞，就選動名詞！8次
技巧 49.「be busy」的後面要接動名詞。1次
技巧 50.「look forward to」的後面不能接原形動詞，而必須接動名詞。

動名詞：
兼具動詞與名詞的功能，在動詞字尾加 -ing，使其名詞化。

技46 動名詞若放在主詞的位置，其後應接單數動詞。

Inspecting assembly machines takes about two hours.
　主詞（動名詞）　　　　　單數動詞
檢查組裝機械約莫需要兩個小時。

require 需要；要求
a lot of 許多
responsibility 責任；職責

1 動名詞的角色
① 作主詞使用
Training new employees requires a lot of responsibilities.
主詞（動名詞）　　　單數動詞　　題4選1
訓練新進員工必須要很有責任感。

② 作及物動詞的受詞使用
The company considered opening a new branch.
　　　　　及物動詞　　受詞（動名詞）
這家公司曾考慮開新的分店。

join 會合；加入

You can receive a discount by joining our membership.
　　　　　　　　　　　　　介系詞 └→ 受詞　題3
　　　　　　　　　　　　　　　　　（動名詞）
加入我們的會員您就能夠享有折扣。

report 報告
daily 每天；天天
題1答2
duty 責任；義務

應用本技巧的題目
Reporting daily sales to the headquarters _____ one of the manager's main duties.
(A) is　　(B) are　　(C) were　　(D) have been

向總公司回報每日銷售量是經理的主要業務之一。
正解 (A)

PART 1_01.mp3　**聽力測驗例題 MP3**

PART 1–4 音檔，請刮開書內刮刮卡，上網啓用序號後即可下載聆聽使用。

網址：https://bit.ly/3d3P7te

或掃描 QR code

反轉迎戰多益的態度
短期間讓多益成績突破 700 分的奇蹟筆記書

47 suggest 後方不能接 to 不定詞，動名詞才是正解。

The technician suggested replacing the broken oven with a new one.
　　　　　　　　　　suggest　動名詞 ┃ 題1

技師建議用新烤箱替換故障的那一台。

broken 壞掉的

將動名詞作受詞使用的動詞 必背★

recommend + V-ing 推薦～；建議～
　　　　　　　題1
consider + V-ing 考慮～
　　　　　　正1題2
suggest + V-ing 提議～
avoid + V-ing 避免～
finish + V-ing 停止做～
enjoy + V-ing 享受～
　　　　題1

▌tip!
「want、need、expect、plan」這幾個動詞會把 to 不定詞當作受詞使用，請確實區分並加以熟記。

應用本技巧的題目

Most nutritionists recommend ＿＿＿＿ a low calorie diet in addition to fruits and vegetables.
(A) eaten　　(B) to eat　　(C) ate　　(D) eating

除了蔬菜水果外，大多數的營養學家還建議攝取低卡路里飲食。

正解 (D)

nutritionist 營養學家
in addition to 除了～還～
　　　　　　還
vegetable 蔬菜

48 空格後方如果有補語或受詞，就選動名詞！

He is qualified for receiving a bonus.
　　　　　　　　　　動名詞　受詞

他有資格領取獎金。

be qualified for 有資格～

1 空格後若有補語或受詞，就選動名詞。

The manager suggested (inviting / invitation) employee's family members
　　　　　　　　　　　　動名詞　　名詞　　　受詞
to the company picnic.

經理提議邀請員工的眷屬一同參加公司的野餐活動。

invite 邀請；招待
invitation 邀請；招待

2 空格前若有冠詞 (a / an / the)，就選名詞。

Johnson Bakery established an online system for the (delivering / delivery)
　　　　　　　　　　　　　　　　　　　　　冠詞　動名詞　　名詞
of its products.

強森麵包坊為了外送產品建構了線上系統。

establish 設立；建立

PART 5

---

4 **出題次數標記略稱**

正：正解

誤：錯誤選項

題：題目

選：選項

試：試題短文內容

數字代表出現於考題之次數。

5 **tip!**

歸納出與考題直接相關的必殺技，只要知道箇中訣竅，就能多破解一道題目。

6 **應用本技巧的題目**

網羅以考古題為基礎編寫的多益實戰考題，讓讀者試著將先前學習到的技巧投入於多益測驗當中。再厲害的技巧不能只是知道就好，必須實際運用才能有效奪分。

LC

RC

奇蹟筆記書

多益 700+
急速奪分祕技

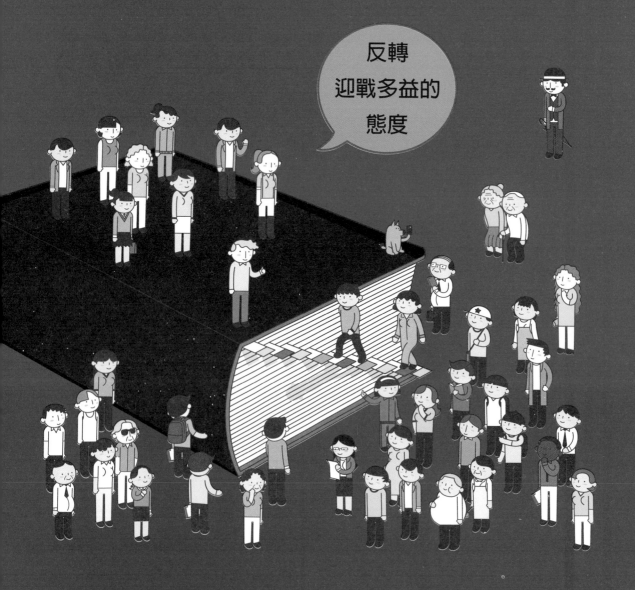

反轉
迎戰多益的
態度

LC
PART 1-4

人物照片

這是出題比重最高的類型。
必須聆聽人物的具體動作和狀態，還有該動作的對象是周遭何許人物，這些是關鍵核心。

高出題率地圖

技巧 **1.** 在以人物為主的照片中，動詞 **(~ing)** 決定答案。
技巧 **2.** 分別確認人物的狀態描述及動作描述。144次
技巧 **3.** 分別確認這些人物的共同動作及個別動作。40次

技巧 **1** 在以人物為主的照片中，動詞 **(~ing)** 決定答案。

▌tip!
請在各選項上標示○
／△／×。選擇的關
鍵不在於找出正解，
而是將錯誤的選項一
個個刪去。

(A) A man is <u>facing</u> the board.
正1
一名男子正面對著白板。

(B) A man is <u>making a presentation</u>.
一名男子正在做簡報。

應用本技巧的題目

 PART 1_01.mp3

▌tip!
單人照片請分別依序
掌握照片中的人物動
作、衣著及背景。

1.

(A)　(B)　(C)　(D)

2.

(A)　(B)　(C)　(D)

錄音內容及解析

1.

(A) The woman is <u>carrying</u> a bag.
誤9
女子正背著包包。

(B) The woman is <u>wearing</u> a hat.
女子正戴著帽子。

shelf 架子
examine 調查；檢查
pave 鋪設（路面等）

(C) The woman is <u>reaching</u> for the shelf.
女子正將手伸向架子。

(D) The woman is <u>examining</u> a product.
誤2
女子正在審視產品。

2.

(A) People are <u>standing</u> in line.
正1誤10
一群人正在排隊。

(B) People are <u>paving</u> the road.
一群人正在鋪路。

(C) People are <u>crossing</u> the street.
誤5
一群人正在過馬路。

(D) People are <u>walking</u> down the steps.
一群人正在下樓梯。

正解 1. (D)　2. (C)

經常被命題的動詞 必背★

看	looking、reviewing、staring、facing、examining、browsing 正5誤5 ／ 誤5
發表	speaking、addressing、making a presentation、giving a speech
工作相關	working on 工作、sweeping 打掃、trimming 修整、wiping 擦拭 正1誤5 ／ 正1誤4
姿勢相關	leaning on/against 倚靠、bending over 俯身於～、kneeling down 跪下 正1誤3 reaching for 伸手 正1誤6

技巧 2 分別確認人物的狀態描述及動作描述。

(A) One of the women is <u>looking</u> at a document.
其中一名女子正看著文件。

document 文件
hold 握；抓；拿

(B) One of the women is <u>holding</u> a cup.
其中一名女子正拿著杯子。

應用本技巧的題目

 PART 1_02.mp3

1.

(A) (B) (C) (D)

2.

(A) (B) (C) (D)

錄音內容及解析

1.
(A) They are putting on hats.
他們正在戴帽子。

(B) They are doing some construction work.
他們正在做建設工程。

(C) They are finishing their work.
他們正準備收工。

(D) They are inspecting the building.
他們正在檢查建築物。

2.
(A) Some people are on the bus.
巴士裡有一些人。

(B) Pedestrians are on the crosswalk.
正1誤4
有一些行人在斑馬線上。

(C) Passengers are waiting for the train.
有幾名乘客正在等火車。

(D) Children are getting on the bus.
有幾名孩童正要搭上巴士。

construction 建設
inspect 檢查；審視
pedestrian 行人
crosswalk 行人穿越道
passenger 乘客

正解 1. (B) 2. (D)

狀態描述 vs 動作描述 必背★

狀態	wearing 穿著（衣服） 正6誤1 holding 拿著（物品） 正4誤8 riding 騎乘著、乘坐著	動作	putting on / taking off 穿 / 脫（衣服）的動作 誤6　　　　　誤5 picking up (lifting) 提起 / 舉起（物品）的動作 誤3 getting on / getting off 上 / 下的動作

技巧 **3** 分別確認這些人物的共同動作及個別動作。

(A) All people are sitting on a bench.
所有人都坐在長凳上。

(B) Two men are looking at each other.
　　　　　　正4誤8
兩名男子正彼此對視。

tip!
如為兩人以上的照片，要留意 "all people"、"both of them" 等字眼。

tip!
如為三人以上的照片，答案有很高的機率會是照片中人物的共同動作。

應用本技巧的題目

 PART 1_03.mp3

1.

(A) (B) (C) (D)

2.

(A) (B) (C) (D)

bookshelf 書架
purchase 購買
performance 表演
hang 懸掛；吊著
microscope 顯微鏡
wipe 擦拭

錄音內容及解析

1.

(A) One of the women is reaching over a bookshelf.
其中一名女子正將手伸向書架。

(B) One of the men is paying for his purchase.　　正1誤7
其中一名男子正在為他所購買的東西付錢。

(C) Some people are waiting in line.
有幾個人正在排隊等候。

(D) Some people are watching a live performance.
有幾個人正在觀賞現場表演。

2.

(A) One woman is removing gloves from a cabinet.　誤4
一名女子正從櫃子裡取出手套。

(B) One man is hanging lab coats in a closet.　正3誤7
一名男子正將實驗袍掛在衣櫥裡。

(C) One woman is looking into a microscope.
一名女子正在使用顯微鏡觀察。

(D) All of the employees are wiping a table.
正1誤3
所有員工都在擦桌子。

正解 1. (C) 2. (C)

Unit 02 物品照片

必須先掌握物品名稱、擺放位置以及排列狀態再聆聽題目內容。

技巧 4. 如果聽到照片中沒有的物品，則該選項即為錯誤選項。
技巧 5. 進行式被動語態 (be being p.p) 是用來描述目前正在發生的動作狀態，故為錯誤選項。22次
技巧 6. 注意 display 這個單字是例外！3次

技巧 4 如果聽到照片中沒有的物品，則該選項即為錯誤選項。

(A) A **bridge** crosses over a **river**.

誤3

有一座橋樑橫跨河流。

(B) A **boat** is **floating** on the **water**.

正1

有一艘船在水上漂著。

經常被命題的物品名詞 必背★

出題頻率高的代表名詞	照片中具體的名詞
vehicle 車輛、**traffic** 交通 正2誤4	**car** 汽車、**taxi** 計程車、**truck** 卡車、**van** 廂型車 誤8　　　　　　　　　　　　正2誤6
heavy machinery 重機械	**forklift** 堆高機、**crane** 起重機
baked goods 烘焙西點類 正1誤4	**bread** 麵包、**rolls** 捲、**pie** 派
beverage 飲料	**coffee** 咖啡、**tea** 茶、**water** 水 　　誤6　　　　　　　正2誤1
musical instrument 樂器 正2誤1	**guitar** 吉他、**piano** 鋼琴
furniture 家具	**chair** 椅子、**sofa** 沙發、**couch** 長沙發 正3誤9
item 物品；商品 正4誤1	**clothing** 衣服、**food** 食物、**fruit** 水果 正6誤5

應用本技巧的題目　　　　　　　　　　🎧 PART 1_04.mp3

1.

(A) (B) (C) (D)

2.

(A) (B) (C) (D)

錄音內容及解析

1.

(A) The table is next to the window.
　　　　　　　正4誤1
　　桌子位於窗邊。

(B) The picture is on the floor.
　　　　　　　誤7
　　畫放在地板上。

(C) The bookshelf is filled with books.
　　　　　　正1誤1
　　書櫃擺滿了書。

(D) The cushions are placed on the sofa.
　　靠墊放在沙發上。

2.

(A) There is a lot of traffic on the road.
　　道路車多壅塞。

(B) People are crossing the street.
　　人們正在穿越街道。

(C) One of the cars is being towed.
　　其中一台車正被拖吊。

(D) The road is empty.
　　道路上完全沒有人車。

正解 1. (D)　2. (A)

floor 地板
fill 裝滿；使充滿
tow 拖拉；牽引
empty 空的

技巧 5 進行式被動語態 (be being p.p) 是用來描述目前正在發生的動作狀態，故為錯誤選項。

動作已經完成的狀態＝ be + p.p / have (has) + been + p.p
動作正在進行的瞬間＝ be + being + p.p

(A) The bicycles have been parked in a row.
　　　　　　　　　　　誤7
　　腳踏車並排停成一列。

(B) The bicycles are being moved.
　　腳踏車正被移動。

📝 tip!
就物品照片類型的考題來說，如果正確答案是進行式被動語態 (be being p.p) 的話，照片當中必定會有正在進行該動作的人物登場。

技巧 **6** 注意 display 這個單字是例外！

如果是有人正在陳列物品，或者是雖然沒有人物出現，但陳列著物品的照片，皆為正解。

(A) Products are on display. (O) → 陳列著＝
正1   陳列展示中

照片中陳列著一些商品。

(B) Products have been displayed. (O)
正1

照片中陳列著一些商品。

(C) Products are being displayed. (O)
正1

照片中有一些商品陳列展示中。

儘管照片中沒有任何動作，也能破例成為正解的一些動詞 必背★

車子被拖吊的照片＝ be being towed
從噴水裝置噴出水來的照片＝ be being watered
覆蓋著陰影的照片＝ be being cast
種植著花木的照片＝ be being grown

應用本技巧的題目

🎧 PART 1_05.mp3

1.

(A)　(B)　(C)　(D)

2.

(A)　(B)　(C)　(D)

3.

(A)　(B)　(C)　(D)

📑 tip!
物品照片的考題只要排除出現人物相關單字的敘述或 "is/are being" 的選項，就能猜出正確答案！

ceiling 天花板
dish 盤子
take away 拿走
install 安裝；設置
sculpture 雕刻品；雕塑品
fountain 噴水池
equipment 裝備；設備
arrange 整理；安排
distance 距離

錄音內容及解析

1.

(A) The flags are hung from the ceiling.
天花板上掛著旗子。

(B) The dishes are being taken away.
正1誤6
盤子正被收走。

(C) Some diners are eating food in the restaurant. 誤3
有幾個客人正在餐廳用餐。

(D) The lamps are being installed. 誤2
照片中正在裝設煤油燈。

2.

(A) There is a sculpture in the lobby.
大廳裡擺放著雕塑品。

(B) There is a fountain near the building.
正1誤2　正2誤2
建築物附近有個噴水池。

(C) The artwork is being carved.
照片中正在雕刻美術作品。

(D) The building is under construction.
建築物正在施工中。

3.

(A) The columns are casting shadows.
柱子上覆蓋著陰影。

(B) The equipment is being arranged.
正2誤7
設備正在整頓中。

(C) The trees are being planted in the 誤10
distance.
遠處正在種植樹木。

(D) A lamp is hanging down from the ceiling.
一盞煤油燈垂掛在天花板上。

正解 1. (A)　2. (B)　3. (A)

人物＋物品照片

儘管照片中有人物登場，但只要是突顯特定事物或背景的照片，各選項就會是人或事物的主詞混合著出題。必須掌握照片裡的場所，並專心聆聽選項的主詞是以什麼開頭。

高出題率地圖

技巧 7. 若正確敘述為現在進行式被動語態 (be being p.p)，則照片中的人物必定正在做該動作。6次
技巧 8. 人物＋物品照片的考題請將注意力集中在各選項開頭的第一個單字。
技巧 9. 就算碰上冗長、難度高的考題，只要將錯誤類型的選項一一排除即可迎刃而解。

技巧 **7** 若正確敘述為現在進行式被動語態 (be being p.p)，則照片中的人物必定正在做該動作。

(A) The shopping basket is being held.
　　　　　　　　　　　　　　正1
有人正提著購物籃。

(B) The man is pushing a shopping cart.
　　　　　　　正2誤3　　　　　　　正4誤3
男子正推著購物車。

應用本技巧的題目

🎧 PART 1_06.mp3

1.

(A)　(B)　(C)　(D)

2.

(A)　(B)　(C)　(D)

> **tip!**
> "is/are being" 之後所接的動詞必須為照片中人物正在進行的動作才行！

録音內容及解析

1.

(A) The man is putting on gloves.
男子正在戴手套。

(B) The lamp is being turned on.
煤油燈正被點亮。

(C) The man is wearing a helmet.
男子正在戴安全帽。

(D) The bread is being sliced.
麵包正被切片。

2.

(A) A woman is trimming a tree.
一名女子正在修剪樹木。

(B) Water is being sprayed from a hose.
水正從水管中噴出。

(C) A woman is repairing a fence.
一名女子正在修理圍籬。

(D) A gardening tool is placed against a wall.
園藝工具正被放置在牆邊。

正解 1. (D)　2. (B)

glove 手套
turn on 開（燈）
slice 切片
trim 修整；修剪
spray 噴；灑
fence 籬笆；圍籬
gardening 園藝

技巧 **8** 人物＋物品照片的考題請將注意力集中在各選項開頭的第一個單字。

(A) Some books are placed on a cart.
正5誤1
有一些書被放在手推車上。

(B) A man is borrowing a book at the library.
一名男子正在圖書館借閱一本書。

應用本技巧的題目　　　　　　　　　　🎧 PART 1_07.mp3

1.
(A) (B) (C) (D)

2.
(A) (B) (C) (D)

錄音內容及解析

1.
(A) The luggage is being removed from
正2誤2
the counter.
正5誤6
行李正被從櫃檯挪開。

(B) Some people are gathered at the carousel.
正1
有一些人聚集在行李輸送帶旁邊。

(C) A suitcase is being picked up.
有一個行李箱正被人取走。

(D) The flight attendants are waiting in line.
誤4
幾名空服員正在排隊等候。

2.
(A) The light is hanging above the people.
正2誤5
燈具吊掛在這群人的頭頂上方。

(B) The picture is being removed from the wall.
畫正被從牆上撤下來。

(C) The door is wide open.
門完全敞開著。

(D) The wall is being repainted.
牆面正被人重新粉刷。

正解 1. (B) 2. (A)

luggage 行李
gather 收集；聚集
carousel 行李輸送帶
suitcase 手提行李箱
pick up 拾起；撿起
remove 移開；去除
repaint 重新粉刷

技巧 **9** 就算碰上冗長、難度高的考題，只要將錯誤類型的選項一一排除即可迎刃而解。

(A) A cash register has been mounted on the counter.　正1誤1
一台收銀機被安裝在櫃檯上。

(B) Boxes are stacked on top of each other.　正4誤9　誤2
幾個箱子被層層堆疊在一起。

▌tip!
只要選項中提及照片上沒有的單字，就請馬上排除該選項！要是打算聽取完整句子再加以分析的話，反倒會讓自己混淆。

應用本技巧的題目　　　🎧💡 PART 1_08.mp3

1.

(A)　(B)　(C)　(D)

2.

(A)　(B)　(C)　(D)

錄音內容及解析

1.

(A) A man is taking boxes out of a car.　誤4
一名男子正從車裡搬出一些箱子。

(B) A wheelbarrow is being pushed to a site.
單輪手推車正被推向工地。

(C) A truck is stopped at an intersection.
卡車停在交叉路口。

(D) Some workers are loading a truck　正1誤2　誤3
with bricks.
幾名工人正將磚塊裝載到卡車上。

2.

(A) Some people are getting off the bus.
有幾個人正在下公車。

(B) Some cars are driving on a bridge.　誤2
有幾台車正行駛在橋上。

(C) Some people are stopped at a traffic light.
有些人在紅綠燈號誌處停下了腳步。

(D) Some trolley tracks run alongside the street.　正1
街道上沿街鋪設有幾條電車軌道。

正解 1. (B) 2. (D)

wheelbarrow 單輪手推車
intersection 十字路口
load 裝載
get off 下（交通工具）
trolley 電車；手推車

PART 2 解題攻略

PART 2 的重點並不是選出一個正確解答,而是要將錯誤的選項一個個刪去。

高出題率地圖

技巧 **10.** 題目的前三到四個單字就能決定答案為何。
技巧 **11.** 如果是疑問詞疑問句的題型,**Yes** 或 **No** 的選項 **100%** 是錯的。67次
技巧 **12.** 相似發音及重複的單字為錯誤選項。217次
技巧 **13.** 若在回覆的選項中出現迴避性質的「萬用正解」,則該選項即為答案。21次

技巧 **10** 題目的前三到四個單字就能決定答案為何。

Q1. <u>When can I come in</u> for my regular check-up?
我什麼時候可以進來? / 做我的定期健康檢查

Q2. <u>Did you decide</u> on the dates for the workshop?
正3題3　　　　　　　　　題8選1
你決定了嗎? / 工作坊的日期

tip!
出題頻率高的相關句型(句首的四個單字)要注意!

應用本技巧的題目　　　　　　　　　　　🎧 PART 2_01.mp3

請聽寫句子開頭的四個單字並分析其文意。

1. _____ _____ _____ _____ are you working on?

2. _____ _____ _____ _____ to the city hall from here?

錄音內容及解析

1. What kind of research are you working on?
題3
你正在做 / 哪一種研究?

2. Is there a bus to the city hall from here?
有沒有公車 / 可以從這裡搭到市政府?

正解 1. What kind of research　2. Is there a bus

技巧**11** 如果是疑問詞疑問句的題型，**Yes** 或 **No** 的選項 **100**% 是錯的。

Q. Who should I talk to about returning this defective item?
我應該找誰反應這個瑕疵商品的退貨事宜？

(A) No, I want a full refund.
不，我想要全額退款。

(B) Someone will be with you soon.
正2
馬上就會有人過來處理。

(C) Be my guest.
請便。

除了 **Yes**、**No** 外，用來表達肯定及否定的用法 必背★

Yes 肯定回覆	No 否定回覆
當然好：Okay、Certainly、Sure 正1選3　　　正18題1選26 　　Absolutely、Definitely、Why not?、No problem. 　　正1　　　　正1 同意：I think (hope) so.、That's right.、That'd be great. 　　正2　　　　　　　　正2選2 　　Not bad.、That's OK. 允許：Go ahead.、Be my guest. 　　選3	I'm afraid not. I don't think so. That's not right. Not really. 選2

應用本技巧的題目　　　　　　　🎧 PART 2_02.mp3

1. Mark your answer.　(A)　(B)　(C)

2. Mark your answer.　(A)　(B)　(C)

錄音內容及解析

1. Why is the road closed to traffic?
正2題1選3

(A) For repair work.
(B) Sure, why not?
(C) Yes, that'd be the best.

1. 為什麼這條路禁止通行？
(A) 為了進行維修工程。
(B) 當然，為什麼不？
(C) 對，這個方法應該是最恰當的。

repair 修理；修補

2. How often do you visit your family?
題1選2

(A) I visit my cousin.
(B) Yes, open it.
(C) Every week.

2. 你多常探望你的家人？
(A) 我去探望我的堂妹。
(B) 是的，請打開。
(C) 每週都會去。

visit 拜訪；訪問

正解 1. (A)　2. (C)

技巧**12** 相似發音及重複的單字為錯誤選項。

Q. The machine isn't working now.
目前機器無法運轉。
(A) Sure, it works. 當然，這很有效。
(B) I'll call the repairman. 我會找維修人員過來。
(C) He's working hard. 他工作很認真。
正1選1

應用本技巧的題目 　　　　　　　　　　　　PART 2_03.mp3

1. Mark your answer. (A) (B) (C)

2. Mark your answer. (A) (B) (C)

錄音內容及解析

1. It looks like it's going to rain tomorrow.
(A) It looks good on you.
(B) The initial training was useful.
正1
(C) Then I should take an umbrella.

1. 看樣子明天應該會下雨。
(A) 這很適合你。
(B) 最初的訓練很有用。
(C) 那我得帶把傘才行。

initial 最初的；開始的
training 訓練；培訓
umbrella 雨傘

2. Could you send me a copy of the contract? 正5題6選3
(A) At the copy machine.
(B) Sure, I'll do it right away.
題1
(C) I'll bring some coffee.

2. 你可以寄合約書的影本給我嗎？
(A) 在影印機那邊。
(B) 當然可以，我現在馬上寄。
(C) 我去拿一些咖啡過來。

copy 影印；影本
contract 合約

正解 1. (C) 2. (B)

技巧**13** 若在回覆的選項中出現迴避性質的「萬用正解」，則該選項即為答案。

Q. Which department does Jade work for?
婕德在哪個部門工作？
(A) She's beautiful. 她很美。
(B) Sorry, I can't remember. 抱歉，我不記得了。
正4題1選7
(C) Five days a week. 一週五天。

department 部門
remember 記得

「我不清楚」、「我不記得了」等萬用正解 必背★

我不清楚 正5	I have no idea. I forgot.	I'm not sure. I wish I knew.
沒聽說過	I haven't heard. I haven't been informed.	
請向～詢問 正3	Ask the manager. Try the receptionist.	
尚未定案 正8	It hasn't been decided. I haven't decided yet. 正12題13選2	
我晚點再回覆您 我確認一下 正5	I'll let you know later. 正1題3選5 Let me check. I'll find out.	
視情況而定	It depends.	

應用本技巧的題目 PART 2_04.mp3

1. Mark your answer. (A) (B) (C)

2. Mark your answer. (A) (B) (C)

錄音內容及解析

1. A lot of customers are responding to
   正2選3
   the surveys, right?
   正1題1選1
   (A) I'll prepare a questionnaire.
   (B) You should ask Bill.
   (C) On the bottom of the receipt.
   正1選2

1. 有許多顧客正在回答問卷調查，對吧？
   (A) 我會準備問卷。
   (B) 你應該去問比爾。
   (C) 在收據的最下面。

respond 作答；回應
prepare 準備
questionnaire 問卷；調查表
bottom 底部；最下面
receipt 收據

2. How many people do you think will attend the seminar?
   (A) I'm not sure yet.
   (B) That'd be great.
   (C) Yes, it'll be informative.

2. 你認為會有多少人來參加研討會？
   (A) 我還不確定。
   (B) 那應該會很棒。
   (C) 是的，這將會很受用。

attend 出席；參加
seminar 研討會
informative 有益的；增廣見聞的

正解 1. (B) 2. (A)

疑問詞疑問句 [Who / When / Where]

若是包含疑問詞的疑問句型，最重要的是要能準確聽出是何種疑問詞。
將各個疑問詞分門別類，來學習與它們相對應的正確解答吧！

技巧 14. 與 Who 疑問詞相對應的正解為人名、職稱或部門名稱。27次
技巧 15. 與 When 疑問詞相對應的正解為時間或時間點的相關描述。32次
技巧 16. 與 Where 疑問詞相對應的正解為場所的相關描述。

技巧14 與 Who 疑問詞相對應的正解為人名、職稱或部門名稱。

Q. Who is responsible for new employees?
新進員工由誰負責？

A. I think the department manager is.
題1選1
我想是由部門經理負責。

tip!
仔細查看在 Who 疑問詞的題型中常見的職稱及部門名稱，掌握 Who 題型的急速得分作答法。

Who 疑問句的題型中經常出現的職稱及部門名稱　必背★

職稱	部門
(vice) president（副）董事長	Human Resources, Personnel 人力資源部
supervisor 主管；監事	Accounting department 會計部 正1題1選2
director 協理 正1題1選2	Maintenance Office 維修部 正3題3選1
manager 經理 department head 部長	Sales division 業務部 正1題1選2
secretary 秘書	Marketing team 行銷部 題2選2
assistant 助理 正1選1	Shipping department 出貨部；物流部

tip!
第三人稱代名詞 "he、she、they" 有很高的機率是錯誤選項！

assign 分配；指派
reject 拒絕

應用本技巧的題目　　　　　　　　　PART 2_05.mp3

1. Mark your answer.　(A)　(B)　(C)

2. Mark your answer.　(A)　(B)　(C)

錄音內容及解析

1. Who's been assigned to the project?
　(A) The sign was broken.
　(B) Someone from Marketing.
　　　正2
　(C) She rejected it.

1. 誰分配到這個專案？
　(A) 號誌燈故障了。
　(B) 某位行銷部的人員。
　(C) 她回絕了。

2. Who will make our flight reservation?

   (A) An early departure.

   (B) No, I don't have my boarding pass.

   (C) Mark from personnel will handle that.
               正1

2. 誰會替我們預定航班？

   (A) 是早航班。

   (B) 不，我的登機證不在手邊。

   (C) 人事部的馬克會處理。

正解 1. (B) 2. (C)

reservation 預約；預訂
departure 出發
boarding pass 登機證
handle 操作；處理

PART 2

技巧**15** 與 **When** 疑問詞相對應的正解為時間或時間點的相關描述。

Q. **When will the new director arrive?**

   新任協理什麼時候會到任？

   (A) Sometime next week. (O)

     下星期之內。

   (B) For two days. (X)

     在兩天期間。

▌tip!
詢問「時間點」的 When 疑問句無法用表達「一段期間」的描述來回應！

When 疑問句的題型中經常出現的時間描述　必背★

介系詞	**at**＋時間：在某個時間點 **in**＋時間：在某個時間點之後 **by**＋時間：截至某個時間點 **within**＋時間：在某段時間範圍內 **on**＋星期幾／日期：在星期幾／在某天
時間名詞 時間副詞	**quarter** 一季 **a month ago** 一個月前 正4題1選5 **last month / next month** 上個月／下個月 **right now** 現在立刻

時間副詞子句連接詞	**not until** 直到～才～
	   正1選2
	as soon as 一～就～
	   正1選1
	(right) after（就）在～之後
	   正1選1
	(right) before（就）在～之前

應用本技巧的題目

🎧 PART 2_06.mp3

1. Mark your answer. (A) (B) (C)

2. Mark your answer. (A) (B) (C)

expect 預期；期待
receive 收到
evaluate 評估；鑑定
region 地區

錄音內容及解析

1. When do you expect to receive the sales report?

(A) By the end of this week.
　　正1選3

(B) I'm evaluating the section.

(C) Yes, just a few more regions.

1. 您希望什麼時候收到銷售報告？

(A) 這個週末之前。

(B) 我正在幫這個部門打考績。

(C) 對，只多了幾個地區。

merchandise 商品
entrance 入口
attach 貼上；附上
price tag 價格標籤

2. When should we put out the new merchandise?

(A) Because the sale hasn't started yet.

(B) How about by the mall entrance?
　　正1選2

(C) As soon as we attach the price tags.

2. 我們應該要什麼時候推出這款新商品？

(A) 那是因為還沒有開始打折。

(B) 在大型購物中心的入口旁怎麼樣？

(C) 等我們一貼完標價就會推出。

正解 1. (A) 2. (C)

技巧 **16** 與 Where 疑問詞相對應的正解為場所的相關描述。

Q. Where can I purchase a train ticket?
我可以在哪裡購買火車票？
(A) From the website. (O) 在網路上。
(B) In 30 minutes. (X) 三十分鐘後。

tip!
務必將注意力集中在疑問詞！
聽錯疑問詞時可能會做的回應，經常會在選項中以陷阱的姿態登場！

Where 疑問句的題型中經常出現的場所與方向描述 必背★

各種介系詞（at / on / in / by / around / across / in front of / next to / to ＋名詞）

at the store 在店裡	by the door 在門旁邊	in front of the lobby 在大廳前面 選2
on the website 在網路上	around the corner 選2 在轉角處	next to the copy machine 正2選8 在影印機旁邊
in the file cabinet 在文件櫃裡	across the street 正1選4 在街道對面	to my office 到我的辦公室

應用本技巧的題目　　🎧 PART 2_07.mp3

1. Mark your answer.　(A)　(B)　(C)

2. Mark your answer.　(A)　(B)　(C)

錄音內容及解析

1. Where is Professor Newton's lecture being held?

　(A) Introduction to marketing.

　(B) The lecture was long.

　(C) In the auditorium.

2. Where are the storage lockers?

　(A) Mr. Klauss will show you around.

　(B) No, by the entrance.
　　　　正2選4

　(C) Until next Friday.

正解 1. (C)　2. (A)

1. 牛頓教授的講座在哪裡舉辦？

　(A) 是行銷入門。

　(B) 這場講座的時間很長。

　(C) 在禮堂舉行。

2. 可上鎖的置物櫃在哪裡？

　(A) 克勞斯先生會帶你四處看看認識環境。

　(B) 不是，在入口處旁邊。

　(C) 到下星期五為止。

🔖 tip!
在 Where 疑問句的題型中，也有可能出現「對象」或「出處」的答案。

professor 教授
lecture 演講；授課
introduction 介紹；引見
auditorium 禮堂

storage 儲藏；保管
locker 儲物櫃

PART 2

若是包含疑問詞的疑問句型，最重要的是要能準確聽出是何種疑問詞。
將各個疑問詞分門別類，來學習與它們相對應的正確解答吧！

高出題率地圖
技巧 17. 若是「What ＋名詞」或「Which ＋名詞」的疑問句型，疑問詞之後所接的單字決定答案。24次
技巧 18. How 疑問句的題型會依據方法或意見來決定答案。30次
技巧 19. How 疑問句的題型會依據其之後所接的形容詞或副詞來決定答案。17次
技巧 20. 在 Why 疑問句的題型當中不見得都會用 because 來應答。21次

技巧 **17** 若是「**What ＋名詞**」或「**Which ＋名詞**」的疑問句型，疑問詞之後所接的單字決定答案。

tip!
疑問詞 Which 是在詢問數個當中的哪一個，然而不指稱特定對象的 "one" 敘述經常就是正確答案！

Q1. What's wrong with the photocopier? 影印機出了什麼問題？
(A) It's out of order. 它故障了。

Q2. Which desk is yours? 哪一張桌子是你的？
(A) The one by the window. 窗戶旁邊的那一張。
正7選1

tip!
詢問價格的疑問句要留意僅回答數字的錯誤選項！

應用本技巧的題目　　　　　　　　　PART 2_08.mp3

1. Mark your answer.　(A)　(B)　(C)

2. Mark your answer.　(A)　(B)　(C)

field 領域；界

錄音內容及解析

1. What field does Mr. Dalton work in?
(A) That's a good point.
(B) Yes, for five years.
(C) Computer programming.

1. 道爾頓先生從事什麼領域的工作？
(A) 說得好。
(B) 對，做了五年。
(C) 電腦程式設計。

expense 支出；費用
approximately 大概
expensive 昂貴的

2. What is the monthly expense for heating? 題4
(A) Approximately 200 dollars.
(B) It was too expensive.
正1題1選5
(C) I'll finish it this weekend.

2. 每個月的暖氣費是多少？
(A) 大約兩百美元。
(B) 太貴了。
(C) 我會在這個週末完成。

正解 1. (C)　2. (A)

技巧 **18** How 疑問句的題型會依據方法或意見來決定答案。

Q1. How did you get the concert ticket? 方法 你是怎麼拿到演唱會門票的？
(A) Through my coworker. 透過我的同事。

through 透過～
presentation 發表；報告
informative 有益的；增廣見聞的

Q2. How was the presentation? 意見 這場簡報怎麼樣？
(A) It was very informative. 獲益良多。

各種詢問意見的 **How** 疑問句所對應之正解型態　必背★

How ＋ be 動詞 題2	How was the company outing? 公司員工旅遊辦得怎麼樣？	It was fun. 很好玩。
How do you like ~ 題3	How did you like the seminar? 你覺得研討會如何？	I found it very helpful. 我覺得獲益良多。
How did ~ go?	How did your interview go? 你的面試進行得怎麼樣？	Really well, thank you. 非常好，謝謝你。

應用本技巧的題目　　　　　　　　🎧 PART 2_09.mp3

1. Mark your answer.　(A)　(B)　(C)

2. Mark your answer.　(A)　(B)　(C)

錄音內容及解析

1. How did you like the resort?
   (A) During my last vacation.
   (B) No, a separate bill.
   (C) It was so nice and relaxing.

1. 你覺得那個度假村怎麼樣？
   (A) 在我上次休假期間。
   (B) 不，拆單各付各的。
   (C) 非常棒，而且很舒適。

vacation 假期；休假
separate 分開的；各自的

2. How did Mr. Allen get to the airport?
   題4
   (A) By express train.
   題1選4
   (B) His plane leaves at 6.
   (C) I don't get it.

2. 艾倫先生是怎麼到機場的？
   (A) 搭乘高鐵。
   (B) 他的班機會在六點起飛離開。
   (C) 我不明白。

express 高速的；特快的
leave 離開

正解 1. (C)　2. (A)

技巧**19 How** 疑問句的題型會依據其之後所接的形容詞或副詞來決定答案。

Q. How many employees have signed up for the event?
有多少員工報名參加這個活動？
(A) More than 50 so far. 截至目前為止已超過五十名。

sign up 註冊；報名登記

各種「**How** ＋形容詞／副詞」的疑問句所對應之正解型態　必背★

期間	How long will the meeting last? 題2選2 會議要開多久？	For an hour, I think. 我想一個小時吧。
價格	How much is this laptop? 題8 這台筆電多少錢？	It's 80 dollars. 八十美元。

last 持續

數量	How many people will attend the event? 題5 多少人將會參加此活動？	About 60 signed up. 大約有六十人報名。
頻率	How often do you work out? 題1 你多常運動健身？	Twice a week. 一星期兩次。

應用本技巧的題目　　　　　　　　　🎧 PART 2_10.mp3

1. Mark your answer.　(A)　(B)　(C)

2. Mark your answer.　(A)　(B)　(C)

錄音內容及解析

1. How long will it take you to get to the office?
   (A) It's Monday.
   (B) Less than an hour.
      正2選2
   (C) The subway is more reliable.

1. 你到辦公室要花費多久時間？
   (A) 是星期一。
   (B) 不到一個小時。
   (C) 地鐵比較可靠。

2. How many boxes of paper did you order?
   (A) I'll sort them in an alphabetical order.
      題2
   (B) The job comes with a lot of paperwork.
      選3
   (C) About a dozen.

2. 你訂了幾箱紙？
   (A) 我會依照字母的順序來分類。
   (B) 這份差事伴隨著許多文書工作。
   (C) 大約十二箱左右。

正解 1. (B)　2. (C)

reliable 可靠的；可信賴的

sort 將～分類
alphabetical 按字母排序的
paperwork 文書工作；書面作業
dozen 一打（十二個）

技巧**20** 在 Why 疑問句的題型當中不見得都會用 because 來應答。

Q. Why did you come in so early this morning?
　　你今天早上怎麼這麼早就來了？
　　(A) To meet my client. (O) 為了見客戶。
　　(B) For submitting the report by noon. (O) 為了在中午之前提交報告。
　　(C) (Because) I have a meeting. (O)（因為）我要開會。

📌tip!
對應的回答並非僅針對理由或原因加以說明，也可能針對目的或必要性來回覆！
不定詞 To：為了做某事
介系詞 For：為了～

應用本技巧的題目　　　　　　　　　🎧 PART 2_11.mp3

1. Mark your answer.　(A)　(B)　(C)

2. Mark your answer.　(A)　(B)　(C)

PART 2

録音内容及解析

1. Why didn't you attend the training session? 題8選1

(A) For an important meeting I had.

(B) Because people are nice.

(C) It was informative.

2. Why can't you finish your assignment?

(A) The computer is down.

(B) Yes, it's in the mail.

(C) Sign a contract, please. 題6選3

正解 1. (A) 2. (A)

1. 你為什麼沒有參加教育訓練講習？

(A) 當時我有個重要的會議。

(B) 因為大家都很親切。

(C) 很受用。

2. 你為什麼沒辦法完成任務？

(A) 電腦當機了。

(B) 對，在郵件裡面。

(C) 請簽署合約。

▌tip!

說明「負面情境」的答覆是 Why 疑問句題型中頗具代表性的正解。例如：

- 故障了
- 延期／取消了
- Too＋形容詞

一般 / 否定 / 附加疑問句

一般肯定問句63 一般否定問句45 附加肯定問句18 附加否定問句30
本單元討論的是不帶有疑問詞的題型。——突破各種疑問句的考法，奪分在望！

高出題率地圖

技巧 **21.** 一般疑問句的主詞和動詞為正解之鑰。
技巧 **22.** 一般疑問句大都會用 **Yes/No** 來回答。41次
技巧 **23.** 否定疑問句和否定附加疑問句一律用肯定疑問句的角度來分析，因為應答方式是一樣的！

技巧 **21** 一般疑問句的主詞和動詞為正解之鑰。

Q. Are <u>you coming</u> to the award ceremony? 你會出席頒獎典禮嗎？
= Do <u>you want</u> to <u>come</u> to the award ceremony? 你要出席頒獎典禮嗎？
= Can <u>you come</u> to the award ceremony? 你能夠出席頒獎典禮嗎？
= Would <u>you like</u> to come to the award ceremony? 你有意出席頒獎典禮嗎？
A. Sure, I'll be there. 當然，我會到場的。

疑問詞 **vs** 一般疑問句的正解型態 必背★

正解型態	疑問詞疑問句	一般疑問句
Yes/No	刪去	正解
發音相似 / 單字重複	刪去	刪去
萬用正解	正解	正解

應用本技巧的題目 🎧 PART 2_12.mp3

1. Mark your answer. (A) (B) (C)

2. Mark your answer. (A) (B) (C)

錄音內容及解析

1. Have you finished the financial report?
　　　　正 2 題 11 選 2　　　　題 1
(A) He reports to Mr. Jones.
(B) I'm almost done.
(C) No, I don't know that song.

1. 你完成財務報表了嗎？
(A) 他向瓊斯先生報告。
(B) 我就快完成了。
(C) 不，我不知道那首歌。

2. Did they review your transfer request?
(A) A moving expense.
(B) Which size of truck would you prefer?
　　　正 4 題 4 選 8
(C) They already approved it.
　　　　正 2 題 1

2. 他們審查過你的調職申請了嗎？
(A) 是移動支出。
(B) 你偏好哪一種大小的貨車？
(C) 他們已經批准了。

正解 1. (B)　2. (C)

📑 tip!
若是以 You（第二人稱）提問，卻以 He/She（第三人稱）應答，就有很大的機率是錯誤選項。

financial 金融的

review 審查；審核
transfer 調動；傳遞
expense 費用；開銷
approve 認可；批准

技巧**22** 一般疑問句大都會用 **Yes/No** 來回答。

Q. Have you met Mr. Peyton's assistant?
你有見過培頓先生的助理嗎？

A. Yes, Jade introduced us.
正1題1
有，婕德介紹過我們認識。

■ tip!
選項中如果出現 "Yes, but ..."，很有可能就是正確答案！

應用本技巧的題目　　　　　　　　　　PART 2_13.mp3

1. Mark your answer.　(A)　(B)　(C)

2. Mark your answer.　(A)　(B)　(C)

錄音內容及解析

1. Did you restock the main product display?
(A) The main entrance.
(B) No, I'll do that now.
(C) On the table.

1. 主要陳列商品你有再進貨了嗎？
(A) 正門。
(B) 沒有，我現在就叫貨。
(C) 在桌子上。

restock 再裝滿；補貨
display 展示；陳列（品）

2. Could you proofread the text for the brochure?
(A) I appreciate your kind words.
選2
(B) Sure, but can it wait until tomorrow?
題3
(C) Customers responded positively.

2. 可否請你校對小冊子的文字？
(A) 我很感激你這番溫暖的話。
(B) 沒問題，但我明天才能給你可以嗎？
(C) 客戶們的反應是正面的。

proofread 校對
brochure（資料或廣告）手冊

正解 1. (B)　2. (B)

技巧**23** 否定疑問句和否定附加疑問句一律用肯定疑問句的角度來分析，因為應答方式是一樣的！

Q1. Isn't the new supermarket closed on Sundays?
正1題2選2　正3題4選6
新開的超市星期天不是沒有營業嗎？

A. No, it opens 24/7.
不，它是 24 小時營業且全年無休。

■ tip!
大多是以 **Yes/No** 來應答！

24/7 24 小時營業且全年無休

Q2. You submitted your application, didn't you?
題3選1
你已經提交申請書了，不是嗎？

A. Yes, I did it last night.
是的，我昨天晚上提交了。

submit 提交
application 申請（書）

應用本技巧的題目　　　　　　　🎧　PART 2_14.mp3

1. Mark your answer. (A) (B) (C)

2. Mark your answer. (A) (B) (C)

錄音內容及解析

1. Aren't you leaving for dinner with us?
   正1題2

   (A) They sent an invitation.
   正1選1

   (B) No, I have another appointment.
   正5題6選2

   (C) Medium-rare, please.

1. 你不跟我們一起去吃晚餐嗎？

   (A) 他們寄了邀請函。

   (B) 不了，我另外有約。

   (C) 三分熟，麻煩你了。

2. We need a business website, don't you agree?
   正5題6選2

   (A) Sure, I'll see you there.

   (B) Yes, that would improve our company's presence.

   (C) It can be purchased on site.

2. 我們需要一個商業網站，你也同意吧？

   (A) 沒問題，我們就在那裡碰面。

   (B) 嗯，網站會提升我們公司的存在感。

   (C) 那可以在現場購買。

正解 1. (B)　2. (B)

leave for（離開某地）到某地
invitation 邀請（函）
appointment（正式的）約會；會面（的約定）

presence 存在；在場
purchase 購買

選擇 / 提議疑問句

選擇問句43 提議問句49

學習應付無疑問詞的疑問句題型，將技巧通通吸收，考場上發揮、奪分！

溫習紀錄

PART 2

高出題率地圖

技巧 24. 若是選擇疑問句的題型，只要選項中聽到兩者之一，就是正確答案。21次

技巧 25. 針對選擇疑問句的題型，只要選項中聽到 "both、either、neither"，即為正解。3次

技巧 26. 遇到提議或請求疑問句的題型，只要選項中有表達允許或拒絕，便是合理的回應。20次

技巧 **24** 若是選擇疑問句的題型，只要選項中聽到兩者之一，就是正確答案。

Q. Do you work as an <u>editor</u> or a <u>reporter</u>? 你的工作是編輯還是記者？
　　　　　　　　　　　　選1　　　　　　選1

A. <u>Reporter</u>, primarily. 以記者工作為主。

應用本技巧的題目　　　　　　　　　PART 2_15.mp3

1. Mark your answer.　(A)　(B)　(C)

2. Mark your answer.　(A)　(B)　(C)

> **tip!**
> 選擇疑問句題型的選項中若出現 "Yes/No"，就有很大的機率是錯誤選項！

錄音內容及解析

1. Are the best seats up front or in the balcony?

   (A) You can see <u>better</u> from the balcony. 正6題1選2

   (B) At the ticket <u>counter</u>. 正1選1

   (C) Yes, around 6 would be good.

1. 最棒的座位是在最前面那一區，還是樓座區？

   (A) 從樓座區看出去的視野比較好。

   (B) 在售票處。

   (C) 對，希望能在六點左右。

2. Would you like coffee for your <u>dessert</u>, 正1選1

   or can I bring you a dessert menu?

   (A) Yes, thank you.

   (B) From a café.

   (C) Coffee with extra sugar, please. 正2題5選7

2. 您的甜點想用點咖啡嗎？還是需要我拿甜點的菜單給您？

   (A) 好的，謝謝。

   (B) 從咖啡館。

   (C) 請給我咖啡，糖多一點。

dessert（餐後）甜品
extra 額外的；附加的

正解 1. (A)　2. (C)

技巧 **25** 針對選擇疑問句的題型，只要選項中聽到 "both、either、neither"，即為正解。

Q. Do you prefer work alone or with a group?
   你比較喜歡自己一個人工作，還是和團隊工作？

A. <u>Either</u> will be fine. 兩種方式都可以。

經常在選擇疑問句當中出現的表達方式 必背★

兩者都選擇	一概拒絕
Either is fine with me. 選4 兩者當中的任何一個皆可。 Both of them. 兩者都要。 正1選1 I don't care. 無所謂（，都可以）。	Neither of them. 兩者都不要。 I don't like either one. 選1 我兩者都不喜歡。

應用本技巧的題目 　　　　　　　　PART 2_16.mp3

1. Mark your answer.　(A)　(B)　(C)

2. Mark your answer.　(A)　(B)　(C)

錄音內容及解析

1. Which would you prefer soup or salad?
   (A) I do. Thanks.
   (B) Neither, thank you.
   (C) In the new restaurant.

1. 你比較想喝湯還是來份沙拉？
   (A) 好啊，謝謝。
   (B) 兩種都不需要，謝謝你。
   (C) 在新開的餐廳。

2. Are you going to send him a card or a gift?
   (A) The car would be nice.
   (B) She sent me a present.
   (C) Both would be nice.

2. 你打算寄卡片給他或是寄禮物？
   (A) 這台車應該不錯。
   (B) 她寄了一份禮物給我。
   (C) 兩種都不錯。

正解 1. (B) 2. (C)

技巧**26** 遇到提議或請求疑問句的題型，只要選項中有表達允許或拒絕，便是合理的回應。

Q1. Why don't you register for the workshop in advance?
　　你何不事先登記報名這場工作坊？
A. Sure, that's a good idea.
　　正19題1選26
　　好啊！這是個好主意。

Q2. Would you like to come to the concert with me?
　　你要不要跟我一起去聽音樂會？
A. I'm afraid I'm quite busy today.
　　我今天恐怕滿忙的。

---

tip!
區分提議疑問句和疑問詞 Why：
[提議]
Why don't you/we ...
[疑問詞]
Why didn't ...
Why doesn't he/she ...

send 寄；發送
present 禮物

register 註冊；登記
in advance 事先；預先
quite 相當；頗

與各型態提議、請求疑問句相對應的正解 必背★

提議、請求疑問句的型態		相對應的正解類型
要不要做〜？	Could/Can you ...? Will you ...? Would you like to ...?	[允許] That's a good idea. 正1選1 Sure、Okay、Certainly 正1選3　選1 I'd love to.、No problem. 正2選1　　　選1 I'd be happy to. 正3題1選2
〜怎麼樣？	Why don't you ...? How about ...? What about ...?	[拒絕] No thanks, ... I'm sorry/afraid .... 正4題7選1 I have other plans.
需要我幫你做〜嗎？	Would you like me to ...?	Thank you. 選7 I'd appreciate that.
介意我做〜嗎？ （＝我可以做某件事嗎？）	Would you mind ...?	Not at all. Of course not.

應用本技巧的題目

🎧 PART 2_17.mp3

1. Mark your answer.　(A)　(B)　(C)

2. Mark your answer.　(A)　(B)　(C)

錄音內容及解析

1. Why don't you take a break and have a snack?

   (A) I left it in the break room.

   (B) Okay, I'll be back in 15 minutes.
   正1題2

   (C) No, some potato chips and a soda.

1. 何不休息一下，吃些點心？

   (A) 我把東西忘在休息室了。

   (B) 好，那我十五分鐘後再回來。

   (C) 不，一些洋芋片跟汽水。

take a break 休息
snack 點心；零食

2. Could I get an ocean-view room?
   選2

   (A) The reviews are helpful.

   (B) You can access the indoor pool for free.

   (C) Sorry, we are fully booked.
   正1選1

2. 可以給我一間海景房嗎？

   (A) 這些評論很有參考價值。

   (B) 您可以免費使用室內游泳池。

   (C) 抱歉，我們的預約都滿了。

access 接近；使用
indoor 室內的
book 預訂

正解 1. (B)　2. (C)

直述句 / 間接疑問句 / 萬用正解

直述句 79 間接疑問句 1

將各種疑問句分門別類,快速掌握相對應的正確答案!

高出題率地圖

技巧 **27.** 直述句題型中若有應聲附和或針對問題狀況提出解決對策的敘述,該選項即為正解!

技巧 **28.** 間接疑問句的答案取決於句子當中出現的疑問詞。

技巧 **29.** 與提問類型無關,只要是萬用正解,都可以是正確答案。21 次

技巧**27** 直述句題型中若有應聲附和或針對問題狀況提出解決對策的敘述,該選項即為正解!

Q1. The security <u>system</u> in our building needs to be inspected.

題 2　　題 2

我們這棟建築物的保安系統有必要進行檢查。

A. <u>You're right.</u> It's urgent. 你說的對,這件事很急迫。

Q2. The <u>projector</u> in the meeting room A doesn't work.

題 4 選 3

會議室 A 裡的投影機沒辦法使用。

A. Maybe <u>it's not plugged in.</u> 也許是插頭沒差。

選 2

tip!

直述句的句尾如果有提出疑問,則聲調會往下掉;其他疑問句句尾的聲調是上揚的,這個關鍵要點必須要區分!

應用本技巧的題目　　　　🎧 PART 2_18.mp3

1. Mark your answer. (A) (B) (C)

2. Mark your answer. (A) (B) (C)

錄音內容及解析

jam 卡住;堵塞;擠滿

1. I think the printer in my office is jammed again.

(A) Let me take a look.

(B) Sorry, because of traffic jam.

(C) A toner cartridge.

1. 我覺得辦公室的影印機又卡紙了。

(A) 我來看看。

(B) 抱歉,因為塞車的關係。

(C) 一個碳粉匣。

headquarter 總部;總公司

apply for 申請;請求得到

incredible 難以置信的;極佳的

2. I was very pleased to <u>hear</u> that Mr.

正 3 題 2 選 4

Blank will be the new manager.

(A) Please send these to headquarters.

(B) I'm interested in applying for it.

正 1

(C) Yes, he has incredible leadership skills.

題 1 選 3

2. 聽到布蘭克先生將成為新任經理一事,我感到十分開心。

(A) 請將這些東西送回總公司。

(B) 我有意申請。

(C) 沒錯,他擁有出色的領導能力。

正解 1. (A) 2. (C)

技巧**28** 間接疑問句的答案取決於句子當中出現的疑問詞。

Q. Can you tell me when the train for Central Station departs?
請問前往中央站的列車何時出發？

A. Maybe in 15 minutes.
正9題3選8
大概再過十五分鐘。

應用本技巧的題目　　　　　　　　　　🎧 PART 2_19.mp3

1. Mark your answer.　(A)　(B)　(C)

2. Mark your answer.　(A)　(B)　(C)

錄音內容及解析

1. Do you know how to do a price adjustment?
(A) No, let's call a supervisor.
(B) The price tag isn't attached.
(C) I don't see one.

1. 你知道要怎麼調整價格嗎？
(A) 不知道，我們請督導過來吧。
(B) 價格標籤沒有貼上。
(C) 我連一個都沒看到。

2. Can you tell me who is in charge of
正1題3
organizing conference?
正2題16選13
(A) No, there will be no charge.
(B) I heard the PR manager.
(C) In the conference hall.

2. 你可以告訴我負責安排會議的是誰嗎？
(A) 不，是免費的。
(B) 我聽說是公關經理。
(C) 在會議廳。

正解 1. (A)　2. (B)

📌 tip!
儘管間接疑問句的答案也同樣取決於疑問詞，但還是可以用 Yes/No 來回答！

adjustment 調整
supervisor 主管；上司

in charge of 負責～
organize 組織；籌劃
conference 會議

merchandise 商品

policy 政策
receive 收到

技巧**29** 與提問類型無關，只要是萬用正解，都可以是正確答案。

Q1. Has the new merchandise arrived at the store?
新商品送到門市了嗎？

A. Ms. Brenner should know.
布瑞納女士應該知道。

Q2. When did the new policy go into effect?
題 3 選 2
新政策是何時開始施行的？

A. Didn't you receive an email from HR?
正 1 題 4 選 2
你沒收到人資部寄的電子郵件嗎？

Q3. Why was the weekly meeting canceled yesterday?
昨天的週會為什麼取消了？

A. I don't know.
我不知道。

各種萬用正解類型 必背★

向～詢問 Ask the manager.	（名字／職稱）should know. ～應該知道。 Doesn't（名字／職稱）know? ～不知道嗎？ （名字／職稱）might know. ～可能知道。 Didn't（名字／職稱）tell you? ～沒有告訴你嗎？
確認看看 Check ...	Here's the (floor plan). 這裡有（樓層平面圖）。 It's posted on the board. 正 2 題 1 已張貼在佈告欄上。 The schedule is on your desk. 正 5 題 4 選 1 行程表在你桌上。 Check your email. 正 11 題 4 選 6 確認一下你的電子郵件。

應用本技巧的題目　　　　　　　　　　PART 2_20.mp3

1. Mark your answer.　(A)　(B)　(C)

2. Mark your answer.　(A)　(B)　(C)

錄音內容及解析

1. How much will it cost to have a dozen roses delivered?

　(A) It depends on the location.

　(B) Make sure you water them every day.

　(C) From the accounting department.

2. The travel reimbursements will be included in this paycheck, right?

　(A) We are still deciding.

　(B) After 30 years with the company.

　(C) Yes, I plan on attending.

1. 代送十二朵玫瑰的話，需要多少費用？

　(A) 費用視配送地點而定。

　(B) 一定要每天幫它們澆水。

　(C) 從會計部。

2. 這次的薪水會包含報銷差旅費，對吧？

　(A) 我們還在商討中，尚未定案。

　(B) 在這家公司服務滿三十年之後。

　(C) 對，我預計會出席。

正解 1. (A)　2. (A)

deliver 配送；投遞

reimbursement 償還；退款；補償
include 包含
paycheck 工資；薪水

高出題率地圖

技巧 **30.** 對話開始之前要迅速掌握該題目在問什麼，並在關鍵字的地方做記號。
技巧 **31.** 要迅速掌握男子／女子的職業及對話場所，並在關鍵字的地方做記號。72次
技巧 **32.** 在詢問場所的題型當中，直接提及場所的相關描述或詞彙決定了答案。
技巧 **33.** 在詢問說話者職業的題型當中，直接提及職業的相關描述或詞彙決定了答案。94次

take place 發生；舉行

技巧**30** 對話開始之前要迅速掌握該題目在問什麼，並在關鍵字的地方做記號。

Q1. What are the speakers mainly discussing? 說話者主要在討論什麼？
Q2. What is scheduled to take place on Thursday? 星期四預計會有什麼行程？
題 14
Q3. What does the woman offer to do? 女子提議要做什麼？
題 9

應用本技巧的題目 掌握下一道題目的用意，並在關鍵字的地方做記號。

1. What problem is being discussed?
2. What does the man apologize for?
題 2
3. What will the woman most likely do next?

題目型態

1. What problem is being discussed? 對話中在討論什麼問題？

2. What does the man apologize for? 男子為什麼理由道歉？

3. What will the woman most likely do next? 女子接下來最有可能會做什麼？

正解 1. problem 問題；缺失　　2. man, apologize 男子道歉
3. woman, do next 女子接下來要做的事

apologize for 為～道歉

技巧**31** 要迅速掌握男子／女子的職業及對話場所，並在關鍵字的地方做記號。

Q1. Who most likely is the man? 男子最有可能是什麼人？
Q2. Where does the conversation take place? 對話是在什麼場所發生的？

應用本技巧的題目 在下一道題目關鍵字的地方做記號，並寫下該題目是在問什麼。

1. What is the man's job?
2. Where does the conversation probably take place?
3. Who is the woman talking with?
4. Where most likely does the man work?
5. Who is the man calling?

conversation 對話

題目型態

1. What is the man's job? 男子的職業為何？

2. Where does the conversation probably take place?
   對話應該是在哪裡發生的？

3. Who is the woman talking with? 女子正在跟誰對話？

4. Where most likely does the man work? 男子最有可能在哪裡工作？

5. Who is the man calling? 男子正在打電話給誰？

正解 1. man's job 男子的職業　2. Where 對話場所
　　 3. woman, with 女子的談話對象　4. Where, man 男子的工作場所
　　 5. man, calling 男子的通話對象

技巧32 在詢問場所的題型當中，直接提及場所的相關描述或詞彙決定了答案。

Q. Where does the man most likely work? 男子最有可能在哪裡工作？
   (A) At a hotel 在飯店
   (B) At a travel agency 在旅行社
      選2
   (C) At a printing company 在印刷廠
      選1
   (D) At a advertising firm 在廣告公司
      選1

tip!
如果是詢問職業或場所的題型，對話前段就會透露答案！

題目型態

M: I heard that we received the tour pamphlets this morning but there was a misprint. The name of one of the hotels we use on the tour is wrong.

男：聽說我們今天早上有收到旅遊手冊，但上面印錯了。我們行程當中會住到的其中一間飯店名稱印錯了。

正解 (B)

pamphlet 小冊子
misprint 印錯；誤植
wrong 錯誤的；搞錯的

經常出題的場所詞彙 必背★

詞彙	意思	詞彙	意思
airport	機場	restaurant	餐廳
hotel	飯店	post office	郵局
library	圖書館	bank	銀行
travel agency	旅行社	pharmacy = drug store	藥局
real estate agency 選1 = realtor	房地產仲介	stationery store = office supply store	文具店；辦公用品店

應用本技巧的題目　　　　　　　　🎧　PART 3_01.mp3

1. Where is the conversation most likely taking place?
   (A) A bank　　　　　　　　(B) A store

2. Where does the man most likely work?
   (A) At a delivery company　　(B) At a furniture store

錄音內容及解析

1. 對話最有可能在什麼地方發生？
(A) 銀行　　　　(B) 商店

M: I'm interested in borrowing some money to start up a business.

W: Well, our specialist isn't in today but I can give you some application forms if you want.

男：我想要借一筆錢來創業。

女：嗯……今天我們的專員不在，但如果有需要的話，我可以先拿一些申請書給您。

2. 男子最有可能在哪裡工作？
(A) 貨運公司　　(B) 家具店

M: Thank you for shopping at Comfort Furniture. Would you like to pick up these chairs now or have them delivered to your office?

W: I'd like to get them delivered. And then, do they require some assembly?

男：感謝您在舒適家居消費，您要現在帶走這些椅子嗎？　選1
　　還是要幫您送到辦公室？

女：用配送的好了。送達之後，這些椅子還需要組裝嗎？

正解 1. (A)　2. (B)

borrow 借；借入
specialist 專員；專家
application 申請（書）

deliver 配送；運送
require 需要；要求
assembly 組裝

技巧**33** 在詢問說話者職業的題型當中，直接提及職業的相關描述或詞彙決定了答案。

Q. Who is the man talking with? 男子正在跟誰對話？
   (A) An assistant 助理
   Ⓑ A job applicant 求職者
   　　選2

題目型態

W: Hello, my name is Tracy Jackson. I'm here for my interview with George Cane.

M: George Cane is in a meeting now. Could you have a seat in a waiting room and wait for a moment?

女：您好，我是崔西・傑克森，我是來找喬治・凱恩面試的。

男：喬治・凱恩目前正在開會，可以麻煩您到休息室稍坐，等他一下嗎？

正解 (B)

PART 3

經常出題的職業詞彙 必背★

詞彙	意思	詞彙	意思
receptionist 選1	櫃檯接待員； 服務台人員	customer = client	顧客；客戶
real estate agent	房地產仲介員	tenant	房客
applicant = candidate	應徵者；候選人	coworker = colleague	同事
manufacturer	製造業者；廠商	repair person 試1	維修人員
flight attendant	空服員	volunteer	志願者；義工

應用本技巧的題目

PART 3_02.mp3

1. Who is the man talking to?
   (A) A doctor   (B) A receptionist
   選1

2. Who most likely is the woman?
   (A) A pharmacist   (B) A dentist
   選2

錄音內容及解析

1. 男子正在跟誰對話？
(A) 醫生　　　(B) 櫃檯接待員

W: Good afternoon, Dr. Clark's office. What can I do for you?

M: Hi, this is Fraser Harper. I have to reschedule my Wednesday appointment.

女：午安，這裡是克拉克醫師的辦公室，有什麼地方可以為您服務？

男：妳好，我是佛雷澤·哈波。我原本有預約星期三，但我必須改時間。

2. 女子最有可能是什麼人？
(A) 藥師　　　(B) 牙科醫師

M: Hello, my name is David Baker. I'm here to pick up my medicine. My doctor sent the prescription to you.

W: Wait a second ... here it is.

男：妳好，我是大衛·貝克。我來領藥，我的醫生有把處方箋傳送給妳。

女：稍等一下……在這邊。

正解 1. (B) 2. (A)

reschedule 重新安排時間；改期

medicine 藥物
prescription 處方；藥方

詢問對話主題或目的的題型

此題型對話前段的內容就會透露答案，因此必須集中注意力聆聽第一位說話者所說的話。

高出題率地圖

技巧 34. 對話開始之前要掌握該考題的用意，並在關鍵字的地方做記號。
技巧 35. 詢問對話主題的題型中 "I'm here to/for ..." 或 "I'm calling to ..." 為正解訊號。59次
技巧 36. 詢問對話主題的題型中 "I'd like to ..." 或 I'm looking for ..." 為正解訊號。61次
技巧 37. 辦公用品或電子產品故障是對話主題題型中常見的正確答案。15次

技巧 **34** 對話開始之前要掌握該考題的用意，並在關鍵字的地方做記號。

Q1. What is the main topic of the conversation?
　　　　　　　　　　　　試 1
對話的主題是什麼？

Q2. What is the problem?
發生了什麼問題？

Q3. Why is the man calling?
男子為何來電？

應用本技巧的題目 掌握下一道題目的用意，並在關鍵字的地方做記號。

1. What are the speakers talking about?
2. What is the purpose of the call?
　　　　　　　　　題 5
3. What problem does the woman mention?

題目型態

1. What are the speakers talking about?
說話者在談論什麼？

2. What is the purpose of the call?
這通電話的目的為何？

3. What problem does the woman mention?
女子提及什麼問題？

正解 1. talking, about 主題　2. purpose 來電目的
　　　 3. problem, woman 女子、問題

技巧**35** 詢問對話主題的題型中 "**I'm here to/for ...**" 或 "**I'm calling to ...**" 為正解訊號。
試3　　　　　　　　試2

Q1. What are the speakers mainly discussing?

說話者主要在討論什麼？

I'm here to talk about the workshop next week.
正解訊號

我是為了討論下週工作坊的事而來的。

正解 The upcoming event 即將到來的活動

應用本技巧的題目　Questions 1-2 PART 3_03.mp3

1. Why is the woman calling?
  (A) To book a room
  (B) To request a schedule change
  選7
  (C) To check on a reservation
  (D) To register for a conference

2. Who most likely is the woman talking to?
  (A) A conference organizer
  (B) An airline employee
  (C) A travel agent
  (D) A hotel receptionist

reservation 預約；預訂
register for 註冊／登記～

organizer 主辦人；組織者

錄音內容及解析

1. 女子為什麼打電話？
  (A) 為了預訂房間
  (B) 為了要求變更行程
  (C) 為了確認預約
  (D) 為了報名一場會議

2. 女子最有可能正在和誰對話？
  (A) 會議召集人
  (B) 航空公司員工
  (C) 旅行社員工
  (D) 飯店櫃檯接待員

W: Hello, this is Gloria Hassle. I'll be attending the conference at your hotel and I'm calling to confirm my room reservation for Friday and Saturday night.

M: Just a moment, Ms. Hassle. Let's see.

女：你好，我是葛洛麗‧哈索。我將要參加在貴飯店舉行的會議，我打電話來是想確認一下我預訂的星期五和星期六的房間。

男：哈索女士，請稍等。我為您確認。

attend 出席；參加
confirm 確認

正解 1. (C)　2. (D)

PART 3

技巧 36 詢問對話主題的題型中 **"I'd like to ..."** 或 **"I'm looking for ..."** 為正解訊號。
試 23   試 5

Q1. What is the <u>conversation</u> mainly about?

這段對話主要與什麼有關？

<u>I'm looking for</u> *Across the Border*, the new novel by Lucas Miller.
正解訊號
I can't seem to find it in the fiction section.

我在找盧卡斯・米勒的小說新作《Across the Border》，

我在小說區找不到這本書。

正解 A book 一本書

應用本技巧的題目 Questions 1-2   🎧 PART 3_04.mp3

1. Why did the woman visit the business?
(A) To exchange an item
(B) To purchase equipment
選 4 試 2
(C) To make delivery
(D) To request a repair

2. What is the woman's occupation?
(A) Graphic designer
(B) Software developer
(C) Interior designer
(D) Laboratory technician

錄音內容及解析

1. 女子為何造訪這間店？
(A) 為了換貨
(B) 為了購買配備
(C) 為了送貨
(D) 為了要求維修

2. 女子的職業為何？
(A) 平面設計師
(B) 軟體研發工程師
(C) 室內裝潢設計師
(D) 實驗室技術人員

W: Good afternoon, I'm interested in buying a new laptop to use for my graphic design business. I need it to be able to run a number of software programs at the same time.

M: Hmm ... what would probably best suit your needs is the Ayon-70.

女：午安，我想購買一台用於平面設計工作的筆電，這台筆電需要能同時運行好幾個軟體程式。

男：嗯……依您的需求，最適合的筆電應該是 Ayon-70。

正解 1. (B) 2. (A)

Glossary (margin):

novel 小說
fiction 小說
section 部分；區域

exchange 交換
equipment 裝備；設備
developer 研發人員
laboratory 實驗室；研究室

be interested in 對～感興趣
suit 合適；相稱
need 需求；需要

技巧**37** 辦公用品或電子產品故障是對話主題題型中常見的正確答案。

Q1. What are the speakers mainly discussing?
<u>題10</u>

說話者主要在討論什麼？

Hi, I bought this camera here last year and it's been great. But recently, the flash stopped working.

正解訊號　　選1試3

你好，我去年在這裡購買了一台相機，而相機的狀況一直都很好，但最近閃光燈不會閃了。

正解 An item is malfunctioning. 產品故障。

應用本技巧的題目 Questions 1-2　　　　　　PART 3_05.mp3

1. Who most likely is the woman?
   (A) The man's friend
   (B) A customer service representative
   (C) A sales clerk
   (D) The man's coworker

2. What problems are the speakers discussing?
   (A) A file cannot be located.
   (B) An employee called in sick.
   (C) An office machine is out of order.
   (D) A telephone number is not listed.

錄音內容及解析

1. 女子最有可能是什麼人？
   (A) 男子的朋友
   (B) 客服專員
   (C) 銷售員
   (D) 男子的同事

2. 說話者正在討論什麼問題？
   (A) 找不到檔案。
   (B) 一名員工請了病假。
   (C) 事務機故障了。
   (D) 有一組電話號碼沒有列在表單上。

M: Emily, the photocopier isn't working very well. The images are all blurry and there's a stripe on the paper.

W: You should tell Carol, the administrative assistant about the problem.

男：艾蜜莉，影印機有點不太對勁，印出來的圖片都很模糊，而且紙上還有條紋。

女：你應該跟行政助理卡蘿反映這個問題。

正解 1. (D)　2. (C)

tip!
機器故障是常見的答案類型，必須熟記故障一詞的各種用語。

recently 最近

representative 代表；負責者

locate 找出～的準確位置（或範圍）
call in sick 請病假
out of order 故障
list 列舉；列入名單

PART 3

高出題率地圖
技巧 38. 在提議或要求的題型中，主詞人物所說的話指向正解。72次
技巧 39. 如果是用被動語態詢問的題型，提出提議或要求的人決定答案為何。9次
技巧 40. 包含特定人名的考題即為三人對話的題型。23次

技巧38 在提議或要求的題型中，主詞人物所說的話指向正解。

ask、request、suggest、offer——對方的台詞不會影響到答案。

Q. What does the **man** **ask** the woman to do?
　　　　　　　　　　題33

男子要求女子做什麼？

We looked over your resume and I'd like to have an interview with you. **Could you come in next week?**
　　　　　　　　　正解訊號
我們看了你的履歷，想和你面談。你下週方便過來嗎？

正解 Drop by his office for a job interview 前往他的辦公室進行職缺面試
　　　　　　　　　　選2

tip!
提議或要求的題型中若出現 "Can/Could you ..." 或 "Why don't you ..."，即為正解訊號。

look over 審視；檢查

Paraphrasing（換句話說）必背★

詞彙	同義詞	意思	詞彙	同義詞	意思
submit	hand in	提交；呈遞	review	go over	審核；查看
call	contact	聯絡	visit	stop by	拜訪；探望
register	sign up 選2試3	註冊；登記	hire	employ	雇用
postpone	put off	延遲；使延期	change	reschedule	變更

應用本技巧的題目 Questions 1-2　　　　　　　　PART 3_06.mp3

1. Where most likely are the speakers?
   (A) In a post office
   (B) In a train station
   (C) At a ticket booth
   (D) In a computer store

2. What does the woman suggest the man do?
   (A) Arrive early
   (B) Cancel the appointment
   (C) Check his schedule
   (D) Complete the form

appointment（正式的）約會；會面（的約定）
complete 完成；填寫

PART 3

錄音內容及解析

1. 說話者最有可能在哪裡？
 (A) 在郵局
 (B) 在火車站
 (C) 在售票處
 (D) 在電腦專賣店

2. 女子建議男子做什麼？
 (A) 早點抵達
 (B) 取消約會
 (C) 確認行程
 (D) 填妥表單

M: Yes, that would be wonderful. And could you please <u>mark</u> the package as <u>fragile</u>? I want to make sure nothing gets broken.

W: Of course. Your total would be 12 dollars and 35 cents. Also <u>why don't you fill out this document for the delivery confirmation service?</u>

男：是的，這樣再好不過了。還有包裹上面可以請妳註明一下這是易碎物品嗎？我想要確保裡面的東西都不會有破損。

女：當然可以。總金額是 **12.35** 美元。另外，麻煩您填寫這份配送服務確認單。

正解 1. (A) 2. (D)

mark 做記號；標記
fragile 易碎的；易損壞的
total 總數；總額
fill out 填寫
document 文件；單據
confirmation 確認

技巧**39** 如果是用被動語態詢問的題型，提出提議或要求的人決定答案為何。

 Q. What is the <u>man</u> <u>asked</u> to do?

 W: <u>Could you show me your ID badge?</u> I can check it in our system
 正確訊號
 manually and then let you into the lab.
 可以麻煩您出示身分識別證嗎？我可以在我們的系統上手動確認，確認後會讓您進入實驗室。

 正解 Present an ID card 出示身分證件

manually 手動地；人工地

present 提出；展現

應用本技巧的題目 Questions 1-2 🎧 PART 3_07.mp3

1. Where most likely do the
 題8
 speakers work?
 (A) At a warehouse
 (B) At a housekeeping service
 (C) At a bakery
 (D) At an electronics store

2. What is the man asked to do?
 (A) Come to work early
 (B) Unpack some supplies
 (C) Confirm an address
 (D) Get pricing details

warehouse 倉庫

unpack 打開（包裹等）取出東西；從（箱／包等）中取出
detail 細節

find out about 發現；
察覺
useful 有用的
foam 泡沫
wipe 擦拭
promising 有前途的；
看好的
cost 要價
decision 決定

錄音內容及解析

1. 說話者最有可能在哪裡工作？
   (A) 在倉庫
   (B) 在家事服務企業
   (C) 在麵包店
   (D) 在電子產品賣場

2. 男子被要求做什麼？
   (A) 早點到班
   (B) 拆箱拿一些物資出來
   (C) 確認地址
   (D) 獲取價格的詳細資訊

M: Gina, I just found out about a product that I think would be useful for our bakery. It's an oven cleaner made by Emery Cleaning.

W: Oh, what makes you think it would be good for us?

M: Well, after spraying on the foam, it's ready to wipe away in just five minutes. For most cleaners, you have to let it sit for an hour.

W: Hmm ... that sounds promising. Could you find out how much it costs? That
試 1
would help us to make a decision for our bakery.

男：吉娜，我剛發現一個產品，應該會對我們的麵包店有所助益，就是艾莫里清潔公司製造的烤箱清潔劑。

女：噢，是什麼原因讓你認為這個產品對我們有幫助？

男：烤箱噴上泡沫之後，只要等五分鐘就可以擦掉了。絕大部分的清潔劑都要靜置一個鐘頭才行。

女：嗯……聽起來很有用。可以麻煩你查一下它多少錢嗎？知道價格有助於我們麵包店做決定。

正解 1. (C) 2. (D)

技巧 40 包含特定人名的考題即為三人對話的題型。

tip!
若考題中提及第三人，則此人的名字即為正解訊號！

on the air 播放中
huge 巨大的
autographed 親筆簽名的

Q. What will Martin most likely receive?
馬丁最有可能將收到什麼？

M1: First caller, you're on the air.
第一位打電話進來的朋友，你在線上了。

M2: Hi, I'm Martin from L.A. I'm a huge fan of your music. But, you haven't visited any cities on the West coast yet.
嗨，我是 L.A. 的馬丁。我是妳的超級大樂迷。妳目前都還沒到訪過任何西岸的城市。

W: I know. Martin, I'll send you an autographed copy of my new album. I want to make it up to you.
正解訊號
我知道。馬丁，我會寄一張我的新專輯簽名 CD 給你，我想給你一點補償。

正解 A music CD 一張音樂 CD

應用本技巧的題目 PART 3_08.mp3

1. Why did Jason send a reminder to the members?
   (A) To ask them to update contact information
   (B) To solicit their feedback on the conference
   (C) To notify a product design deadline
   (D) To send a fax to the department heads

reminder 提醒
contact information
聯繫資訊
solicit 請求
notify 通知；告知
deadline 最後期限；
截止日期

PART 3

錄音內容及解析

1. 傑森為什麼要寄提醒通知給會員？
   (A) 為了要求會員們更新通訊地址
   (B) 為了徵求會員們對於會議的意見
   (C) 為了通知產品設計的最後期限
   (D) 為了發送一封傳真給部長們

M1: The invitations to next month's conference will be ready on Wednesday.

invitation 邀請（函）
association 協會

W: Jason, how about the address labels?

M2: They will be ready by then. I sent an email reminder to the association
members to update their mailing address. 選1試1

男 1：下個月的會議邀請函會在星期三備妥。

女： 傑森，那地址標籤名條呢？

男 2：到時候也會準備好。我已經寄了電子郵件提醒協會會員們要更新
通訊地址。

正解 1. (A)

高出題率地圖

技巧 **41.** 「時間點、場所、第三人」等既是考題的關鍵字，也是正解訊號。106次
技巧 **42.** 如果是詢問下一步行動的題型，答案會在對話後段出現。97次
技巧 **43.** 詢問下一步行動的題型中若出現 "I'll ..."、"Let me ..." 或 "Why don't I ..."，即為正解訊號。85次

技巧 **41** 「時間點、場所、第三人」等既是考題的關鍵字，也是正解訊號。

Q. From when is breakfast served on Saturday?
星期六幾點開始供應早餐？

serve 提供飲食
continue 繼續

It's served starting at 7:00 A.M. on weekdays and 8:00 A.M. on weekends. And it continues until 1:00 P.M. 正解訊號
平日早上七點開始供應，週末早上八點開始，都會持續供應到下午一點。

正解 At 8:00 A.M. 早上八點

應用本技巧的題目 Questions 1-2　　　　　🎧 PART 3_09.mp3

1. What is the conversation mainly about?
   題2
   (A) A company outing
   (B) A music festival
   選5試1
   (C) A theater performance
   (D) A sporting event

2. What will the man look for on the website?
   選4試1
   (A) An event schedule
   (B) A direction to a venue
   (C) A reservation deadline
   (D) An order form
   選2

company outing 公司員工旅遊
direction 方向；路線
venue 發生場所；舉行地點
reservation 預約；訂位

錄音內容及解析

1. 這段對話主要與什麼有關？
   (A) 公司員工旅遊
   (B) 音樂節
   (C) 劇場表演
   (D) 體育活動

2. 男子將在網站上找什麼？
   (A) 活動時程
   (B) 前往會場的交通方式
   (C) 預訂截止日
   (D) 訂單

extra 額外的；附加的
perform 演出；表演
interesting 有趣的

M: Laura, I have an extra ticket to the music festival in St. John's Park and I was wondering if you wanted to go this evening. There is a good singer performing, Joey Maroni.
試1

W: Oh, I've heard of Joey Maroni. He really is good. I'd love to go but I have to work late tonight.

M: That's too bad. Well, the tickets are good for any night of the week. Let's look at the website and see if there's another concert that looks interesting.
選2

男：蘿拉，音樂節要在聖約翰公園舉行，我有多一張票，想問妳今天晚上想不想去看。有實力派歌手喬依·馬洛尼的表演。

女：噢，我有聽過喬依·馬洛尼，他真的很棒。我很想去，但我今晚得加班。

男：真不湊巧。不過，這門票在這個禮拜每晚都能使用，我們再查詢一下網站，看有沒有其他我們感興趣的演唱會吧。

正解 1. (B) 2. (A)

技巧42 如果是詢問下一步行動的題型，答案會在對話後段出現。

Q. **What is the woman going to do next?**
女子接下來會做什麼？

Unfortunately, they're out of stock at the moment. Let me call another store nearby and see if they have anything in stock. _{正解訊號}
很可惜這項產品目前缺貨。我打電話問一下附近的其他門市，看他們有沒有庫存。

正解 **Make a phone call** 打一通電話
_{選3試1}

▎tip!
說話者使用未來時態時，經常會直接講出自身接下來要做的事！

unfortunately 不幸地；不湊巧
out of stock 沒有庫存；缺貨
nearby 附近的

應用本技巧的題目 Questions 1-2 　　🎧 PART 3_10.mp3

1. Why is the woman not available this Saturday?
   (A) She will be out of town.
   (B) She is taking visitors to the airport.
   (C) She has to work at the office.
   (D) She has to attend a meeting.

2. What does the man say he will do next?
   (A) Complete some work
   (B) Organize an event
   (C) Plan a vacation
   (D) Get some information

_{選1}

out of town 出城
visitor 訪客
vacation 假期
information 資訊

錄音內容及解析

1. 這個星期六女子為什麼沒空？
   (A) 屆時她不在城裡。
   (B) 屆時她要送訪客到機場。
   (C) 屆時她必須在辦公室工作。
   (D) 屆時她必須參加一個會議。

2. 男子說他接下來會做什麼？
   (A) 完成工作
   (B) 籌備活動
   (C) 計畫假期
   (D) 獲取資訊

M: Christina, my sister and I are planning to go to the museum this weekend. Can you join us?

W: Oh, I can't. I have family visiting and have to take them to the airport on Saturday. But I'd really like to see the woodwork exhibits there. You don't know how long it'll be on display, do you? _{選5試5}

M: No, I don't. But I'll get you a schedule of events while I'm there. It lists the exhibits and their days.

plan 計畫
museum 博物館
woodwork 木工
exhibit 展示；展覽

男：克莉絲汀，這個週末我和我妹妹打算去博物館，妳要跟我們一起去嗎？

女：噢，我沒辦法去。星期六我的家人來訪，我得送他們去機場。可是我真的很想去看木工工藝展。你知道這個展覽會展出多久嗎？

男：我不知道。我到那邊時再幫妳拿活動時程，上面有列出各個展覽活動和它們的檔期。

正解 1. (B) 2. (D)

技巧 **43** 詢問下一步行動的題型中若出現 "I'll ..."、"Let me ..." 或 "Why don't I ..."，即為正解訊號。

Q. What will the man have to do later?
男子後續必須做什麼？

I'm not sure if the shipment has already been sent out. I'll check with the
選4試2　　　　　　　　　　　　　　　　　　　　　　　正解訊號
shipping department.
選6試4

我不確定貨品是否已經配送出去，我再跟出貨部確認一下。

正解 Contact another office 聯繫其他部門

shipment 運送／裝載的貨物
shipping department 運輸部門

應用本技巧的題目　Questions 1-2　　　　　　　　　PART 3_11.mp3

1. What are the speakers discussing?
   (A) A newspaper article
   　　選8試3
   (B) A presentation
   (C) A magazine
   　　選4試6
   (D) A new book

2. What will the woman do next?
   (A) Make a copy of the document
   (B) Purchase a book
   (C) Meet with the author
   (D) Review the report

article 文章
presentation 發表；報告
author 作者；作家

錄音內容及解析

1. 說話者在討論什麼？
   (A) 一則新聞報導
   (B) 一場簡報
   (C) 一本雜誌
   (D) 一本新書

2. 女子接下來會做什麼？
   (A) 影印文件
   (B) 購買書籍
   (C) 與作者會面
   (D) 審視報告

M: Have you read Geraldine Brook's new novel?
　　　　　　　　　　　　　　　　試1

W: No, I was too busy these days finishing my report.

M: You should read it. I think it's the best story ever, and it is one of the best-selling books now.

W: OK, I believe you. Why don't I stop by at the bookstore now and get a copy?
　　　　　　　　　　　試1

stop by 順道造訪
copy 份（書籍、CD等的計量單位）

男：潔蘿汀・布魯克的新小說妳看了嗎？

女：還沒有，我這幾天太忙了，要把報告完成。

男：妳一定要看。我覺得它的故事情節是史上最棒的，而且這本書現在也在暢銷排行榜上。

女：好，我相信你。不如我現在就順道到書店買一本怎麼樣？

正解 1. (D) 2. (B)

14 換句話說／說話者意圖題型

高出題率地圖

技巧 44. **Paraphrasing**（換句話說）就是作答的關鍵。83次
技巧 45. 具有代表性或概括性含意的詞彙即為正解。55次
技巧 46. 當考題詢問說話者某句話的言下之意時，答案就在前一句話中。48次

🔖 tip!
解答常常不是對話中曾經提及的詞彙，而是換句話說，以其他的形式出現！

forget 忘記
reserve 預約；預訂

improve 改善
quarterly 每季的
transfer 調職；轉任
overseas 在海外；向海外
host 主辦；主持

be concerned about
對～有所疑慮／感到擔心
ceremony 儀式；典禮
train 訓練
select 選擇
site 用地；場所

popular 受歡迎的
contract 合約（書）

技巧 **44** Paraphrasing（換句話說）就是作答的關鍵。

Q. What did the man forget to do? 男子忘了做什麼？

I'm attending the Annual Technology Convention in Seoul this weekend, and I forgot to reserve a hotel room.

正解訊號

我即將參加本週末在首爾舉行的年度技術大會，但我忘記訂飯店了。

正解 Book accommodations 預訂住宿

應用本技巧的題目 Questions 1-3　　🎧　PART 3_12.mp3

1. What is the conversation mainly about?
   (A) Attending an event
   (B) Improving quarterly sales
   (C) Transferring overseas
   (D) Hosting a workshop
   選6試9

2. What is the man concerned about?
   (A) Organizing a ceremony
   (B) Training new employees
   (C) Selecting a factory site
   (D) Finding a place to live

3. What does Theresa plan to give the man?
   (A) A popular book
   (B) Some contact information
   (C) Some sample contracts
   (D) An updated schedule

錄音內容及解析

1. 這段對話主要與什麼有關？
   (A) 出席一項活動
   (B) 增加季營收
   (C) 轉職至海外
   (D) 舉辦一場工作坊

2. 男子在擔心什麼？
   (A) 籌備一場典禮
   (B) 訓練一批新進員工
   (C) 挑選一塊工廠用地
   (D) 找個地方住

3. 泰瑞莎打算給男子什麼？
   (A) 一本暢銷書
   (B) 一些聯繫資訊
   (C) 一些合約樣本
   (D) 一份最新行程

PART 3

W1: Jacob, I heard that <u>you're transferring to the branch in Tokyo next quarter.</u>

M: That's right, in mid-September. It'll be my first time living abroad.

W2: But the company will provide you with everything you need, right?

M: Well, they've arranged temporary accommodations for the first six weeks. After that, <u>I have to find my own housing, and I'm worried that it will be difficult.</u>

W2: Yes, that would be a challenge.

M: Theresa, haven't you traveled to Tokyo quite a few times? Maybe you could give me some advice.

W1: I can do something even better. My friend is a real estate agent in Tokyo. I have her business card at home. I can give it to you on Monday.

女 1：雅各，我聽說你下一季被調任到東京分公司。

男：　沒錯，九月中旬過去。這將是我第一次在海外生活。

女 2：公司應該會提供你一切需要的東西，對吧？

男：　這個嘛，公司已經幫我安排好了前六週的臨時住所，但六週後我必須自己另外找地方住，有點擔心住的地方會不好找。

女 2：嗯，這確實是一項挑戰。

男：　泰瑞莎，妳不是曾經到東京旅遊過好幾次嗎？也許妳可以給我一些建議。

女 1：我能夠做的還超乎你的預期！我的朋友在東京做房屋仲介，她的名片我放在家裡，星期一帶來給你。

正解 1. (C) 2. (D) 3. (B)

branch 分公司；分店；分行
quarter 季度
provide 提供
arrange 安排；準備
temporary 暫時的
accommodation 住處；艙位
challenge 艱難的事；挑戰

技巧 45 具有代表性或概括性含意的詞彙即為正解。

Q. What is the conversation mainly about?
這段對話主要與什麼有關？

Matthew, <u>are we ready for tomorrow's award ceremony?</u>
正解訊號
麥修，明天的頒獎典禮都準備好了嗎？

正解 Company event 公司活動

award ceremony 頒獎典禮

經常出題的概括性詞彙及具象詞彙 必背★

概括性詞彙	意思	具象詞彙
electronics、appliances 選2試2	家電產品	TV、radio、refrigerator
furniture	家具	table、chair、sofa
beverage	飲料	coffee、tea、juice
vehicle	車輛	car、taxi、bus、van
event	活動	anniversary、reception、award ceremony

應用本技巧的題目　　🎧 PART 3_13.mp3

offer an apology 道歉
request 要求；請求
refund 退款

1. What does the man suggest doing?
   (A) Offering an apology
   (B) Requesting a refund
   (C) Using public transportation
   選7試2
   (D) Rescheduling a client meeting
   選5試3

2. What does the woman want?
   (A) A menu
   (B) A beverage
   (C) A newspaper
   (D) A business card

錄音內容及解析

1. 男子建議做什麼？
   (A) 道歉　　　　　　　(B) 要求退款
   (C) 利用大眾運輸工具　(D) 變更與客戶開會的行程

far 遠的
plenty of 大量的

M: Thanks for the call. I was thinking, maybe it's best for us to just take the subway. Westbrook Station is not far from my house, and there's plenty of space to park. I could meet you there.　試3

男：謝謝你的來電。我剛正在想搭地鐵可能是我們最好的選擇。衛斯特布魯克站離我家不遠，停車位也很多，我們可以在那裡碰面。

2. 女子需要什麼？
   (A) 菜單　　　　　　　(B) 飲料
   (C) 報紙　　　　　　　(D) 名片

M: We've reserved a table near the window for your group. Let me show you the table.

W: OK. And I'd like to have some hot tea while I'm waiting.

男：我們已經為您們保留了窗邊的座位，我來幫您帶位。

女：好的，候餐時我想先喝點熱茶。

正解 1. (C) 2. (B)

技巧**46** 當考題詢問說話者某句話的言下之意時，答案就在前一句話中。

Q. What does the woman mean when she says, "I've never been there before"?

當女子說 "I've never been there before" 時，言下之意是什麼？

M: Can you stop by Dr. Hamilton's office tomorrow morning?

正解訊號

明天早上妳可以順道去漢米爾頓博士的辦公室一趟嗎？

W: Sure. But, I've never been there before.

當然沒問題，不過我沒有去過那裡。

正解 She wants to get some information. 她想獲取一些資訊。

應用本技巧的題目 Questions 1-2　　　　　　PART 3_14.mp3

1. What does the woman say is a problem?
   (A) A supplier did not send a
   　選5試2
   shipment.
   (B) A delivery truck broke down.
   (C) A product sells out quickly.
   (D) A sale event has ended.

2. What does the woman imply when she says, "I'll take care of that"?
   (A) The scanner did not recognize a sale price.
   (B) She will put an item back where it belongs.
   (C) There is more of a product in the stock room.
   (D) She will request larger shipments from a supplier.

supplier 供應商；提供者
quickly 快速地

recognize 認出；識別；認可
belong 屬於
stock room 倉庫

録音內容及解析

1. 女子提及的問題是什麼？
   (A) 供應商沒有出貨。
   (B) 送貨的卡車拋錨了。
   (C) 產品很快就賣完了。
   (D) 特賣活動結束了。

2. 當女子說 "I'll take care of that." 時，言下之意是什麼？
   (A) 掃描設備無法辨識折扣價格。
   (B) 她會將商品放回原位。
   (C) 倉庫裡有更多存貨。
   (D) 她會要求供應商提高供貨量。

W: I'm sorry, but we're all out of organic milk right now. We usually sell out of it by the afternoon.

M: Is that so? In that case, I think I'll go put back this box of cereal.

W: I'll take care of that. Would you like to pay by cash or credit?

女：很抱歉，目前有機牛乳全都賣完了。通常都是到下午就會賣完。

男：是嗎？這樣的話，那我去把這盒穀片放回架上好了。

女：我來處理就可以了。您要用現金還是信用卡結帳？

正解 1. (C) 2. (B)

organic 有機的
usually 通常；一般
take care of 照顧／負責處理～

技巧 **47.** 在表格類的題型中，備選答案及其相關資訊就能決定答案為何。22次

技巧 **48.** 在地圖與平面圖的題型中，場所介系詞片語就能決定答案為何。17次

---

tip!
聆聽時視線不能停留在選項上，要看著表格才行！

技巧 **47** 在表格類的題型中，備選答案及其相關資訊就能決定答案為何。

Floor	Room
4th	Cafeteria 題 1 選 2 試 3
3rd	Meeting Space
2nd	Conference Room 選 4 試 5
1st	Lobby

Q. Look at the graphic. Where will the speakers meet?
請看圖表。說話者們會在哪裡碰面？
(A) 4th floor 四樓
(B) 3rd floor 三樓
(C) 2nd floor 二樓
(D) 1st floor 一樓

M: Where should we meet?
我們要在哪裡碰面？
W: The lobby will be crowded around lunch time, so how about the
conference room? 正確訊號
中午的時候大廳會很擁擠，我們在會議室見怎麼樣？
M: Sounds good.
這個主意不錯。

正解 **(C) 2nd floor**

crowded 擠滿人群的

應用本技巧的題目 Questions 1-2　　　　　PART 3_15.mp3

Refrigerator Model	Storage Capacity (in cubic feet)
Sabina	18
Lottie	14
Marion	16
Amber	20

1. Why is the business holding a sale?
   (A) To celebrate an anniversary
   (B) To introduce a new brand
   (C) To promote a relocation
   <u>選 1 試 1</u>
   (D) To recognize a national holiday

2. Look at the graphic. Which model does the woman plan to buy?
   (A) Sabina
   (B) Lottie
   (C) Marion
   (D) Amber

celebrate 慶祝；祝賀
anniversary 週年紀念日
introduce 介紹；引進
promote 宣傳
relocation 遷移；搬遷
recognize 認出；認可；承認

PART 3

錄音內容及解析

冰箱型號	儲藏容量（立方英呎）
Sabina	18
Lottie	14
Marion	16
Amber	20

1. 該店為何舉辦特賣活動？
   (A) 為了週年慶
   (B) 為了介紹一個新品牌
   (C) 為了宣傳搬遷一事
   (D) 為了彰顯一個國定假日

2. 請看圖表。女子打算購買哪一種型號的冰箱？
   (A) Sabina
   (B) Lottie
   (C) Marion
   (D) Amber

W: Hi, I read in the newspaper that your store is having a big sale because you've <u>relocated</u> to the Lakewood <u>neighborhood</u>.
<u>試 2</u>

M: That's right. We are offering special deals all week.

W: I'm interested in purchasing a refrigerator.

M: May I recommend the Marion model? It has 16 cubic feet of storage space, and it's half off.

W: Hmm ... I'm not sure that will be large enough.

M: We've got one with 20 cubic feet of space.

W: <u>Perfect! I'll stop by the store later this week.</u>

女：嗨！我看報紙上寫說因為你們搬遷到萊克伍德附近，所以你們店在舉行大特賣。

男：沒錯，我們這一整週都有做商品特惠活動。

女：我想買一台冰箱。

男：我推薦您 Marion 型號的冰箱。它的儲藏容量有 16 立方英呎，而且現在是半價。

女：嗯……我不太確定這個容量夠不夠大。

男：我們也有儲藏容量 20 立方英呎的型號。

女：太棒了！我這星期晚點會再順道來賣場一趟。

relocate 遷移；搬遷
refrigerator 冰箱
storage 保管；儲藏
space 空間
enough 足夠的；充分的

正解 1. (C) 2. (D)

技巧**48** 在地圖與平面圖的題型中，場所介系詞片語就能決定答案為何。

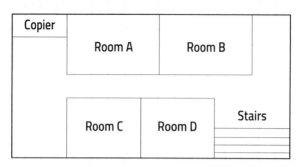

Q. Look at the graphic. Which room will the new staff use?
請看圖表。新進員工將使用幾號室？
(A) Room A A 號室
(B) Room B B 號室
(C) Room C C 號室
(D) Room D D 號室

M: Have you decided where the new staff will work? Room C is currently occupied.
選1
妳決定好新進員工要在哪裡工作了嗎？C 號室目前有人使用。

W: Right. How about one of the bigger rooms? Probably, the one near the photocopier since they handle jobs using the machine. 正解訊號
正1選1
沒錯。選一間空間大一點的怎麼樣？或許離影印機比較近的那一間，畢竟他們使用影印機工作。

正解 **(A) Room A**

經常出題的場所介系詞片語 必背★

場所介系詞片語	意思	場所介系詞片語	意思
next to	在～旁邊	close to 選1試4 near	在～附近；靠近～
across from opposite to	在～對面	on the left/right	在左邊／右邊
in the front row	在第一列／排	in the center/middle of	在～中央／中間

currently 現在
occupy 占（時間／空間）；占用
handle 操作；處理

應用本技巧的題目　　　　　　　　　🎧 PART 3_16.mp3

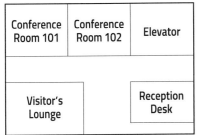

Conference Room 101	Conference Room 102	Elevator
Visitor's Lounge		Reception Desk

1. Look at the graphic. Where should the man wait for Rick Goldman?
   (A) At the <u>reception</u> desk
   <small>選1</small>
   (B) In the visitor's lounge
   (C) In Conference Room 101
   (D) In Conference Room 102

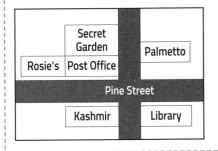

	Secret Garden	Palmetto
Rosie's	Post Office	
Pine Street		
	Kashmir	Library

2. Look at the graphic. Which business does the woman recommend?
   (A) Kashmir
   (B) Rosie's
   (C) Secret Garden
   (D) Palmetto

錄音內容及解析

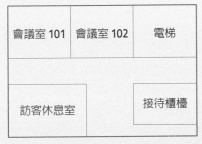

會議室 101	會議室 102	電梯
訪客休息室		接待櫃檯

1. 請看圖表。男子應於何處等候瑞克‧高德曼？
   (A) 接待櫃檯
   (B) 訪客休息室
   (C) 會議室 101
   (D) 會議室 102

W: I've <u>arranged</u> for a colleague to go over the contract with you instead.
<small>選4試5</small>

　His name is Rick Goldman. He's one of our department heads.

M: Okay. Should I come up to your office and ask for him once I arrive?

W: No, just check in at reception and have a seat <u>inside the room beside the elevator. Rick will come down and meet with you there.</u>

女：我已經另外安排一位同事和您一起審閱合約。他叫作瑞克‧高德曼，
　　是我們公司的其中一位主任。

男：好的。我一抵達就直接上樓到妳的辦公室找他嗎？

女：不，請至接待櫃檯登記，然後到電梯旁邊的房間裡稍坐一下。瑞克會
　　下樓到那個房間找你。

go over 審核；查看
instead 作為替代
department head 部門主管

PART 3

vegetarian 素食主義者
directly 直接地
give a try 嘗試

2. 請看圖表。女子推薦哪一間店？
(A) Kashmir
(B) Rosie's
(C) Secret Garden
(D) Palmetto

W: Great. How do you like working here so far?

M: A lot, but, um ... I'm not sure where to go to eat. I'm a vegetarian.

W: Well, on Pine Street directly across from the post office, there's a restaurant
試2
with several vegetarian options on the menu. You might give that a try.

女：很好。到目前為止，你喜歡在這裡工作嗎？

男：很喜歡。不過，嗯⋯⋯其實我不太清楚該去哪裡吃飯，因為我吃素。

女：嗯⋯⋯松木街上郵局正對面有間餐廳提供多種素食主義者可選擇的餐點，你可以去吃吃看。

正解 1. (D) 2. (A)

技巧 **49** 詢問職業、產業或場所的題型中若出現自我介紹的用語，即為正解訊號。

〔語音通話〕 說話者—This is 名字＋calling from＋產業／公司名
聽者—This message is for＋名字
〔語音訊息〕 You have reached＋名字／產業／公司名
試1
Thank you for calling＋名字／產業／公司名

Q. What kind of company does the speaker work for?
說話者在什麼業別工作？

Ms. Sally, this is Danny calling from Bella auto garage.
試21　　　　　試4　　　　正解訊號
莎莉小姐，我是貝拉汽車維修中心的丹尼。

正解 Car repair shop 汽車維修中心

應用本技巧的題目　　　　　　　　　　　PART 4_01.mp3

1. Who most likely is the speaker?
(A) A doctor
正1
(B) An instructor
(C) A receptionist
(D) An author

2. Where does the caller work?
(A) At the marketing department
(B) At the accounting department
(C) At the facility department
(D) At the Human Resources department　選3試5

錄音內容及解析

1. 說話者最有可能是什麼人？
(A) 醫生　　(B) 講師　　(C) 接待員　　(D) 作家

This is Hannah from Dr. McGreek's office. I'm calling to remind your 3 o'clock appointment with Dr. McGreek on Monday.　試1

我是麥葛瑞博士辦公室的漢娜，來電提醒您星期一的三點與麥葛瑞博士有約。

remind 提醒

PART 4

facility 設備；設施
personnel department
人事部
properly 適當地；正確
地

2. 撥打電話者是在哪裡工作？
(A) 行銷部　　(B) 會計部　　(C) 總務部　　(D) 人資部

Hi, this is a message for the facility manager. This is Joe Brown from the personnel department. I'm calling to let you know my printer has not been working properly since yesterday.　　試2

嗨，以下是要向總務部經理傳達的訊息。我是人事部的喬·布朗，來電告知您我的列表機從昨天開始就沒辦法正常運作。

正解 1. (C)　2. (D)

技巧50 詢問談話主題的題型中若出現 "I'm calling ..."、"I'd like to let you know ..."，即為正解訊號。

Q.　What is the purpose of the call?
　　這通電話的目的是什麼？

be supposed to 應該～；
預期～
be able to 能夠～
make it 成功；及時趕到

Hi, this is Jack. I'm calling because I have to change my appointment.
　　　　　　　　　　　　試1　　　　　　　正解訊號
I'm supposed to come in this afternoon, but I won't be able to make it.
　　試3

嗨，我是傑克。我必須更改會面時間，所以打電話過來。原本我應該今天下午過去，但我無法前往。

正解 To reschedule the appointment 更改約定會面的時間
　　　　選4試3

應用本技巧的題目　　　　　　　　　　　　　　　PART 4_02.mp3

passport 護照
verify 證明；核實
personal information
個人資料
ask for 要求～
assistance 協助
confirm 確認
arrangement 安排；準
備工作

banquet hall 宴會廳
catering service 外燴業
者

1.　What is the message about?
　　(A) Requesting a passport
　　(B) Verifying personal information
　　(C) Asking for assistance
　　　　　正2選3
　　(D) Confirming travel arrangements
　　　　　選9

2.　What kind of business is the speaker calling?
　　(A) A farm
　　(B) A banquet hall
　　(C) A catering service
　　　　　正1試1
　　(D) An event planner

錄音內容及解析

1.這則訊息與什麼有關？
(A) 申請護照
(B) 核對個人資料
(C) 請求協助
(D) 確認旅遊安排

Hello, Mr. Roberts. This is Zoe calling from Top Travel. I am calling to let you know that we have confirmed seats for you and your friend on Friday's flight to Madrid.

羅伯茲先生您好，我是頂尖旅遊的佐伊。來電通知您星期五前往馬德里的班機我們已經為您和您的朋友確保了機位。

2. 說話者正在打電話給什麼業者？
   (A) 農場
   (B) 宴會廳
   (C) 外燴服務
   (D) 活動企劃

Hi, I'm calling about food options for an event my company is going to hold
_{試7}
in Plymouth Park. An associate of mine recently attended an event that was catered by your business and he said that everything was delicious.

嗨，我們公司即將在普利茅斯公園舉辦活動，因此來電詢問餐點的選擇有哪些。我同事最近有參加過一場由貴公司提供外燴服務的活動，他說所有的餐點都很美味。

正解 1. (D) 2. (C)

option 選項；選擇（權）
associate 同事；（生意）夥伴
cater 提供飲食；承辦宴席
delicious 美味的

技巧51 提議或要求的題型中若出現 "**Please ...**"、"**I ask you ...**"、"**Could you ...**"、"**Let me know if ...**"，即為正解訊號。

Q. What does the <u>speaker ask</u> the listener to do?
   說話者要求聽者做什麼？

   Please <u>call me back</u> at 2334-8870 so that we can <u>reschedule</u> the meeting.
   _{試50　正解訊號}　　　　　　　　　　　_{試2}
   Thank you.
   煩請回電至 2334-8870，好讓我們重新約會議時間，謝謝。
   正解 Return a call 回電

▌tip!
頻出的提議／要求題型：
含有 ask、recommend、suggest、request、encourage 或 invite 等詞彙的這類考題，也經常出現在其他類型的談話內容中，而正確答案會在談話的後段出現！

應用本技巧的題目　　　　🎧　PART 4_03.mp3

1. What does the speaker ask the listener to do?
   (A) Contact a restaurant
   _{選3}
   (B) Meet a new colleague
   (C) Make dinner for a friend
   (D) Return a call
   _{正3}

2. What is the listener asked to do?
   (A) Provide contact information
   _{正1選3}
   (B) Make a new appointment
   (C) Change a menu option
   _{選2}
   (D) Look into seat availability

contact 聯絡
colleague 同事
return 回應；返回

make an appointment 敲定會面時間
look into 調查；研究
availability 可利用性；可獲得性

PART 4

ride 騎乘；搭乘

録音內容及解析

1. 說話者要求聽者做什麼？
(A) 聯繫餐廳
(B) 見新同事
(C) 為朋友做晚餐
(D) 回電

Lily and I will be driving to the restaurant together and there is room in my car if you would like a ride. <u>Please call on my mobile if you get this message.</u> Hope to see you tonight.

我會開車載莉莉一起前往餐廳，車裡還有位子，看你要不要搭我的車。聽到這則訊息，請回電至我的手機，希望今晚能見到你。

2. 聽者被要求做什麼？
(A) 提供聯絡資訊
(B) 約定新會面時間
(C) 變更菜單選項
(D) 打聽是否還有位子

include 包含
dietary restriction 飲食限制
instead of 作為～的替代

There's just one thing. My friend said that a lot of pork was included, but I'm concerned about dietary restrictions. <u>Please call me back at 555-3125 to let me know if you can provide vegetarian options instead of pork.</u>

我只有一件事想確認。我朋友說菜單裡有很多含有豬肉的料理，我擔心有些東西我不能吃，請回電至 555-3125 給我，告知是否能提供素食的選擇以取代豬肉料理。

正解 1. (D) 2. (C)

Unit 17 說明／公告事項題型

【大眾廣播的結構】廣播的目的－細節－要求事項
【公司公告的結構】公告或議案的主題－細節－要求事項

高出題率地圖

技巧 52. 機場或火車站：經常出現有關交通工具延遲或取消的考題。11次

技巧 53. 經常出現各種商店在進行特賣的相關考題。15次

技巧 54. 公司公告類的題型經常出現有關維修工程的考題。13次

技巧 **52** 機場或火車站：經常出現有關交通工具延遲或取消的考題。

Q. What is the **purpose** of this announcement? 這則廣播的目的是什麼？

Attention, passengers for Train 768 to Paddington Station. The train was
試5

originally scheduled to depart at Platform 2. But there will be 30 minutes
選2試3

delay due to a fallen tree on the railroad.
正2選7　　　　　正解訊號

搭乘 768 車次前往柏靈頓站列車的乘客請注意，原定從二月台出發的列車由於鐵道上發生樹木塌落事故，因此將延遲三十分鐘。

正解 To inform about train delays 為了通知列車誤點

passenger 乘客
originally 原本
depart 出發
delay 延遲
railroad 鐵路

應用本技巧的題目 Questions 1-2　　　🎧　PART 4_04.mp3

1. Where is the announcement probably taking place?
   (A) In an airport
   試3
   (B) On a tour bus
   (C) On an airplane
   (D) At a train station

2. What has caused delays?
   (A) Heavy traffic
   (B) Broken equipment
   (C) Inclement weather
   (D) Staff shortage

🔖 tip!
如果是問主題、身分或場所的題型，正確答案會在談話內容的頭一、兩句內出現，因此音檔一播放就必須集中注意力聆聽！

heavy traffic 交通壅塞
inclement weather 惡劣的天候
shortage 缺乏

錄音內容及解析

1. 這則廣播可能出現在什麼地方？
   (A) 在機場
   (B) 在觀光巴士上
   (C) 在飛機上
   (D) 在火車站

2. 是什麼原因導致誤點？
   (A) 交通堵塞
   (B) 設備故障
   (C) 天候惡劣
   (D) 人力不足

Attention, all passengers waiting to **board** Sun Jet flight 56 to Miami. We regret to announce that several of our flights have been rerouted to avoid heavy snowfall affecting the mid-western region of the country.

所有等候搭乘陽捷航空 56 號班機前往邁阿密的旅客請注意，很遺憾在此通知各位，為了避開影響中西部地區的暴雪，本公司數個航班已變更航線。

board 搭乘
regret 遺憾；懊悔
reroute 變更路線
avoid 避免
heavy snowfall 暴雪
affect 影響
region 地區

正解 1. (A) 2. (C)

customer 顧客；客戶
fantastic 極好的
bargain 特價商品；便宜貨

技巧 **53** 經常出現各種商店在進行特賣的相關考題。

Q. What is the purpose of the announcement?
這則廣播的目的是什麼？

Attention all Retro Fashion customers. This weekend, we are having our second anniversary sale with fantastic bargains in every department.
　　　　正解訊號　　　　　　　　　　　　　　　　　　　　　　試3
Retro Fashion 的顧客請注意，本週末 Retro Fashion 各門市將舉行兩週年紀念特賣活動，提供超棒的優惠價格給各位。

正解 To announce a special discount 為了公告特惠折扣
正2選10試4

appliance 器具；設備
grocery 食材；雜貨

last 持續

應用本技巧的題目 Questions 1-2　　🎧　PART 4_05.mp3

1. What kind of business does the speaker most likely work for?
   (A) A restaurant
   (B) An appliance store
   (C) A grocery store
   (D) A flower shop

2. How long will the sale last?
   (A) For one week
   (B) For two weeks
   (C) For three days
   (D) For two days

錄音內容及解析

1. 說話者最有可能在什麼業別工作？
   (A) 餐廳
   (B) 家電賣場
   (C) 雜貨店
   (D) 花店

2. 特賣活動會進行多久？
   (A) 一週
   (B) 兩週
   (C) 三天
   (D) 兩天

produce 產品；農產品
grapefruit 葡萄柚
fresh 新鮮的
ground 磨碎的
available 可利用的；可獲得的；有空的

Attention all shoppers. We have some great deals for you in the store. In the produce section, we're offering delicious yellow and red grapefruit at a bargain price of two for a dollar. Over in the meat department, fresh ground beef is at the low, low price of 99 cents a pound. These offers are available only today and tomorrow.

買家們請注意，本店提供部分超值優惠商品，農產品區的美味黃皮紅肉葡萄柚特價兩顆一美元，肉品區的新鮮牛絞肉給您破盤價，一磅只賣 99 美分。以上優惠僅限今明兩天。

正解 1. (C) 2. (D)

技巧**54** 公司公告類的題型經常出現有關維修工程的考題。

Q. What is the announcement about?

這則公告與什麼有關？

May I have your attention, please? This is Mark Brian, the Maintenance

試2

manager. I have an important announcement for all employees. The

正2選3試8

interior work on the lobby will start tomorrow.

正解訊號

各位請注意，我是維修部的經理馬克‧布萊恩，這邊有重要事項要向
全體職員宣布，明天起大廳將開始進行裝潢工程。

正解 A building remodeling work 建物整修施工

正1選1試1

應用本技巧的題目 Questions 1-2 PART 4_06.mp3

1. What is the main topic of the talk?
   (A) Offering scholarships
   (B) Renovating a school
   正2選3試3
   (C) Planning a class reunion
   (D) Recruiting qualified teachers

2. What problem does the speaker mention?
   (A) Construction contract
   正4選6試8
   (B) Classroom space
   (C) Scheduling conflicts
   選3試2
   (D) Delayed permits

scholarship 獎學金
class reunion 同學會
qualified 有資格的；合格的

permit 許可證

錄音內容及解析

1. 這段談話的主題是什麼？
   (A) 提供獎學金
   (B) 翻修校園
   (C) 策劃同學會
   (D) 招募合格教師

2. 說話者提及什麼問題？
   (A) 建設合約
   (B) 教室空間
   (C) 行程撞期
   (D) 許可延遲

Thanks for coming to this meeting of the Westbury Education Board. You have all heard about the plan to renovate our town's elementary school. We want to do all the work over the summer while school is out. The problem is, the permits for the construction work are taking longer than we expected to process.

感謝蒞臨本次韋斯特伯里教育委員會的會議，各位都有聽說關於我們村裡
小學翻新計畫的事了，本校想要在暑假期間進行所有工程，但問題是申請
工程許可所需的時間比我們預期的還要久。

正解 1. (B) 2. (D)

PART 4

技巧 **55** 會出現詢問交通堵塞原因的考題。

塞車＋... due to / because of ＋堵塞的事由
　　　　　試2　　　　　　試3

Q1. What's causing traffic delays?

交通堵塞的原因是什麼？

There is a delay on the highway. Two lanes of the highway 15 have been
　　　　　　　　　　　　　　　　選2試1

closed due to the road repair.
正1選2試6　　　　正解訊號

由於 15 號高速公路正在進行路面維修工程，因而封閉了其中兩線車道，導致目前車多壅塞。

正解 A road construction 道路建設

traffic 交通；車流量
repair 修理；修補
construction 建設；建築

tip!
在詢問交通堵塞原因的題型當中，答案是「道路工程」的機率很高！

應用本技巧的題目　　　　　　　　　　　PART 4_07.mp3

1. What caused the problem?
   (A) A road repair
   (B) A bad weather
   　　正1選1
   (C) An accident
   (D) An event

2. What is causing the problem?
   (A) Maintenance work
   (B) Car accidents
   (C) City events
   (D) Bad weather

錄音內容及解析

1. 是什麼原因導致問題發生？
   (A) 修路工程
   (B) 天候惡劣
   (C) 交通事故
   (D) 活動

Good afternoon everyone, I'm Jeff Marshall with your traffic report. There
is heavy traffic for several hours now due to an accident that occurred this
morning on King's Cross Intersection.

大家午安，我是傑夫‧馬歇爾，為您進行路況報導。由於今天上午在國王交叉路口發生了一起交通事故，目前車流嚴重回堵已持續了好幾個小時。

accident 意外；事故
occur 發生；出現
intersection 十字路口

2. 是什麼原因導致問題發生？
(A) 維修工程
(B) 車輛事故
(C) 城市活動
(D) 天候惡劣

Good morning. This is Liz Clarkson with your hourly traffic update. We are
_{選1}
experiencing more serious backups than usual today. Especially if you're
_{試1}
driving southbound on highway 60, you should be ready for traffic congestion
because a construction work is being done on two of the lanes.
_{選1試1}

congestion 擁擠

早安，我是莉姿‧克拉克森，為您播報整點即時交通路況。我們今天正在經歷比往常還要嚴重的交通堵塞，尤其是 60 號高速公路南下方向的駕駛朋友們，因為有兩線車道正在進行維修工程，您要有車流回堵的心理準備。

正解 1. (C) 2. (A)

技巧 **56** 會出現與特定時間天候狀態有關的考題。

Q1. What will the weather be like this week?
_{正2選6試8}

這星期的天氣怎麼樣？

You can put your heavy clothes away for a while because we won't be seeing anymore cold weather for the rest of the week. Starting this
_{試2}   _{試5}
afternoon, we can expect to enjoy some warm and sunny weather.
_{試3}   _{正解訊號}

本週接下來幾天的天氣不會再變冷，可以暫時將厚重的衣物收納起來。預計從今天下午開始，就會是溫暖和煦的天氣了。

正解 It will be warm and sunny. 將會是溫暖而晴朗的天氣。

應用本技巧的題目 Questions 1-2 🎧 PART 4_08.mp3

1. When is it expected to rain?
   (A) This morning
   (B) This afternoon
   (C) Tomorrow morning
   (D) Tomorrow evening

2. What kind of weather is expected on Saturday?
   (A) Cold and windy
   (B) Warm and foggy
   (C) Warm and drizzling
   (D) Hot and sunny

PART 4

錄音內容及解析

1. 預測什麼時候會下雨？
   - (A) 今天上午
   - (B) 今天下午
   - (C) 明天上午
   - (D) 明天晚上

2. 星期六預測會是什麼樣的天氣？
   - (A) 風大寒冷
   - (B) 溫暖起霧
   - (C) 溫暖微雨
   - (D) 晴朗炎熱

Now, let's check the weather for this week, we can expect lots of sunshine today in the high 20's but this evening, it should cool down a bit. And tomorrow, a light drizzle in the evening with temperatures in the low 20's. Thursday and Friday we
試 1
should see a fair bit of sunny spell. Saturday, we expect high temperatures combined with sunshine so please go outdoors and enjoy yourself while you can.

現在我們來看一下本週的天氣預報，今天白天預估會十分晴朗，並且有 20 度以上的高溫，但入夜後氣溫會稍微變涼。明天晚上氣溫預估會降到 20 度以下，還會下一點毛毛雨。星期四和星期五，陽光應該會露臉一段時間。星期六則預計會是高溫晴朗的天氣，請趁著好天氣走出戶外，享受美好時光。

正解 1. (D) 2. (D)

drizzle（下）毛毛雨
temperature 溫度

技巧57 依談話類型的不同，會出現不同要求事項的考題。

Q1. What advice does the speaker give?
   說話者提供了什麼建議？

Even though the road workers have been working several hours to clean
選 2
up the mess, it looks like the congestion won't finish until this afternoon.
試 7
For those of you who intend to go this way, I advise you to take an alternate route.   正解訊號
試 1

儘管道路工程人員已經花了好幾個小時來清理現場的一片狼藉，但交通堵塞的情形看來要等到今天下午才能夠解除。建議打算走這條路的駕駛朋友們改走替代路線。

正解 Use a different road 利用其他道路

tip!
〔路況報導〕
假使交通阻塞→請繞道
〔天氣預報〕
倘若晴朗→請走出戶外
倘若寒冷→請穿保暖一點
倘若會降雨→請攜帶雨具

road 道路
clean up 打掃；清理
advise 勸告
alternate 供選擇的；供替換的

應用本技巧的題目 Questions 1-2   🎧 PART 4_09.mp3

1. What are the listeners advised to do?
   - (A) Stay indoors
   - (B) Take a walk
   - (C) Cover flowers and plants
   - (D) Wear warm clothes

2. What will the listeners hear next?
   - (A) Local news
   - (B) Advertisements
   - (C) A discussion program
   - (D) A music program

録音內容及解析

1. 聽眾被建議做什麼？
 (A) 待在室內
 (B) 去散個步
 (C) 覆蓋花朵及植物
 (D) 穿得保暖一點

2. 聽眾接下來會聽到什麼？
 (A) 地方新聞
 (B) 廣告
 (C) 談話性節目
 (D) 音樂節目

But the bad news is this change in the weather will only last for a few days as the temperature will rise again. Weather experts are advising people to stay out of
正1試1
the heat if possible. Stay tuned for our updated news coming up right after this commercial break.

但壞消息是這樣的天氣變化僅會持續短短幾天，接下來氣溫又會再度升高。氣象專家建議民眾儘可能避免在這種炎熱天氣之下活動。我們先進一段廣告，廣告過後緊接的是最新消息，請繼續鎖定收聽。

正解 1. (A) 2. (B)

rise 增加；提升；上漲
expert 專家
commercial 商業的

PART 4

廣告 / 介紹文題型

【廣告文的結構】廣告商品或企業介紹─提及特性、優點─誘導購買─購買方式或優惠方案說明
【介紹文的結構】問候─說明本次要介紹的人物─人物經歷與詳細事項─該人物接下來要做的事

高出題率地圖

技巧 **58.** 會出現詢問該段內容是什麼廣告的考題。11次
技巧 **59.** 有些考題會詢問該廣告商品或企業的特性、優點。16次
技巧 **60.** 有些考題會詢問出現該談話的場所在哪裡或詢問活動目的為何。32次

技巧 58 會出現詢問該段內容是什麼廣告的考題。

Q1. What is the advertisement about?

這則廣告與什麼有關？

Do you travel internationally? Are you looking for ways to communicate with your customers in their native language? The Ashton Institute can help. You can learn French, Mandarin, Japanese, and more with the help of our experienced instructors.　　　正解訊號

選3試1

您會到海外出差嗎？您正在想方設法用客戶的母語和他們溝通嗎？讓艾希頓機構助您一臂之力！我們經驗豐富的講師群能協助您學習法語、漢語、日語以及更多其他語言。

正解 Some language classes 語言課程

▌tip!

詢問是何種廣告的題型中若出現 "Are you looking for ..."、"Would you like to ..."，即為正解訊號。

internationally 在國際間
communicate 溝通
native language 母語
instructor 教練；講師

應用本技巧的題目 Questions 1-2　　　　　PART 4_10.mp3

1. What is Green Table?
   (A) A farmers' association
   (B) A meal plan service
   (C) A grocery store
   (D) A restaurant

2. What does the speaker mean when she says, "No one has time for that"?
   (A) A task requires too much time and effort.
   (B) A team needs to recruit more members.　選1
   (C) An application deadline has passed.　選8
   (D) An event has been canceled.

錄音內容及解析

1. Green Table 是什麼？
   (A) 農會
   (B) 餐飲服務業者
   (C) 雜貨店
   (D) 餐廳

2. 當說話者說 "No one has time for that!" 時，言下之意是什麼？
   (A) 任務需要花費太多的時間和心力去做。
   (B) 組內必須招募更多成員才行。
   (C) 申請的截止期限已經過了。
   (D) 活動已經被取消了。

Do you wish you could have fresh, home-cooked meals on a daily basis? Normally that requires planning, grocery shopping, food prep, looking up recipes ... *No one has time for that*! With Green Table, you can select from a variety of different meal plans. We will select a recipe and deliver all of the ingredients to your doorstep.

選1試2

你希望每天都能享用新鮮的家庭料理嗎？一般而言，那必須先擬定菜單，然後出門採買、備料、找食譜……，沒人有這種閒工夫的！只要有「綠餐桌」，你就能享有多樣化的菜色選擇，我們會選定食譜，然後將一切所需食材配送到你家門口。

正解 1. (B) 2. (A)

normally 通常；一般地
select 選擇
variety 多樣化；變化
recipe 食譜；料理方法
ingredient（食品的）成分；材料

技巧**59** 有些考題會詢問該廣告商品或企業的特性、優點。

Q1. According to this advertisement, why do customers like this business?

根據這則廣告，顧客為什麼喜歡這間企業？

We are globally loved by our customers due not only to our good location but also to our top level of customer services.

正解訊號　　　　　　選6試3

我們之所以廣受全球顧客的喜愛，不僅是因為我們擁有好的據點，還有我們頂級的客戶服務。

正解 It provides high-quality service. 其提供優質服務。

應用本技巧的題目 Questions 1-2　　　　🎧 PART 4_11.mp3

1. What is being advertised?

題4

(A) A kitchen appliance

選2

(B) A power tool
(C) A software program
(D) A smartphone app

2. What does the speaker highlight about the product?

(A) Its lightweight design
(B) Its low price
(C) Its generous warranty

選6試1

(D) Its long-lasting battery

錄音內容及解析

1. 這是什麼廣告？
(A) 廚房用具
(B) 電動工具
(C) 軟體程式
(D) 手機應用程式

2. 關於此產品，說話者強調什麼？
(A) 輕巧的設計
(B) 低廉的價格
(C) 充裕的保固期
(D) 續航力強的電池

When you're working on repairs at your home, you need the right tools to get the job done. The 6S cordless drill from Mayer Electronics is the perfect solution. Its battery lasts for four hours, much longer than many other models on the market.

tool 工具；器具
cordless 無線的

當你在家中修理某些東西的時候，你需要對的工具來完成工作。美亞電子出品的 6S 無線電鑽是你最理想的選擇，電池可持續使用四小時，續航力比許多市面上其他型號的產品還要優秀得多。

正解 1. (B) 2. (D)

技巧60 有些考題會詢問出現該談話的場所在哪裡或詢問活動目的為何。

Q1. What is the purpose of the event?
活動的目的是什麼？

正解訊號
Good evening, everyone, and thanks for being here. We're here to welcome the newest member of our team, Evelyn Simmons. She is joining us from Upton Incorporated, where she served as the marketing director for five years.　試2

各位晚安，感謝大家的蒞臨。我們聚在此地是為了歡迎我們組內的新進成員伊芙琳·席夢思。她過去五年在厄普頓公司擔任行銷部主任一職，現在離開前公司加入我們。

正解 To introduce a new employee 為了介紹新員工

應用本技巧的題目 Questions 1-2　　　　　　　PART 4_12.mp3

1. What is the purpose of this talk?
   (A) To announce a retirement
   (B) To introduce new rules
   (C) To announce a promotion
   (D) To introduce a new staff member

2. What will Ethan probably do next?
   (A) He will give a talk.
   (B) He will applaud.
   (C) He will serve dinner.
   (D) He will receive an award.

錄音內容及解析

1. 這段談話的目的是什麼？
   (A) 為了宣布退休
   (B) 為了介紹新規定
   (C) 為了宣布升遷
   (D) 為了介紹新進職員

2. 伊森接下來可能會做什麼？
   (A) 他將發表一段談話。
   (B) 他將鼓掌喝采。
   (C) 他將為大家上晚餐。
   (D) 他將獲得一個獎項。

Hello everyone, I'm glad you could all make it to this meeting. I'm very happy to introduce Ethan Hull, the new chosen director of design team. I will hand the microphone over Ethan now. He's going to talk to us about his vision for our company. Please join me in welcoming Mr. Ethan Hull.

哈囉！非常高興你們都能來參加這次會議，很開心能夠向各位介紹設計團隊這次新推選出來的伊森·赫爾組長，現在我就把麥克風交給伊森，他將分享自己對公司所抱持的願景，請大家和我一同歡迎伊森·赫爾先生。

正解 1. (D) 2. (A)

視覺資料相關／說話者意圖題型

"Look at the graphic." 開頭的題目必須找出符合視覺資料的敘述。

溫習紀錄

高出題率地圖

技巧 **61.** 在出現圖表或示意圖的題型當中，「最高級」的敘述是常見正確選項。6次
技巧 **62.** 在出現圖表或示意圖的題型當中，備選答案與其他資訊就能決定答案。5次
技巧 **63.** 當考題詢問說話者該句話言下之意為何時，答案就在其前一句話當中。36次

PART 4

技巧 **61** 在出現圖表或示意圖的題型當中，「最高級」的敘述是常見正確選項。

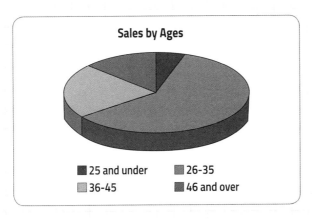

Sales by Ages

■ 25 and under ■ 26-35
□ 36-45 ■ 46 and over

Q1. Look at the graphic. Which age group does the speaker suggest focusing on?

請看圖表。說話者建議聚焦在哪個年齡層？
(A) 25 years old and under 25 歲及 25 歲以下
(B) 26 to 35 years old 26～35 歲
(C) 36 to 45 years old 36～45 歲
(D) 46 years old and over 46 歲及 46 歲以上

So, here are the results for last quarter's travel magazine sales. Now, what I'd like to do—I mean, to discuss—is, how we can improve sales to our least selling groups.　　　　　　　　　　正解訊號

因此，這就是上一季的旅遊雜誌銷售成果，我現在想做的是……我的意思是我想討論的是我們要怎麼做才能針對銷量最低迷的年齡層來提升銷售量。

正解 (A)

tip!
"The most/least …" 或 "The highest/lowest …" 等最高級的用法很重要！

result 結果；成果
magazine 雜誌
discuss 討論

應用本技巧的題目 Questions 1-2 PART 4_13.mp3

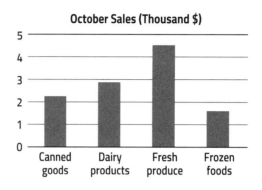

1. What kind of business does the speaker work at?
   題1試1
   (A) A dairy farm
   (B) A grocery store
   (C) A food cannery
   (D) A market research firm

2. Look at the graphic. According to the speaker, which section will be expanded?
   選5試2
   (A) Canned goods
   (B) Dairy products
   (C) Fresh produce
   (D) Frozen foods

錄音內容及解析

1. 說話者在什麼產業工作？
   (A) 酪農業
   (B) 雜貨店
   (C) 罐頭食品工廠
   (D) 市場調查公司

2. 請看圖表。根據說話者所言，哪個分區將會被擴大？
   (A) 罐頭製品
   (B) 乳製品
   (C) 新鮮農產品
   (D) 冷凍食品

Upon reviewing our grocery store's sales figures from last month, I found that our top-selling category made over $4,000 in profits. That's great news. I think we
選2試2
can increase that number in the upcoming months. We can do so by expanding the most profitable section.
試1

仔細看完我們雜貨店上個月的銷售額之後，我發現銷售量最好的類別創造了超過四千美元的收益。這是個好消息，我認為接下來的幾個月透過擴大收益最好的區塊就能讓這個數據更上一層樓。

正解 1. (B) 2. (C)

figure 數字
profit 利潤；盈利
increase 增加
upcoming 即將來臨的
expand 擴展
profitable 有利的；有益的

技巧**62** 在出現圖表或示意圖的題型當中，備選答案與其他資訊就能決定答案。

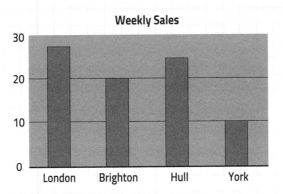

Weekly Sales

Q1. Look at the graphic. In which city is the company's most profitable location?

請看圖表。該公司在哪個城市獲益最多？

(A) London 倫敦
(B) Brighton 布萊頓
(C) Hull 赫爾
(D) York 約克

If you look at it, this dealership with <u>sales of only 20 vehicles per week is actually our most profitable one.</u>　　　　正解訊號

您看了就知道，一週只賣二十台的這個經銷門市，其實是我們獲利最好的點。

正解 **(B)**

■tip!
聆聽時視線不能停留在四選項上，要看著圖表才行！

dealership 經銷店；經銷權
vehicle 車輛；（陸上）交通工具

PART 4

應用本技巧的題目 Questions 1-2　　　🎧　　PART 4_14.mp3

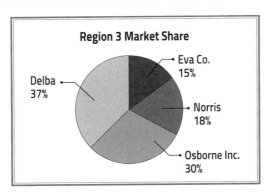

Region 3 Market Share

Eva Co. 15%
Delba 37%
Norris 18%
Osborne Inc. 30%

1. Why did Mr. Renner travel to Philadelphia?
   (A) To participate in a negotiation
       選1試1
   (B) To tour a headquarters site
       選1
   (C) To present a new product
   (D) To attend an industry conference
       選3試4

2. Look at the graphic. Which company may be purchased soon?
   (A) Eva Co.
   (B) Norris
   (C) Osborne Inc.
   (D) Delba

録音內容及解析

1. 雷納先生為什麼去了一趟費城？
   (A) 為了參與協商
   (B) 為了巡視總公司用地
   (C) 為了介紹新產品
   (D) 為了出席產業會議

2. 請看圖表。哪一家公司可能即將被收購？
   (A) 艾瓦公司
   (B) 諾里斯
   (C) 奧斯本公司
   (D) 德爾巴

Troy Renner just got back from Philadelphia, where he was negotiating an acquisition deal with one of our competitors. It's not finalized yet, but if it goes through, we'll benefit from that company's eighteen-percent share of the market in Region 3. I'll keep you updated as things unfold.

特洛伊‧雷納先生剛從費城回來，他去那裡協商我們其中一個競爭企業的收購交易事宜。雖然事情尚未談妥，但順利的話，我們將受益於那家公司在第三區所占有的 18％ 市場占有率。一有最新發展，我會隨時向各位報告。

正解 1. (A) 2. (B)

技巧 63 當考題詢問說話者該句話言下之意為何時，答案就在其前一句話當中。

Q1. What does the speaker imply when she says, "This is a critical time for us"?

當說話者說 "This is a critical time for us." 時，言下之意是什麼？

As department managers, I'm sure you have some advice that may be helpful, so I'd like you to email me any ideas you may have. *This is a critical*
選 1 試 1   正解訊號
time for us.

各位身為部門經理，想必都有一些具有建設性的建言。因此，我希望你們可以把任何你們能想到的點子用電子郵件告訴我，畢竟現在這個時期對我們來說至關緊要。

正解 She wants all listeners to provide suggestions. 她希望所有聽者都能提出建言。

---

negotiate 談判；協商
acquisition 收購；取得
competitor 競爭者；對手
finalize 完成；結束
benefit 利益；好處

critical 關鍵性的；危急的

suggestion 建議；提議

應用本技巧的題目 Questions 1-2 PART 4_15.mp3

1. What kind of business does the speaker work at?
   (A) A university
   (B) A pharmacy
   (C) A medical clinic
   選3
   (D) A research laboratory
   選3

2. What does the speaker imply when he says, "we might not get to you by your appointment time"?
   (A) He needs more staff members.
   (B) He asks the listeners to be patient.
   (C) He cannot accept any more people.
   (D) He recommends returning at a later date.

錄音內容及解析

1. 說話者在什麼產業工作？
   (A) 大學
   (B) 藥局
   (C) 醫療診所
   (D) 研究實驗室

2. 當說話者說 "we might not get to you by your appointment time" 時，言下之意是什麼？
   (A) 他需要更多工作人員。
   (B) 他拜託聽者要有耐心。
   (C) 他無法再接收更多人了。
   (D) 他建議聽者日後再來。

May I have your attention, please? Thank you for visiting Maple Health Clinic this morning. As you can see, there are quite a few of you here for regular health checkups. We're going to do our best to process you all quickly and efficiently. *However, we might not get to you by your appointment time.*

麻煩各位聽我說一下。感謝大家在今天上午來到楓葉保健診所。如各位所見，在場有相當多人是為了做定期健康檢查而來的。我們將竭盡所能為各位進行迅速而有效率的檢查，但還是有可能無法在您預約的時間準時為您服務。

正解 1. (C) 2. (B)

quite 相當；頗
regular 固定的；經常性的
checkup 健康檢查
process 處理；辦理

奇蹟筆記書
多益 700+
急速奪分祕技

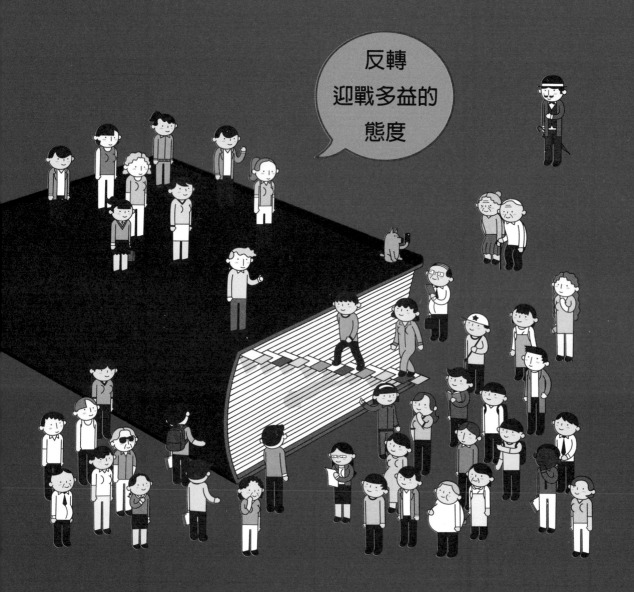

RC
PART 5-7

高出題率地圖

技巧 **1.** 冠詞與介系詞之間要放名詞。7次
技巧 **2.** 所有格之後要放名詞。4次
技巧 **3.** 形容詞之後要放名詞。21次
技巧 **4.** 人物名詞之前必須有冠詞或本身是複數形式，才有可能是正確答案。5次
技巧 **5.** 不可數名詞之前不能加 a / an，也不可採用複數形式。3次

be responsible for 負責～
distribution 分發
goods 商品；貨物
seaport 海港（城市）

技巧**1** 冠詞與介系詞之間要放名詞。

Highland Trucking is responsible for the distribution of goods that arrive at the seaport.
　　　　　　　　　　　　　　　　　　　　　　冠詞　名詞 正3　介系詞
高地貨運負責抵達此海港的商品物流。

① 冠詞的種類：a / an / the
② 名詞的型態 必背★

🔖 tip!
帶有例外字尾的名詞
會出現在考題中。
字尾為 -tive 或 -al 等
的形容詞，實際上也
可以作為名詞使用的
詞彙：

• representative
　正1題4
　具代表性的；代表
• alternative
　替代的；替代方案
• objective
　客觀的；目標
• potential
　正1題4選4
　潛在的；潛力
• original
　題3
　原先的；原作

字尾	例字	字尾	例字
-tion -sion	distribution 分配；散發 permission 許可；允許 正1題1選2	-er -or	employer 雇主 supervisor 監督者；上司 題4選1
-ance -ence	assistance 協助 difference 差異	-ment	agreement 協定；協議 正1選3 development 開發 正1題8
-sure -dure	closure 關店；關閉 procedure 手續；程序	-ness -age	decisiveness 果斷 storage 儲藏 正1題8
-ty -cy	productivity 生產率 題2 agency 代理商、代理機構	-ist	technologist 科學技術人員
-ant -cian	applicant 申請人 題2 politician 政治人物	-ee	attendee 出席者；參加者 題2

應用本技巧的題目

Because of the _____ of land for farming, residents of the island rely on imported goods.
(A) shorter　　(B) shortest　　(C) shortage　　(D) shortening

由於務農所需的土地匱乏，因此這個島上的居民依賴進口商品。
正解 (C)

farming 農業
resident 居民
　題2
rely on 依靠～
imported goods 進口商品
shortage 不足；短缺
　題1選1

技巧 2 所有格之後要放名詞。

Your donation is always welcome. 歡迎您隨時捐贈。
　所有格　　名詞

donation 捐贈

　① 所有格人稱代名詞：my、your、his、her、its、our、their
　② 一般名詞或固有名詞的所有格：名詞＋'s（例如：manager's、Ms. Allen's）
　③「所有格＋ own」或「所有格＋形容詞」之後的空格也應是名詞。

應用本技巧的題目

Critics expect that Ms. Hilton's _____ will be recognized at the next awards ceremony.
(A) performs　　(B) performed　　(C) performing　　(D) performance

評論家們預測希爾頓女士的表演將會在下一次頒獎典禮獲得肯定。
正解 (D)

perform 演出
performance 表演
　　題4

技巧 3 形容詞之後要放名詞。

形容詞扮演修飾名詞的角色。

　① 當形容詞前面有冠詞或所有格時：

The successful candidates will start to work on July 1.
定冠詞　形容詞　　名詞 題6
獲選的求職者將於七月一日起開始上班。

successful candidate
獲選的應徵者／候選人

　② 當形容詞前面沒有冠詞或所有格時：

AT Motors offers competitive salaries.
　　　　　　　　形容詞　　名詞
AT 汽車提供具有競爭力的薪資。

competitive
　正 2 題 1
競爭的；具有競爭力的
salary 薪水
　　題3

多益考古題當中常見的「形容詞＋名詞」好拍檔 必背★

complete descriptions 完整的描述 正1題9選3	pragmatic solution 務實的解決方案 題1選1
successful resolution 成功的決議	competitive market 競爭市場
considerable increase 大幅的增加 正2題16	collective effort 集體努力 題2

應用本技巧的題目

Since the ads began airing, Panther Footwear has enjoyed significant _____ .
(A) grows　　(B) to grow　　(C) growth　　(D) grown

自從廣告開始播出之後，黑豹鞋履就有了顯著的成長。
正解 (C)

air 廣播；播送
significant 重大的；顯著的

PART 5

apply 適用；起作用
policy 政策

editor 編輯

▌tip!
如果人物名詞與事物
／抽象名詞同時出現
在選項中，正確區別
它們則成為考點。

技巧 **4** 人物名詞之前必須有冠詞或本身是複數形式，才有可能是正確答案。

The company applied the vacation policy to interns.
　　　　　　　　　　　　　　　　　　　　　無冠詞 / intern 的複數形 題3

這家公司的休假制度適用於實習員工。

Any articles will be reviewed by the editor.
　　　　　　　　　　　　　　　　冠詞 單數形 題3

所有文章都會經由編輯審閱。

人物名詞──事物／抽象名詞 必背★

an applicant / applicants 申請人──**application** 申請（書）
　　　　　　　　　　　　　　　　　　　題7選2
a founder / founders 創辦人──foundation 建立；基礎
an investor / investors 投資人──investment 投資
an analyst / analysts 分析師──**analysis** 分析
　　題3　　　　　　　　　　正1題1
an assistant / assistants 助理──assistance 援助；協助
　　　題4
a resident / residents 居民──residence 住宅；居住
a user / users 使用者──use / usage 使用
　　題3　　　　　　　　　題2
an operator / operators 經營者──operation 營運
a contributor / contributors 貢獻者；捐贈者──**contribution** 貢獻；捐贈
　　　正1　　　　　　　　　　　　　　　　　　　正1
a supervisor / supervisors 督導；管理人──supervision 監督；管理
a negotiator / negotiators 協商者；交涉者──**negotiation** 協商；交涉
　　　　　　　　　　　　　　　　　　　　題2
an architect / architects 建築師──architecture 建築物
　　題2
a representative / representatives 代表；代理人──representation 代表
a distributor / distributors 分銷商──distribution 分配
a journalist / journalists 記者──a journal / journals 雜誌；期刊
──journalism 新聞工作；新聞業
an employer / employers 雇主；老闆──an employee / employees 職員；員工
──employment 雇用　　　　　　　題46
　　　題3
an attendant / attendants 侍者──an attendee / attendees 出席者
──attendance 出席；出席人數　　題2

應用本技巧的題目

_____ working at the information booth offer assistance to event attendees.
(A) Volunteered　　(B) Volunteering　　(C) Volunteers　　(D) Volunteer

在詢問處服務的志工們為參加活動的人提供協助。
正解 (C)

volunteer
正1
志願者；自願做／無
償做

技巧 **5** 不可數名詞之前不能加 **a / an**，也不可採用複數形式。

Mr. Hans is looking for <u>employment</u> in New York City.
     不可數名詞（an employment 或 employments 為誤）
漢斯先生正在紐約市找工作。

employment 工作；雇用

📑 **tip!**
會出現測驗區分不可數名詞與可數名詞的考題。

1 可數名詞 **vs** 不可數名詞　必背★

可數 名詞	〈正確用法〉－ **a / an / the /** 所有格＋可數名詞 　　　　　　－複數形式：可數名詞～**s /** ～**es** 〈經常出題的可數名詞〉**a refund / refunds** 退款 **the price / prices** 價格、**a discount / discounts** 折扣 　　_{題12} **the rate / rates** 費用、**a regulation / regulations** 規定 　　_{題5}　　　　　　　_{正1題2選1} **an instruction / instructions** 指示；使用說明 　　_{正1題1選1} **a request / requests** 要求、**a rule / rules** 規則 　　_{正3題8選1}
不可數 名詞	〈正確用法〉－ **the /** 所有格＋不可數名詞 　　　　　　－不可數名詞可單獨使用 〈經常出題的不可數名詞〉**advice** 建議、**access** 接近；使用 　　　　　　　　　　　_{題4選1}　　　_{正1題4} **information** 資訊、**notice** 通知、**clothing** 衣服、**consent** 同意 　_{題6}　　　_{正1題2} **equipment** 設備、**luggage / baggage** 行李、**news** 新聞；消息 　_{題9}　　　　_{題2}

2 區分含意或型態相近的可數名詞與不可數名詞

空格前若有冠詞或所有格，則可數名詞為正解；若沒有，則不可數名詞為正解。

可數名詞		不可數名詞
product / item / goods 產品；商品	－	**merchandise** 商品 　_{題4選1}
approach 接近；方法		
permit 許可證 _{題1選2}	－	**access** 接近；使用
	－	**permission** 許可；允許
account 帳戶；帳號 _{題1選2}	－	**accounting** 會計 　_{題3}

應用本技巧的題目

The brand manager gave _____ to post ads on social media.
(A) permit　　(B) permits　　(C) permitted　　(D) permission

該品牌經理已批准在社群媒體上張貼廣告。
正解 (D)

post 張貼；（在網路上）發布訊息
ad 廣告
permit 許可證
permission 許可；允許

PART 5

高出題率地圖

技巧 6. 動詞前面選主格；及物動詞或介系詞之後選受格；名詞前面選所有格。25次
技巧 7. 一個完整的句子如果有空格要填空，則反身代名詞即為正解。4次
技巧 8. 代名詞 those 之後若出現修飾語，則 those 就是指 people。2次
技巧 9. 空格前如果是 "one of the"，則答案應選複數名詞選項。4次
技巧 10. no 是形容詞，not 是副詞，none 是代名詞。

技巧 **6** 動詞前面選主格；及物動詞或介系詞之後選受格；名詞前面選所有格。

exercise 運動

He recommended 20 minutes of exercise for me.
介系詞 └→ 受格

他建議我做二十分鐘的運動。

tip!
必須掌握空格前後緊接的詞彙是何種詞性。

1 人稱代名詞的種類 必背★

人稱	單複數/性別	主格 7次	所有格	受格	所有格代名詞	反身代名詞
第一人稱	單數	I	my	me	mine	myself
	複數	we	our	us	ours	ourselves
第二人稱	單數	you	your	you	yours	yourself
	複數					yourselves
第三人稱	單數 男性	he	his	him	his	himself
	單數 女性	she	her	her	hers	herself
	單數 事物	it	its	it	—	itself
	複數	they	their	them	theirs	themselves

2 所有格人稱代名詞 15次

① 所有格人稱代名詞與名詞之間可以是形容詞。

train 訓練

We train our current employees every six months.
└ 所有格 形容詞　名詞
題4　　正1題4選1

我們每隔六個月訓練我們的在職員工。

② 所有格人稱代名詞也可以和 own 一起使用。

my own；his own；their own 等

We train our own employees every six months.
　　　　所有格 own
我們每隔六個月訓練自家公司員工。

3 受格人稱代名詞 2次 **vs** 所有格代名詞 1次

① 受格要放在及物動詞或介系詞之後。

② 所有格代名詞是用來取代「所有格＋名詞」，可放在主詞、受詞或補語的位置。

Your order just arrived, yet mine has not been delivered.

正1題5　　　　主詞 (mine = my order)　　正2題2

你訂的東西剛送到，而我訂的還沒有出貨。

應用本技巧的題目

Mr. Chase will present ＿＿＿＿＿ perspectives on the new building code.
(A) he　　(B) his　　(C) him　　(D) himself

present 提出；展現
題7

perspective 觀點；想法
building code 建築法規
題3

蔡斯先生將提出他對於新建築法規的見解。

正解 (B)

PART 5

技巧 **7** 一個完整的句子如果有空格要填空，則反身代名詞即為正解。

Mr. Walton (himself) fixed the problem. 沃爾頓先生（自行）解決了問題。

就算不加 himself，也是一個完整的句子

fix 修理

1 反身代名詞的強調用法：「自己一個人」或「親自」 2次

① 主詞或受詞欲強調某一行為時，反身代名詞可放在要強調的名詞之後或句子末尾。

② 若反身代名詞用於強調用法，就算該句子不加反身代名詞，也會是一個完整的句子。

2 反身代名詞的反身用法：主詞＝受詞時，反身代名詞應置於受詞的位置。

Newly elected board members introduced themselves to the stockholders.

主詞　　　　　　　　題3　　　　受詞
(newly elected board members =
themselves)

elect 選舉；推選
board member 董事會
董事
stockholder 股東

新推選出來的董事會董事們向這些股東自我介紹。

① 若反身代名詞用於反身用法，該反身代名詞就不能在句中省略。

② 頻出片語：**devote oneself to** 專注於～

familiarize oneself to 讓自己熟悉～

commit oneself to 致力於～
題2選2

help oneself to 自行取用～

3 介系詞與反身代名詞合成的片語 必背★

by oneself (= alone, on one's own) 獨力；靠自己一人、**for oneself** 為自己
of itself 自動地；自然而然地、**in itself** 就其本身而言；本質上

test drive 試駕

Ms. Stanton wanted to test drive the new Wesson Automobiles sedan _____ .

(A) she   (B) her   (C) hers   (D) herself

史坦頓女士想親自試駕威森汽車的新型轎車。
正解 (D)

技巧 **8** 代名詞 **those** 之後若出現修飾語，則 **those** 就是指 **people**。

valid 有效的

Those [with a valid coupon] will receive a 10% discount.
              題2   正2題15
    介系詞片語（修飾語）
持有效折價券者將獲得 10% 的折扣。

🔖 tip!
請將 "those who" 視為
片語一併背起來。

1 those + who / p.p. / -ing / 介系詞片語：～的人

① 若指示代名詞 **those** 並非用於指稱前面曾出現過的特定名詞，就是用來表示「～的人」。

② 在這種情況下，其後必定是接介系詞片語、分詞片語或關係代名詞子句等型態的修飾語。

③ 當 **those** 之後出現關係代名詞子句時，由於 **those** 是複數，因此整個句子的動詞皆須使用複數形。

2 指示代名詞 that / those

① 一般而言，**that / those** 用於替代比較句型前面曾出現過的名詞時，主要會以 **that of / those of** 的型態出現。

② 前面出現過的名詞如果是單數就用 **that**，如果是複數就用 **those**。

Our bid for the contract is much lower than that of our competitors.
    題2   題12選2   替代前面的 bid
我們在這份合約所開出的投標價格遠低於我們同業競爭對手的（投標價格）。

clinic 診所
fill out 填寫

Before seeing a doctor, _____ who visit our clinic for the first time will be asked to fill out a form.
(A) those   (B) they   (C) them   (D) these

在給醫生看診之前，前來本院就醫的初診病患會被要求填寫表格。
正解 (A)

技巧 **9** 空格前如果是 **"one of the"**，則答案應選複數名詞選項。

One of the wholesale stores was open early in the morning.
　　　　　　　　　　　　複數名詞　題2

其中一間批發店一大早就開始營業。

wholesale 批發的

1 以代名詞表示**整體當中的一部分**──視為單數的代名詞

one of the ＋複數名詞：～當中的一個 **each of the** ＋複數名詞：～當中的每一個 1次 **either of the** ＋複數名詞：～兩者當中的任一個皆～ 正2題2選9 **neither of the** ＋複數名詞：～兩者當中的任一個皆不～ 題1選2 **much of the** ＋不可數名詞：～當中有許多 **little of the** ＋不可數名詞：～當中幾乎沒有	＋單數動詞

2 以代名詞表示**整體當中的一部分**──視為複數的代名詞

several of the ＋複數名詞：～當中的好幾個 題7選2 **both of the** ＋複數名詞：～兩者皆～ **many of the** ＋複數名詞：～當中的多數 1次 **few of the** ＋複數名詞：～當中幾乎沒有 **a few of the** ＋複數名詞：～當中的少數 **fewer of the** ＋複數名詞：～當中的較少數	＋複數動詞

Few of the volunteers have experience in sales.
正1題1選2　　複數名詞　複數動詞

這群志工當中幾乎沒有人有銷售方面的經驗。

experience 經驗

3 以代名詞表示**整體當中的一部分**──可視為單數或複數的代名詞

all of the ＋名詞：～當中的全部 **most of the** ＋名詞：～當中的大部分 1次 **some of the** ＋名詞：～當中的一部分 **any of the** ＋名詞：～當中的一些／任何一個 **half of the** ＋名詞：～當中的一半 **the rest of the** ＋名詞：～當中剩餘的部分	複數名詞＋複數動詞 不可數名詞＋單數動詞

tip!
動詞的單複數變化必須與 of 之後的名詞一致。

All of the information about the membership is posted on our website.
　　　　　不可數名詞　　　　　　　　　　　　單數動詞

所有與會員相關的資訊都已 po 在我們的網站上了。

post 張貼；（在網路上）發布訊息

PART 5

be capable of 有做某
事的能力
distance 距離

fee 費用
cash 現金
withdrawal 提款

supplementary 補充
的；追加的
insurance 保險
rental 租賃的
mandatory 義務性
的；強制的

candidate 應徵者；候
選人

應用本技巧的題目

_____ of the electric cars on the market are capable of travelling long distances.
(A) Much　　(B) Little　　(C) Each　　(D) Several

市面上的電動車當中，有好幾種車款都能夠長途行駛。
正解 (D)

技巧 **10** no 是形容詞，**not** 是副詞，**none** 是代名詞。

There is no fee for cash withdrawal.
　　　　 形容詞（放在名詞之前）
提領現金不會收取手續費。

Supplementary insurance for rental cars is not mandatory.
　　　　　　　正1題4　　　　　　　　　副詞 正1題2選1
　　　　　　　　　　　　　　　　（放在形容詞之前）
租賃車的附加保險並非強制性的。

None of the employees are in the office.
代名詞
沒有任何一個職員在辦公室。

1 由於 **none** 是代名詞，因此就如同名詞一般，可置於主詞、受詞或補語的位置。

2 **none** 可視為單數，也可視為複數，經常以「**none of the** 複數名詞＋複數／單數動詞」或「**none of** 所有格＋複數名詞＋複數／單數動詞」的結構出現。

None of our meeting rooms is big enough for the orientation session.
　　　　　　複數名詞　　單數動詞　　選3
我們沒有任何一間會議室大到足以舉辦新人培訓講習。

應用本技巧的題目

We had five candidates for the marketing manager position, but _____ of them had enough experience.
(A) every　　(B) else　　(C) none　　(D) much

我們有五位行銷經理一職的候選人，但當中卻沒有任何一個人具備充分的資歷。
正解 (C)

高出題率地圖

技巧 **11.** 空格後若為名詞，則答案應選形容詞選項。22次
技巧 **12. be** 動詞之後的空格應填入形容詞。13次
技巧 **13.** 在「主詞＋及物動詞＋受詞（名詞）＋受詞補語」句型中，受詞（名詞）之後的空格應填入形容詞（受詞補語）。3次
技巧 **14. every** 和 **each** 之後必須接單數的可數名詞。7次
技巧 **15.** 若選項當中同時出現一般形容詞和分詞形容詞，請優先在空格處代入一般形容詞來分析。19次

技巧 **11** 空格後若為名詞，則答案應選形容詞選項。

The managers are asked to bring innovative ideas to reduce the monthly spending.

　　　　　　　　　形容詞　名詞　　　　　　　　　題2
　　　　　　　　　正1題1選1

經理們被要求提出一些革新的構想以減少每月的支出。

innovative 創新的；有創意的
reduce 減少；降低
monthly 每月的
spending 開銷；花費

1 形容詞最基本的角色：放在名詞前修飾名詞

① 冠詞＋形容詞＋名詞

a successful entrepreneur 一個成功的企業家

　正1題7選2

successful 成功的
entrepreneur 企業家

② 冠詞＋副詞＋形容詞＋名詞

a highly competitive market 一個高度競爭的市場

　　　正2題1

③ 所有格＋形容詞＋名詞

your recent application 你最近的申請書

　　　正1題4選1

recent 最近的

④ 限定詞＋形容詞＋名詞

any important information 任何重要的資訊

　　　題6

important 重要的

2 形容詞的型態

① 一般形容詞的字尾

字尾	例字	字尾	例字
-tive -sive	competitive 競爭的；具有競爭力的 extensive 廣闊的；廣泛的 正1題1選1	-al	exceptional 優秀的；傑出的 題2 functional 實用的
-ful	successful 成功的 helpful 有幫助的 題2選1	-cial -tial	beneficial 有益的；有利的 substantial 大量的；豐盛的 正1

PART 5

字尾	例字	字尾	例字
-ous	various 不同的；各式各樣的 選2 serious 嚴重的	-ic -tic	specific 具體的；明確的 正1選1 dramatic 戲劇性的
-able -ible	affordable（價格）負擔得起的 正3題1 accessible 可接近的；可取得的 題1選2	-ary	necessary 必要的；必需的 temporary 一時的；暫時的 題1選1

② 「-ly」結尾的形容詞　必背★

形容詞字尾加上 ly 的單字大部分都是副詞，但在名詞字尾加上 ly 的單字則會是形容詞。不要只看單字型態就誤將形容詞判斷為副詞，這點要留意。

likely 很可能的	friendly 友善的；親切的	costly 昂貴的 題1選1
timely 及時的 正1選1	leisurely 悠閒的；從容不迫的	orderly 整齊的

應用本技巧的題目

Professor Hahn is conducting a study on the _____ effects of napping during the day.
(A) benefits　　(B) beneficial　　(C) beneficially　　(D) benefited

韓恩教授正在進行一項在白天小睡片刻會帶來正面影響的相關研究。
正解 (B)

conduct 進行；處理
題3
effect 影響
nap 打盹；午睡
beneficial 有益的

技巧 **12** be 動詞之後的空格應填入形容詞。

Tips for drawing oil paintings are helpful. 一些畫油畫的訣竅很有幫助。
be 動詞　└─ 形容詞（主詞補語）

tip 指點；提示
draw 畫；繪製
oil painting 油畫
helpful 有幫助的

1 形容詞擔任主詞補語的角色

在「主詞＋不及物動詞＋主詞補語」句型中，後接形容詞作為主詞補語的動詞：

be 是～ 題9	remain / stay 剩下／保持～的狀態 題4　　題4	become / grow / get 成為～ 題4　　題4
seem / look / appear 看起來～ 題2　　題2　　題3	prove 證明～；表現出／顯示為～	

主詞補語：補充說明主詞

2 在「主詞＋不及物動詞＋主詞補語」句型中，動詞之後也可接名詞。
當「主詞＝補語」時：

Jerry's Farm has become a famous tourist attraction.
　　　　　　　　└─ 名詞（主詞補語）
　　　　　　└─「主詞＋不及物動詞＋主詞補語」句型的動詞
傑瑞農場已成為知名的觀光景點。

famous 有名的
tourist attraction 觀光景點

應用本技巧的題目

Thanks to technology advancements, mobile devices have become _____ to most people.
(A) afford　　(B) afforded　　(C) affording　　(D) affordable

拜科技進步所賜，行動裝置已成為大多數人都負擔得起的消費了。
正解 (D)

advancement 發展；進展
afford 買得起；有時間做
affordable（價格）負擔得起的

技巧 **13** 在「主詞＋及物動詞＋受詞（名詞）＋受詞補語」句型中，受詞（名詞）之後的空格應填入形容詞（受詞補語）。

Members of the HR team found the new intern productive.
　　　　　　　　　　　　名詞（受詞）　　形容詞（受詞補語）
　　　　　　　　　└─「主詞＋及物動詞＋受詞＋受詞補語」句型的動詞
人資部的同仁們認為這個新進的實習員工很有效率。

productive 多產的；有成效的

1 形容詞擔任受詞補語的角色

在「主詞＋及物動詞＋受詞＋受詞補語」句型中，受詞之後接形容詞作為受詞補語的動詞：

受詞補語：補充說明受詞

make 使成為某種狀態 題5	**consider** 將～視為～ 選4
keep 使維持某種狀態 題2	**leave** 使處於某種狀態
find 認為／發現～處於某種狀態	**deem** 認為；將～視為～

2 在受詞補語的位置也可能會出現名詞。當「受詞＝補語」時：

The board of directors considers Mr. Choi the department head.
　　　　　　　　　　　　名詞（受詞）　名詞（受詞補語）
　　　　　　　　　└─「主詞＋及物動詞＋受詞＋受詞補語」句型的動詞
董事會成員們將崔先生視為部長。

board of directors 董事會；董事會成員
department head 部門主管；主任

在「主詞＋及物動詞＋受詞＋受詞補語」句型中，受詞之後接名詞作為受詞補語的動詞：

appoint 任命／指派～為～	**consider** 將～視為～	**call** 稱～為～ 選3
elect 推選～為～		

應用本技巧的題目

Their first collaboration work will make the partnership between two companies _____.
(A) strong　　(B) strongly　　(C) strength　　(D) strengthen

他們的首度合作將會強化兩家公司之間的夥伴關係。
正解 (A)

collaboration 合作
正1選1

PART 5

remove 移開；去除
belongings 個人物品；
所有物

技巧14 every 和 each 之後必須接單數的可數名詞。

Each worker removed their belongings to the new office.
　　單數可數名詞　題1選1
每位員工都把自己的個人物品移至新辦公室了。

Every employee should attend the meeting.
　　單數可數名詞
每一個職員皆應出席這場會議。

tip!
考題會問數量形容詞
之後所接的名詞是單
數或複數。

1 數量形容詞＋單數名詞 必背★

each 各自的 正2	**every** 全部的 題8	
another 另外的 題2	**a single** 單一的 題2	＋單數名詞

2 數量形容詞＋複數名詞 必背★

many 許多的 正2題8	**both** 兩者都	**several** 好幾個的 題7選2
a few 幾個	**few** 幾乎沒有 正1	**fewer** 較少的
numerous 很多的 正1	**a number of** 若干；一些	
the number of ～的數量 題2	**a series of** 一系列的	＋複數名詞
various 各種不同的 選2	**a variety of** 各式各樣的 題1	

a number of vs
the number of:
「a number of ＋複數名
詞」須搭配複數動詞，
而「the number of ＋複
數名詞」則須搭配單數
動詞。

automobile 汽車
on display 陳列著；展示
中

Various automobiles are on display.
　　　複數名詞
各式各樣的汽車正在展示中。

A number of bestselling books were exhibited in the show.
　　　　複數名詞　　複數動詞　正1選2
許多暢銷書在這場活動當中展出。

The number of bestselling books is increasing.
　　　　複數名詞　　單數動詞
暢銷書的數量正在增加。

3 數量形容詞＋不可數名詞 必背★

much 許多的 題3選9	**a little** 一點點	**little** 極少的
less 較少的	**least** 最少的	＋不可數名詞
a great deal of 許多的	**a large amount of** 大量的	

spend 花費

He spends much money on clothing. 他在服飾上花很多錢。
　　　題1　　　不可數名詞

4 數量形容詞＋複數可數名詞／不可數名詞 必背★

當選項中同時出現可數名詞與不可數名詞時，首先要確認動詞的單複數變化！如果是單數動詞，則不可數名詞即為正解。

all 所有的 正1	**other** 其他的 題4	**some** 一些 題7	
more 較多的 正1題6	**most** 大部分的 題2選3		＋複數可數名詞／不可數名詞
a lot of / lots of / plenty of 許多的			

應用本技巧的題目

Five additional days off will be given to ＿＿＿＿ employee who has worked for more than three years.
(A) all   (B) every   (C) some   (D) these

additional 額外的
正3題6

每一位工作超過三年的員工將會額外獲得五天的休假。
正解 (B)

技巧 **15** 若選項當中同時出現一般形容詞和分詞形容詞，請優先在空格處代入一般形容詞來分析。

Our company has survived in a competitive market.
　　　　　　　　　　　　　　　　一般形容詞（competing 為誤）
本公司在競爭激烈的市場中存活了下來。

■ tip!
大部分的一般形容詞都會是正確答案。

survive 存活

一般形容詞與分詞形容詞的含意有何不同 必背★

extensive 廣闊的；廣泛的——extended 延伸的；長的
understandable 可理解的——understanding 善解人意的
last 上一個的；最後的——lasting 持續的
complete 完整的——completed 完成的
　　正1選2
impressive 令人印象深刻的——impressed 感動的
informative 有益的；增廣見聞的——informed 見多識廣的

應用本技巧的題目

Users complimented the ＿＿＿＿ battery life of the new cellphone.
(A) impress   (B) impressed   (C) impressing   (D) impressive

compliment 讚美

新手機令人印象深刻的電池壽命讓使用者們稱許。
正解 (D)

PART 5

高出題率地圖

技巧 16. 副詞要放在形容詞前或不及物動詞之後。17次
技巧 17. 空格若出現在助動詞與原形動詞之間，則副詞選項即為正解。32次
技巧 18. 由於動名詞帶有動詞的特性，故修飾動名詞要用副詞。4次
技巧 19. 數字前面若出現 about 一字，是指「大約」的意思。4次
技巧 20. 表達增減的動詞之後會伴隨著增減副詞一同出現。5次

技巧 **16** 副詞要放在形容詞前或不及物動詞之後。

remarkably 明顯地；非常地
stylish 時髦的；漂亮的

The new product has a remarkably stylish design.

　　　　　　　　　　　　　　副詞 題1選2　形容詞

新產品的設計非常時尚。

We should work closely with the new interns.

　　不及物動詞 ——」 副詞 正2選4

我們應與新進的實習員工們密切合作。

1 副詞可修飾形容詞

① 放在「形容詞＋名詞」之前加以修飾

多益考古題當中常見的「副詞＋形容詞」必背★

highly 非常；很
refundable 可退還的

highly competitive 高度競爭的 正1題1	fully refundable 可全額退款的 正1題1
extremely popular 極受歡迎的 選2	surprisingly short 驚人地短 正2
remarkably high 非常高的 fairly optimistic 相當樂觀的 正1題1	exceptionally positive 特別正面的 markedly successful 明顯成功的 immediately available 馬上可用的 正3題2
directly applicable 直接可應用的	

② 修飾形容詞補語

－在「**be/become** ＋＿＿＿＿＋形容詞」的句型結構中，空格內應填入副詞。

Your ticket is fully refundable within 24 hours of purchase.

　　be 動詞 ——」 副詞　形容詞

你可以在購入票券後的二十四小時內辦理全額退款。

－在「**make / find / keep / consider** ＋受詞＋＿＿＿＿＋形容詞」的句型結構中，空格內應填入副詞。

He found the website highly informative.

　　find　　受詞　　副詞　　形容詞

他覺得這個網站十分有用。

2 副詞可修飾不及物動詞

多益考古題當中常見的「不及物動詞＋副詞（＋介系詞）」必背★

work closely with 與～密切地合作	act professionally 專業地行動
work diligently 勤奮地工作	behave responsibly 負責地行動
work remotely 遠距工作	listen carefully/attentively 仔細地聆聽
work cooperatively 合作	正1題1選2
progress smoothly 順利進行	drop/decrease considerably
正1題2	大幅下降 / 減少
function reliably 可靠地運行	rise/increase significantly
正3	大幅上升 / 增加

應用本技巧的題目

Audiences have responded _____ to the new cast of the musical *Au Revoir*.

(A) favor　　(B) favorable　　(C) favorably　　(D) favored

觀眾們對於《**Au Revoir**》音樂劇的新卡司反應很不錯。

正解 **(C)**

cast 卡司；演出陣容
favorable 贊同的；正面的
favorably
　正1
贊同地；正面地

技巧 **17** 空格若出現在助動詞與原形動詞之間，則副詞選項即為正解。

I will completely finish my report by noon.
助動詞　副詞 正2　原形動詞

我會在中午以前把報告全部完成。

completely 完整地；完全地；齊全地

1 副詞置於動詞與動詞之間

① be 動詞＋副詞＋ -ing

The number of customers is continually increasing.
　　　　　　　　　　be 動詞　　副詞　　　-ing

顧客數正不停地增加。

continually 不停地；一再地
increase 增加

② be 動詞＋副詞＋ p.p.

The office is fully furnished.
　　　be 動詞　副詞　p.p.

這間辦公室設備齊全。

fully 完全地；充分地
furnished 配有家具的

③ have ＋副詞＋ p.p.

I have recently moved to Sydney for work.
　　have　副詞　p.p.
　　　　正1題2

我近期因為工作的關係搬到雪梨了。

④ 助動詞＋副詞＋原形動詞

PART 5

2 副詞可置於動詞的前面或「及物動詞＋受詞」之後。

① 空格之後若為動詞，無須區分該動詞是不及物動詞或及物動詞，正確答案 100% 就是副詞。

We <u>promptly</u> <u>respond</u> to our customer's complaints.
　　副詞 正3　不及物動詞
我們立即回應顧客的抱怨。

promptly 立即地；迅速地
respond 回應；作出反應
complaint 抱怨；投訴

② 副詞可放在「及物動詞＋受詞（代名詞或名詞）」之後，用以修飾動詞。

You should <u>remove</u> <u>the device</u> <u>safely</u>.
　　　及物動詞 受詞（名詞）└→副詞 正1
你應該安全地移除此裝置。

device 裝置
safely 安全地

應用本技巧的題目

At Yun's Law Firm, staff members must ＿＿＿＿ announce their resignation two weeks in advance to receive a severance package.
(A) form　　(B) formally　　(C) formal　　(D) formation

在尹氏律師事務所，員工離職必須預先在兩週前正式告知才能領到解僱金。
正解 (B)

announce 公告；宣布
resignation 辭職
in advance 事先；預先
severance package 資遣費；離職金

技巧 18 由於動名詞帶有動詞的特性，故修飾動名詞要用副詞。

The consultant recommended <u>reducing</u> the travel cost <u>significantly</u>.
　　　　　　　　　　　　動名詞　　　　　　　　副詞
顧問建議大幅縮減旅遊支出。

consultant 顧問
significantly 顯著地

1 副詞的角色：修飾動名詞

① 動名詞是由動詞變化而來，故帶有動詞的特性，因此修飾動名詞要用副詞。

Mr. Han is in charge of <u>successfully</u> <u>organizing</u> the company retreat.
　　　　　　　　　　　　副詞 正1選1　　動名詞
韓先生負責成功籌備公司員訓之旅。

〈比較〉名詞必須用形容詞來修飾。

successfully 成功地
company retreat 公司員工培訓旅遊

② 若動名詞扮演的是介系詞之受詞，副詞即可置於介系詞與動名詞之間。

Thank you for <u>promptly</u> <u>sending</u> me the document.
　　　　　　　介系詞 副詞　　動名詞
謝謝你迅速地把文件寄給我。

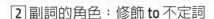

2 副詞的角色：修飾 to 不定詞

① 副詞放在 to 不定詞之後加以修飾的情況

We are planning to work closely with other departments.
       to 不定詞　副詞

我們正在計畫與其他部門密切合作。

② 副詞放在 to 與原形動詞之間加以修飾的情況

The HR division decided to randomly assign interns.
          副詞

人資部決定隨機指派實習生。

3 副詞的角色：修飾分詞

① 置於現在分詞或過去分詞之前加以修飾

We carry a wide variety of reasonably priced items.
        副詞　過去分詞

我們備有豐富多元且經過合理定價的商品。

② 若為分詞構句，則副詞可放在分詞的前或後來加以修飾。

Recently joining the company, Mr. Park has helped achieve its goals.
  副詞　 分詞

最近才剛進公司的朴先生已協助公司達成目標。

Situated perfectly in the downtown area, the hotel provides convenient
  分詞　 副詞 正1選1

airport-to-hotel transportation service.

飯店座落於市中心區的絕佳地點，並提供往返機場及飯店的便利交通服務。

應用本技巧的題目

We are committed to working _____ with the government.
(A) cooperation   (B) cooperatively   (C) cooperate   (D) cooperative

我們正致力於與政府合作。
正解 (B)

---

tip!
在 to 不定詞句型中，由於 to 和原形動詞之間無法插入其他詞性的字，因此正確答案 100% 就是副詞。

randomly 隨機地

a variety of 各式各樣的～
reasonably 合理地

achieve 達成
goal 目標

situated in 位於～
convenient 方便的

be committed to 致力於～
government 政府
cooperation 合作；協力
cooperatively 配合地
cooperate 合作；協力
cooperative 配合的

PART 5

vendor 小販；攤商
regional 地區的；區域的

技巧**19** 數字前面若出現 about 一字，是指「大約」的意思。

There were about 1,000 vendors in the regional festival.
大約
大約有一千個攤商參與了這個地方節慶。

1 與數字用語搭配使用的副詞 必背★
可放在數字相關描述前修飾的副詞是固定的。

approximately / about / around / roughly 大概 正1	at least 至少 正1題8
almost / nearly 幾乎 正1選1	up to 至多；直到～ exactly 精確地
more than / over 比～多；多於～ 題4	正1題1選5

應用本技巧的題目

_____ 100 meters of water pipe go into building a townhouse.
(A) Heavily　　(B) Highly　　(C) Roughly　　(D) Consistently

建造連棟屋大約需要用到 100 公尺左右的輸水管。
正解 (C)

drop（使）降低

技巧**20** 表達增減的動詞之後會伴隨著增減副詞一同出現。

The sales dropped significantly.
增減動詞　　副詞
銷售量大幅下降。

1 用來修飾「增加、減少或變化之動詞」的副詞

表增加、減少或變化的動詞	修飾「增加、減少或變化動詞」的副詞
rise / increase / soar / go up / advance 上升；增加；驟升；升高；上漲 decrease / fall / drop / decline 減少；下降；下跌；降低 gain 獲得 lose 失去 boost 提高；增加 change 改變；變化	substantially / significantly / considerably / 　　　正1選1　　　　　　　　　　正3 noticeably / remarkably 大幅地；顯著地；相當地；明顯地；非常 dramatically / drastically / radically / sharply 　　　　　　　　　　　　　　　　　選4 戲劇性地；急遽；徹底地；激烈地 slightly 輕微地 steadily 穩定地 gradually 逐漸地 　　正1選1

應用本技巧的題目

Average cost per vehicle is expected to rise _____ next year.
(A) substantially   (B) roughly   (C) reluctantly   (D) only

明年每台汽車的平均價格預計將大幅上漲。
正解 **(A)**

average 平均（值）
substantially 很大程度
上；相當
roughly 大致上
reluctantly 不情願地；
勉強地

PART 5

介系詞

介系詞文法考題出現了 10 次，詞彙考題出現了 71 次。

高出題率地圖

技巧 **21.** 介系詞置於名詞、代名詞、動名詞或名詞子句之前。81 次
技巧 **22. since** 之後須接時間名詞、**within** 之後須接期間名詞。12 次
技巧 **23.** 介系詞 **by** 與帶有完成或結束意味的動詞是最佳拍檔，而 **until** 的好夥伴則是帶有持續意味的動詞。1 次
技巧 **24.** 不及物動詞與介系詞總是「出雙入對」。2 次
技巧 **25. regarding** 也是介系詞。10 次

介系詞：
又稱前置詞，顧名思義是指置於前方的詞彙，會放在名詞、代名詞、動名詞或名詞子句的前面。

weather 天氣

有可能出現在介系詞之後的代名詞包括：受格、所有格代名詞、反身代名詞

survey 調查

技巧 21 介系詞置於名詞、代名詞、動名詞或名詞子句之前。

Her flight was delayed due to the weather.
　　　　　　　　　　　介系詞　名詞
　　　　　　　　　　　題3
她的班機由於天候的緣故延遲了。

1 介系詞的位置：名詞（名詞片語）的前面
　① 介系詞＋名詞
　② 介系詞＋代名詞

Ross asked you to wait for him until 2 P.M.
　　　　　　　　　介系詞└•代名詞
　　　　　　　　　正3
羅斯請你等他到下午兩點。

　＊補充：介系詞＋名詞＝介系詞＋名詞片語／介系詞片語，
　　在句子當中扮演的是副詞或形容詞的角色。
During the meeting, they discussed the survey results.
修飾之後的整個句子（副詞作用）
正2題8
他們在會議的過程中討論了調查的結果。

2 介系詞的位置：動名詞的前面
扮演名詞角色的動名詞可置於介系詞之後。
You are able to change your flight without paying extra fees.
　　　　　　　　　　　　　　　介系詞　動名詞
　　　　　　　　　　　　　　　題5
你可以不用支付額外的費用來變更航班。

tip!
與名詞子句搭配使用的介系詞當中，帶有「針對～」、「就～而言」、「與～有關」之意的詞彙 about、as to、regarding、concerning 等的出題率相當高。

3 介系詞的位置：名詞子句的前面
All staff members were concerned as to how the company could save money.
　　　　　　　　　　　　　　　　介系詞　　　　　　　名詞子句
全體工作人員都很擔心公司要怎樣才能節流。

應用本技巧的題目

_____ their hard work, they were not able to meet the deadline.
(A) Although   (B) Only   (C) Despite   (D) Forward

儘管他們工作認真，卻還是趕不上期限。
正解 (C)

技巧**22** **since** 之後須接時間名詞、**within** 之後須接期間名詞。

He has served as the marketing manager <u>since</u> <u>2015</u>.
　　　　　　　　　　　　　　　　　　　　　　　　　時間

他自 2015 年以後擔任行銷部長至今。

serve as 擔任～工作

1 時間介系詞 **vs** 期間介系詞 必背★

時間介系詞	**by** 在～之前 **until** 直到～ 　正1題4 **since** 自～以後 　正2題3 **from** 從～開始 **before / prior to** 在～之前 　正4題11 **after / following** 在～之後 　正5題11	＋時間描述 星期幾、 時刻、日期
期間介系詞	**for** 計；達（一段時間） **during** 在～期間 **within** 在～之內 　正6題5 **throughout** 在某段期間始終～ 　正1題1 **around** 大約～（某個時間範圍內） **in** 在某個時間點（以後或以內） **over** 歷時～；在～期間	＋期間描述 時間 (hours)、 年 (years)、 週 (weeks)

應用本技巧的題目

My favorite café is scheduled to reopen _____ a week.
(A) on   (B) in   (C) at   (D) of

我最喜愛的咖啡館預計將在一週後重新開幕。
正解 (B)

PART 5

report 報告

技巧**23** 介系詞 **by** 與帶有完成或結束意味的動詞是最佳拍檔,而 **until** 的好夥伴則是帶有持續意味的動詞。

Please submit the report by tomorrow. 請在明天之前提交報告。

提交(帶有完成之意)

1 **by**(最晚在~之前)**vs until**(直到~)

與 **by** 一同使用的動詞(帶有完成之意)	**finish** 完成;結束 題3選1	**complete** 使完整;完成 正1題8	**submit** 提交 正3題8
	turn in 呈交	**inform** 通知 題2	**notify** 告知 正2題2
	deliver 運送;投遞 正3題2	**arrive** 抵達;到達 正2題5	**cancel** 取消
與 **until** 一同使用的動詞(帶有持續之意)	**wait** 等待 題1	**continue** 繼續 題6	**last** 持續　　**stay** 保持
	be open(會議、活動)召開　　**postpone** 延遲;使延期 **work** 工作		

表期間的名詞:
holiday season 度假季節
summer vacation 暑假
peak season 旺季
business hours 營業時間

2 **for vs during**(在~期間)

「**for**」後接有具體數字的期間描述,而「**during**」之後則是接表期間的名詞。

Sales have doubled for the last ten years.

題1　　　　　有具體數字的期間描述

在過去十年間銷售量已增長一倍。

Our restaurant will remain open during the holiday.

表期間的名詞

本餐廳在節日期間將照常營業。

🔖 tip!
between 的後面經常會出現 A and B 型態的考題。

3 **between vs among**(在~之間)

正4題6　　正4

要表達在兩者之間用「**between**」,要表達在三者或三者以上之間就用「**among**」。

Please stop by my office between 1 P.M. and 3 P.M.

麻煩請於下午一點到三點之間來我的辦公室一趟。

divide 分發;分配

She divided chocolates among three children.

她把巧克力分給了三個小朋友。

應用本技巧的題目

serving staff 服務業從業人員
extra shift 加班

All of the serving staff members are requested to work extra shifts _____ the peak season.
(A) beside 　　**(B) during** 　　**(C) beyond** 　　**(D) for**

所有的服務人員都被要求在旺季期間加班。
正解 (B)

技巧24 不及物動詞與介系詞總是「出雙入對」。

All visitors should comply with the security procedures.
　　　　　　　不及物動詞 └•介系詞
所有訪客都應遵守保全措施。

多益考古題當中常見的「不及物動詞＋介系詞」 必背★

comply with 遵守～	**focus on** 聚焦在～；集中注意力在～
benefit from 得益於～	正1題1
interfere with 妨礙～	**register for / enroll in** 註冊～；登記～
specialize in 專攻～	題1
題1	**contribute to** 捐贈～；貢獻～
depend on 依靠～；取決於～	題1選2
rely (up)on 依靠～；依賴～	**appeal to** 吸引～；引起～的興趣
qualify for 具備～的資格	**collaborate on/with** 在～方面合作／與～合作
	選4

就算不及物動詞變成名詞，原先放在之後的介系詞依舊不變。

contribute to
→ contribution to
　　　正2

collaborate on
→ collaboration on

應用本技巧的題目

This item will appeal _____ customers in China.
(A) to　　(B) on　　(C) with　　(D) in

這項商品將引起中國顧客的興趣。
正解 (A)

技巧25 regarding 也是介系詞。

The details regarding the new coffee machine are written in the manual.
　　　　　　　　題3
說明書上寫著關於這台新咖啡機的詳細資料。

detail 細節

1 表「與～有關」之意的介系詞

about	on	regarding
concerning	pertaining to	as to
正2題2		
in/with regard to	with respect to	with/in reference to

2 分詞介系詞

字尾是 **-ing** 或 **p.p.** 這類分詞型態的介系詞

following 在～之後	**considering** 考慮到～
正2題3選5	
given 如果～；有鑑於～	**including** 包含～在內
正1題3選2	
pending 在～期間；直到～時為止	**excluding** 除了～之外

feature 特色；特點
wireless 無線的
transfer 調動；傳遞
enable 使能夠

應用本技巧的題目

New features _____ wireless file transfer enable users to upload photos directly to social media.

(A) against   (B) including   (C) before   (D) than

包含檔案無線傳輸在內的新功能讓使用者能夠直接將照片上傳至社群媒體。

正解 (B)

動詞的種類與單複數變化

Unit 06

動詞種類的考題出現了 92 次，動詞單複數變化的考題出現了 14 次。

高出題率地圖

技巧 26. 及物動詞之後須接名詞，不及物動詞之後可接副詞或形容詞。92次
技巧 27. 如果主詞是單數，就用 **is/was**；如果主詞是複數，就用 **are/were**。3次
技巧 28. **There is** 後接單數名詞，而 **There are** 之後則接複數名詞。
技巧 29. 如果主詞是第三人稱單數且時態為現在式，則動詞的時態變化為字尾加上 **-(e)s**。7次
技巧 30. 主格關係代名詞之後接的動詞必須符合先行詞的單複數。

技巧 26 及物動詞之後須接名詞，不及物動詞之後可接副詞或形容詞。

The staff gathered to discuss the agenda for the conference.
　　　　　　　　　　　及物動詞　　名詞 題2選1
員工聚集在一起討論會議的議程。

Customers can enroll online for the cooking class.
　　　　　不及物動詞　　副詞　　　介系詞片語
顧客可以在網路上登記報名料理課程。

1 「主詞＋不及物動詞」句型：不及物動詞 Part 5 8次 Part 6 5次

　　由於此句型中的動詞不能直接有受詞，故之後緊接著是介系詞片語或副詞。

　　Mr. Martin came to the headquarters yesterday.
　　　不及物動詞　　　介系詞片語 選2
　　馬丁先生昨天來總公司了。

2 「主詞＋不及物動詞＋主詞補語」句型：不及物動詞
　　在此句型中，動詞之後接補充說明主詞的主詞補語。
　　① 形容詞作主詞補語
　　　Mr. Clark is highly competent.
　　　不及物動詞　　　主詞補語（形容詞）
　　　克拉克先生非常能幹。

　　② 名詞作主詞補語
　　　Kevin Bacon's latest novel has become a bestseller.
　　　　　　　正2題5選1　　　不及物動詞　　主詞補語（名詞）
　　　凱文·貝肯的最新小說成了暢銷書。

3 「主詞＋及物動詞＋受詞」句型：及物動詞 Part 5 56次 Part 6 20次
　　在此句型中動詞之後有受詞，而受詞的位置可以是名詞、代名詞、to 不定詞、動名詞或名詞子句。
　　Ms. White agreed [that she will volunteer to work extra hours].
　　　　　及物動詞 題2選4　　　　　　受詞（名詞子句）　　題5
　　懷特女士同意將自願加班。

gather 收集；聚集
agenda 議程；待議議案
enroll in 註冊；登記

🔖 tip!
在詞彙題中會出現區分及物動詞和不及物動詞的考題。

🔖 tip!
考題中會出現其後須接名詞補語的動詞，例如：**be**、**become**、**remain**。

PART 5

帶有「給予」意味的動詞通常會出現在「主詞＋及物動詞＋間接受詞＋直接受詞」句型中。

4 「主詞＋及物動詞＋間接受詞＋直接受詞」句型：及物動詞

在此句型中，動詞之後必須接表「對象」的間接受詞與表「物品」的直接受詞。

The manager gave him a cash bonus.

　　　　　　及物動詞　└ 間接受詞　└ 直接受詞

經理給了他現金分紅獎勵。

5 「主詞＋及物動詞＋受詞＋受詞補語」句型：及物動詞 Part 5 2次 Part 6 1次

在此句型中，及物動詞後面必須接受詞與受詞補語（用於補充說明受詞）。

① 形容詞作受詞補語

Davis found the article informative.

　　及物動詞　受詞　　受詞補語（形容詞）

戴維斯發現這篇文章很有用。

通常用以表達「稱 A 為 B」或「將 A 視為 B」的意思。

② 名詞作受詞補語

The board members appointed Ms. Kim a new director.

　　　　　　及物動詞　　受詞　受詞補語（名詞）

正 1 題 13 選 1

董事會的董事們任命金女士為新任處長。

應用本技巧的題目

enclosed 圍住的
　題 1
compete 競爭
　題 1 選 2
refer 參考；提及
feature 以～為特色
正 1 題 1 選 1

Foster's Café _____ an enclosed play area for small children.
(A) arrives　　(B) competes　　(C) refers　　(D) features

福斯特咖啡館的特色是有個圍起來的遊戲區供小朋友們遊玩。
正解 (D)

技巧 **27** 如果主詞是單數，就用 **is/was**；如果主詞是複數，就用 **are/were**。

A variety of teas are on display.

　複數主詞　　　　　題 1

有各式各樣的茶陳列著。

be 動詞隨主詞的單複數變化

	現在式	過去式
單數主詞	am / is	was
複數主詞	are	were

應用本技巧的題目

Nearly 50 boxes of toys and clothes _____ during the community event.
(A) were collected　　(B) is collecting　　(C) collectables　　(D) to collect

在這次的社區活動期間募集到了將近五十個裝有玩具和衣服的箱子。
正解 (A)

nearly 幾乎
community 社區
題5
collect 收集
題3選1

技巧 **28** There is 後接單數名詞，而 There are 之後則接複數名詞。

There are some boxes on the desk.
　　　　　複數名詞
有一些箱子在桌子上。

1 在 There 開頭的句型中，主詞是在動詞之後出現的名詞。

2 在 There 之後出現的動詞和名詞兩者的單複數變化必須一致。

① **There is / There was / There has been** ＋單數名詞
　　題1　　　　題1

② **There are / There were / There have been** ＋複數名詞
　　選1　　　　題1

3 在 There 的句型中經常使用的動詞：**be** 動詞、**exist**、**remain**

There remains one glass bottle on the shelf.
　　　　　　　　　單數名詞
架子上還剩下一個玻璃瓶。

在 There 句型中，be 動詞之後不能加現在分詞、過去分詞或形容詞。

應用本技巧的題目

There _____ detailed information on our website.
(A) is　　(B) are　　(C) have been　　(D) would

在我們的網站上有詳細的資訊。
正解 (A)

detailed 詳盡的
正1題1選2

技巧 **29** 如果主詞是第三人稱單數且時態為現在式，則動詞的時態變化為字尾加上 **-(e)s**。

He teaches American history at Vincent High School.
單數主詞 └→ 單數動詞 -(e)s
他在文森高中教美國史。

1 視為單數的主詞：

單數可數名詞、不可數名詞、第三人稱單數代名詞、固有名詞、動名詞、名詞子句的主詞、「**one / every / each** ＋單數名詞」、「**every / any / some / no** ＋ **-thing / -body / -one**」

Incorrect information misleads people to invest in wrong companies.

不可數名詞　　　單數動詞 -(e)s　　　選5

不正確的資訊會誤導人們投資錯誤的公司。

2 視為複數的主詞：

複數可數名詞、「A and B / Both A and B」形式的主詞、「many / several / few / a few / both ＋複數名詞」、「a variety of / a range of ＋複數名詞」、「a series of ＋複數名詞」、「a number of ＋複數名詞」

Several customer service managers handle customer complaints.

several ＋複數名詞　　　　複數動詞　　　　正1
題4選1　　　　　　　題3選1

有好幾名客服經理在處理客訴。

應用本技巧的題目

To keep up with customer demand, Coffey Inc. _____ employees for its assembly lines.

(A) is recruiting　　(B) recruiting　　(C) recruit　　(D) have recruited

為了跟上顧客的需求，柯菲公司正在為他們的生產線招募員工。

正解 (A)

技巧**30** 主格關係代名詞之後接的動詞必須符合先行詞的單複數。

We will meet a distributor [who supplies goods to grocery shops in Boston].

單數先行詞　　　單數動詞　　題4

我們將與在波士頓供貨給雜貨店的經銷商會面。

1 「單數先行詞＋主格關係代名詞＋單數動詞」、「複數先行詞＋主格關係代名詞＋複數動詞」

All employees [who work in the New York branch office] must park their

複數先行詞　　　複數動詞　　　　題3選2

cars in a reserved lot.

所有在紐約分公司工作的員工都必須將他們的車子停在指定停車場。

應用本技巧的題目

Rainbow Travel provides an airport taxi service to anyone who _____ a VIP tour package.

(A) purchase　　(B) purchases　　(C) to purchase　　(D) purchasing

彩虹旅行提供機場計程車服務給每位購買 VIP 旅遊套裝行程的顧客。

正解 (B)

keep up with 跟上～
demand 要求；需求
題4選2
assembly line 組裝線
題2
recruit 徵募；招收
正1題2選2

distributor 經銷商；批發商
supply 供給；供應
grocery shop 雜貨店

關係代名詞：
包含 who、that、which 等的代名詞兼連接詞，用來代替前面出現的名詞（先行詞），同時也連接後面所接的關係子句。

主動語態與被動語態

相關考題在 Part 5 出現了 26 次，在 Part 6 出現了 19 次。

技巧 31. 在「主詞＋及物動詞＋受詞」句型中，動詞之後如果沒有受詞，則答案應選被動語態選項。36次
技巧 32. 不及物動詞無被動語態。1次
技巧 33. 在「主詞＋及物動詞＋間接受詞＋直接受詞」句型中，即使動詞為被動語態，其後仍應接上受詞（名詞）。3次
技巧 34. 假如情緒動詞前面的主詞是人，則被動語態選項即為正解。1次
技巧 35. 在「主詞＋及物動詞＋受詞＋受詞補語」句型中，動詞若為被動語態，其後須接形容詞或名詞。

技巧 **31** 在「主詞＋及物動詞＋受詞」句型中，動詞之後如果沒有受詞，則答案應選被動語態選項。

The new machine will be installed next week.

題2　副詞片語

「主詞＋及物動詞＋受詞」句型中的被動語態動詞

下週會安裝新機器。

1 被動語態的基本形式：**be + p.p.**（過去分詞）

2 在「主詞＋及物動詞＋受詞」句型中，動詞如果是被動語態，後面就不會接受詞。

〈「主詞＋及物動詞＋受詞」句型主動語態〉 James | obtained | approval .

〈「主詞＋及物動詞＋受詞」句型被動語態〉 Approval | was obtained | (by James) .

被動語態的動詞之後不會有受詞

詹姆士獲得了許可。

3 「主詞＋及物動詞＋受詞」句型中的動詞題常考 必背★

establish 建立；創辦	regulate 調節；控制
題1	題1選2
detail 詳述；詳細說明	notify 告知
predict 預言；預料	release 釋出；發表
題2選2	題1選1
install 安裝；設置	maintain 維持
illustrate 說明	close 關閉
serve 有用；供應（飯菜）	report 報告；報導
題2選2	題3選2
generate 產生；造成	construct 建設；建造

be 動詞會依主詞的單複數和時態來變化。

PART 5

initiative
正1題1選1
（為解決問題的）倡
議；新措施
go into effect 開始生
效／實施
waste disposal 廢物處
理
regulate 調節；控制

tend to 傾向～；易
於～
occur 發生；出現
warning 警告；預告

應用本技巧的題目

Since the initiative went into effect last year, all waste disposals _____ by Maine's Nature Department.
(A) have been regulated
(B) were regulating
(C) had regulated
(D) will be regulating

自從去年開始新措施實行以來，廢物處理全都由緬因州自然部控管。
正解 (A)

技巧**32** 不及物動詞無被動語態。

Storms tend to <u>occur</u> without warning.
　　　　　　　不及物動詞
　　　　　無被動語態 (be occurred)
暴風雨往往毫無預警就發生。

1 不及物動詞無法轉換為被動語態
　① 由於不及物動詞之後不需要受詞，因此沒有被動語態。
　② 在被動式「**be + p.p.**」中，**p.p.** 的位置若是不及物動詞，即為錯誤選項。
　③ 頻出不及物動詞 必背★

<u>rise</u> 上升	<u>appear</u> 出現 題3選2	<u>exist</u> 存在
<u>remain</u> 維持；餘留 題4選2	work 工作	<u>depart</u> 出發；離開 題1選2
proceed 繼續進行 last 持續	consist 組成 <u>participate</u> 參與 正1選3	arrive 抵達；到達
<u>occur</u> / happen / <u>take place</u> 發生 題5		

2 「不及物動詞＋介系詞」可使用被動語態
　① 由於此句型之後可接受詞，因此有被動語態。
　② 經常出題的「不及物動詞＋介系詞」

<u>deal with</u> 處理；對待 → be dealt with
　題1選1
account for 說明 → be accounted for
refer to 參考；提及 → be referred to
carry out 執行 → be carried out
take care of 照顧；負責處理 → be taken care of

應用本技巧的題目

We _____ at our destination soon, so please follow the flight attendants' instructions.
(A) are arrived　　(B) will arrive　　(C) arrival　　(D) to arrive

我們即將抵達目的地，請各位聽從空服員的指示。

正解 (B)

技巧**33** 在「主詞＋及物動詞＋間接受詞＋直接受詞」句型中，即使動詞為被動語態，其後仍應接上受詞（名詞）。

Montgomery Construction <u>was awarded</u> <u>the contract</u>.

↓
直接受詞

「主詞＋及物動詞＋間接受詞＋直接受詞」句型的被動語態動詞

蒙哥馬利營造取得了這紙合約。

1 在「主詞＋及物動詞＋間接受詞＋直接受詞」句型中，無論主動或被動語態的動詞，之後皆應接受詞。

間接受詞　　直接受詞

〈主動語態〉 The company ｜ gave ｜ them ｜ a cash bonus .

〈被動語態〉 They ｜ were given ｜ a cash bonus ｜ by the company .

被動語態動詞之後留有直接受詞

公司給了他們現金獎勵津貼。

必背★

2「主詞＋及物動詞＋間接受詞＋直接受詞」句型中的動詞題經常出現

give 給	**send** 發送；寄	**offer** 提供
題5選1	正2題10	正1題23選16
award 授予；頒發	**grant** 給予	**sell** 賣；販售
		正1題5選4

應用本技巧的題目

Any visiting kids _____ a free mini-sized chocolate bar every Sunday.
(A) are offered　　(B) has offered　　(C) offer　　(D) was offered

每逢星期日所有到訪的小朋友都可以獲得一條免費的迷你巧克力棒。

正解 (A)

右側註解：

destination 目的地
follow 聽從；跟隨
flight attendant 空服員
instructions 使用說明；指示

award 授予；頒發
contract 合約（書）

當直接受詞移到主詞的位置時，被動語態動詞之後不一定會接受詞。

〈間接受詞移作主詞〉
They were offered a 10% discount.
〈直接受詞移作主詞〉
A 10% discount was offered to them.

PART 5

satisfy 使滿足；使滿意

技巧 **34** 假如情緒動詞前面的主詞是人，則被動語態選項即為正解。

Mr. Klein is satisfied with the new TV.

主詞（人）情緒動詞被動語態

克萊因先生對這台新電視很滿意。

可透過「空格後是否有受詞」來判斷應該用主動或被動語態。

1 在「主詞＋及物動詞＋受詞」句型中，所有情緒動詞都是及物動詞。

2 區分情緒動詞為主動或被動語態的要訣：

① 若主詞為事物而且是賦予情緒者，則須使用主動語態。

The performance delighted the audience.

主詞（表演）→ 給予觀眾喜悅

這場表演讓觀眾看得很開心。

② 若主詞為人而且是感受情緒者，則須使用被動語態。

The audience were delighted with the performance.

題5選1

主詞（觀眾）→ 感受到喜悅

觀眾對這場表演感到很開心。

3 頻出情緒動詞 必背 ★

interest 使感興趣 正1題2選2	excite 使興奮 選1	concern 使擔憂
delight 使高興	satisfy 使滿意 題1選1	please 使開心 正2題2
disappoint 使失望	surprise 使驚訝 題1選3	amuse 使發笑
tire 使疲倦	fascinate 使著迷	

應用本技巧的題目

Many recent graduates _____ in job openings at Hudson Financial Group.
(A) interest　　(B) are interested　　(C) interested　　(D) have interested

recent 最近的
graduate 畢業生
job opening 職缺

最近有許多畢業生對哈德森金融集團的職缺感興趣。

正解 (B)

技巧 **35** 在「主詞＋及物動詞＋受詞＋受詞補語」句型中，動詞若為被動語態，其後須接形容詞或名詞。

secure 安全的
encryption 數據加密

Client information should be kept secure with digital encryption.

形容詞

「主詞＋及物動詞＋受詞＋受詞補語」句型中的被動語態動詞

客戶資料應採用數位加密來確保安全。

elect 選舉；推選
chairperson 主席
committee 委員會
judge 裁判；評審

Ms. Perez was elected chairperson of the committee by the judges.

名詞

「主詞＋及物動詞＋受詞＋受詞補語」句型中的被動語態動詞

培瑞茲女士被評審委員推選為委員會主席。

1 當被動語態動詞的後面是形容詞時

〈「主詞＋及物動詞＋受詞＋
受詞補語」句型主動語態〉

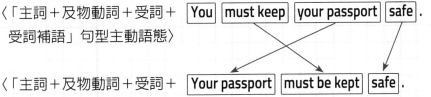

〈「主詞＋及物動詞＋受詞＋
受詞補語」句型被動語態〉

被動語態動詞之後留有形容詞

你必須確保你的護照是安全的。

① 在「主詞＋及物動詞＋受詞＋受詞補語」句型中，可於受詞補語的位置放形容詞的動詞 必背★

make 做；製造	**keep** 使維持某種狀態	**find** 認為；發現
題6選2	題2	題2選4
consider 將～視為～	**deem** 認為；將～視為～	

2 當被動語態動詞的後面是名詞時

〈「主詞＋及物動詞＋受詞＋
受詞補語」句型主動語態〉

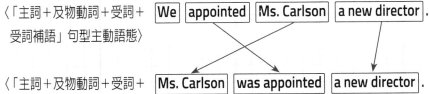

〈「主詞＋及物動詞＋受詞＋
受詞補語」句型被動語態〉

被動語態動詞之後留有名詞

我們任命卡爾森女士為新任處長。

① 在「主詞＋及物動詞＋受詞＋受詞補語」句型中，可於受詞補語的位置放名詞的動詞 必背★

call A B 稱 A 為 B
elect A B 將 A 推選為 B
appoint A B 將 A 任命為 B
consider A B 將 A 視為 B；將 A 當作 B
name A B 將 A 任命為 B；將 A 指定為 B

應用本技巧的題目

Barney Holliday _____ the new director of Houston Security's main branch.

(A) named　　(B) has named　　(C) is naming　　(D) was named

巴尼‧哈勒戴被任命為休士頓保全總公司的新任處長。

正解 (D)

---

tip!

動詞 keep 會使用在「主詞＋及物動詞＋受詞＋受詞補語」句型中，且考題經常會搭配形容詞補語，並問應使用主動語態還是被動語態的動詞。

director 部長；處長；主任
main branch 總部；總公司

<table>
<tr><td rowspan="5">高出題率地圖</td><td>技巧 36. 頻率副詞與現在式是「天生一對」。1次</td></tr>
<tr><td>技巧 37. 只要看到 last 就知道答案是過去式，只要看到 next 就知道答案是未來式。5次</td></tr>
<tr><td>技巧 38. 只要看到「since＋過去的時間」就知道答案是現在完成式。8次</td></tr>
<tr><td>技巧 39. 如果是時間副詞子句或條件副詞子句，則應使用現在式代替未來式。</td></tr>
<tr><td>技巧 40. 在義務、命令、要求或提議動詞之後所接的 that 子句中必須使用原形動詞。1次</td></tr>
</table>

assistant 助理
take care of 照顧／負責處理～

技巧36 頻率副詞與現在式是「天生一對」。

My assistant usually takes care of arranging my schedules.
　　　　　　　正2題2選5　└→ 現在式
　　　　　　　頻率副詞

通常是由我的助理負責安排我的行程。

1 現在式的動詞型態：動詞的基本形／第三人稱單數現在式

2 現在式用以表示現在的狀態、反覆的動作或一般普遍的事實

3 可看出時態應為現在式的線索 必背★

表「現在」的時間用語	now 現在　currently 當前　presently 目前
	題1選3　　　　正1選2

頻率副詞	usually 通常；一般　commonly 通常；經常　**often** 經常 　　　　　　　　　　　　　　　　　　　　題3選4 generally 通常　normally 通常　frequently 頻繁地；屢次地 正1選2　　　　　　　　　正1選2 sometimes 有時　occasionally 偶爾 regularly 有規律地；定期地　periodically 週期性地；定期地 正2選3 each/every month [year] 每個月（每年）

He inspects the machine every week.
他每週都會檢查機器。

photographer 攝影師

應用本技巧的題目

Ms. Miller occasionally _____ as a freelance photographer.
(A) working　　(B) works　　(C) will work　　(D) to work

米勒小姐偶爾會做自由接案的攝影師。
正解 (B)

技巧**37** 只要看到 **last** 就知道答案是過去式，只要看到 **next** 就知道答案是未來式。

The stock prices <u>dropped</u> dramatically <u>last</u> week. 上週股價暴跌。
　　　　　　　過去式

Sharon <u>will retire</u> <u>next</u> month. 莎朗下個月即將退休。
　　　　未來式

stock price 股價
dramatically 戲劇性地；誇張地
retire 退休

⬚1 過去式

① 過去式的動詞型態：「原形動詞＋**(e)d**」、不規則動詞（如 **spend**—**spent** 等）

② 過去式用以表過去已結束的動作或狀態

③ 可看出時態應為過去式的線索 必背★

yesterday 昨天	recently 最近	once 昔日；曾經
時間用語＋**ago**：～前	**last**＋時間用語：上個～	
in＋過去的年度／時間：在～		

He <u>missed</u> the meeting <u>yesterday</u>.
他錯過了昨天的會議。

⬚2 未來式

① 未來式的動詞型態：「**will**＋原形動詞」、**is/are going to** 不定詞

② 未來式用以表對未來將發生的事加以預測、計畫或表達意志

③ 可看出時態應為未來式的線索 必背★

tomorrow 明天　**shortly / soon** 馬上；很快地　**next**＋時間用語：下個～
　　　　　　　　　　正 1 題 1 選 5

as of / effective＋未來的時間：自～起

starting / beginning＋未來的時間：自～起
　題 2　　題 1 選 3

upcoming / following＋名詞：即將到來的（名詞）／在（名詞）之後
　題 2 選 2

As of next year, we will implement a new policy.
從明年開始，我們將實行一項新政策。

應用本技巧的題目

Pennington Chemicals ＿＿＿＿ local bands and musicians to the upcoming annual picnic.
(A) will invite　　(B) had invited　　(C) was inviting　　(D) invitation

local 當地的；地方的
upcoming 即將來臨的
annual 一年一次的；每年的

彭寧頓化學製藥公司將邀請一些當地樂團和音樂家出席即將到來的年度野餐會。

正解 (A)

PART 5

技巧**38** 只要看到「**since** ＋過去的時間」就知道答案是現在完成式。

fresh 新鮮的
founding 成立；創辦

Emily's Orchard <u>has supplied</u> local restaurants with fresh fruits
現在完成式
<u>since its founding in 2010</u>.
愛蜜麗果園自 2010 年創立以來就持續供應新鮮水果給當地的餐廳。

1 現在完成式的動詞型態：have/has ＋ p.p.
2 現在完成式用以表持續、完成或經驗

① 表持續（一直）之意時所使用的詞彙 必背★

for ＋期間：計；達（一段時間）	always 總是
during / for / over / in ＋ the last [past] ＋期間：在過去某段期間	
since ＋主詞＋過去式動詞 / since ＋過去的時間：自～以後	

假如 since 是作表「理由」的副詞子句連接詞使用，則主要子句中可能會出現各種時態。
He <u>was</u> late <u>since</u> he missed the bus.

We <u>have worked</u> at Paris branch <u>for three years</u>.
我們在巴黎分公司上班已經三年了。

② 表完成（做完）之意時所使用的詞彙 必背★

just 剛才	already 已經	now 現在
	正2題2選6	

He <u>has already finished</u> the marketing proposal.
他已經完成了行銷提案。

③ 表經驗（曾做過）之意時所使用的詞彙 必背★

ever 曾經做過某事	never 從未做過某事
	題2
recently 最近	lately 最近
	題1選2

I <u>have never worked</u> at overseas branches.
我從未在海外分公司工作過。

應用本技巧的題目

develop 開發
development 開發；發展

Over the past two quarters, Mr. Flynn _____ the new store membership program.
(A) developing　　(B) has developed　　(C) develops　　(D) development

過去兩季間，佛林先生一直在開發新的商店會員程式。
正解 (B)

技巧**39** 如果是時間副詞子句或條件副詞子句，則應使用現在式代替未來式。

Someone will pick you up when you arrive at the airport tomorrow.

時間副詞子句連接詞 └→ 現在式 (will arrive)

你明天抵達機場的時候會有人去接你。

▌tip!
在時間副詞子句與主要子句的時態題中，問時間副詞子句之動詞時態的題目出題比重較高。

1 時間／條件副詞子句的動詞時態與主要子句的動詞時態

若時間／條件副詞子句與主要子句皆表未來的事情，則時間／條件副詞子句用現在式、主要子句用未來式。

2 頻出時間／條件副詞子句連接詞 必背★

時間副詞子句 連接詞	**when** 當～的時候 **after** 在～之後 **by the time** 到～的時候 **while** 在～期間	**before** 在～之前 **as soon as** 一～就～ 正3題1 **once** 一旦、一經～便～
條件副詞子句 連接詞	**if** 假如～ **unless** 除非～ 正4選6 **provided／providing (that)** 以～為條件；假如～	**as long as** 只要～

If another store opens, he will hire a store manager.

條件副詞子句   ~~will open~~
連接詞

如果另一家店開了，他將會雇用一位門市經理。

應用本技巧的題目

Ms. Dorsey will attend the training after she _____ from her business trip next week.
(A) returning   (B) will return   (C) returns   (D) to return

business trip 出差
return from 從～回來

朵希小姐下週出差回來之後會出席教育訓練。
正解 **(C)**

技巧**40** 在義務、命令、要求或提議動詞之後所接的 **that** 子句中必須使用原形動詞。

The technical support asks that the printer be replaced with a new one.

要求動詞   原形動詞（is 為誤）

技術支援部要求更換一台新的印表機。

replace 替換

在「It ... that」虛主詞
一真主詞的句型中，
若有使用「帶有義務
意味的形容詞」，則
無關乎 that 子句中的
主詞是第幾人稱或單
數複數，一律皆須使
用原形動詞。

important 重要的
necessary 必要的；
必需的
imperative 必要的
essential 必要的；不
可缺的
vital 極其重要的；必
不可少的
mandatory 義務性
的；強制的
advisable 可取的；明
智的

recommend 推薦；建
議
production cost 生產
成本

1 義務、命令、要求或提議動詞之後的 that 子句動詞時態

that 子句的動詞時態無須配合主詞是第幾人稱或單數複數，一律都使
用原形動詞。

2 頻出義務、命令、要求或提議動詞 必背★

mandate 命令	order 命令	insist 堅持
demand 要求	require / request / ask 要求	
urge 極力主張；強烈要求	suggest / propose / recommend 建議；提議；勸告	
	題3選1　　　　題3選2	

3 多益常考類型

① 文法題：透過 that 子句前的動詞來判斷其後之動詞的問題

The labor union <u>insisted</u> that the company (~~hires~~ / hire / ~~hired~~) more workers.
工會堅決要求資方應雇用更多員工。

② 詞彙題：看到 that 子句使用未搭配主詞做單複數變化的原形動詞
來判斷主句動詞的問題

MJ Insurance (mandates / ~~interviews~~) that an agent <u>investigate</u> all claims thoroughly before issuing payouts.
MJ 保險公司下令在支付理賠金之前，專員要先徹底調查所有的理賠申請。

應用本技巧的題目

The consultant recommends that the product design team _____ a way to reduce the production cost.
(A) finding　　(B) finds　　(C) to find　　(D) find

顧問建議產品設計團隊想辦法降低生產成本。
正解 (D)

to 不定詞

相關考題在 Part 5 出現了 13 次。

高出題率地圖

技巧 41. 帶有未來意味的動詞之後必須接 to 不定詞。2次
技巧 42. 空格前的單字若為 opportunity，則 to 不定詞選項即為正解。3次
技巧 43. to 不定詞和虛主詞 it 是「好麻吉」。
技巧 44. to 不定詞前面會出現的形容詞是固定的。1次
技巧 45. 如果是「行為誘發動詞」，則受詞補語的位置會是 to 不定詞。3次

技巧 **41** 帶有未來意味的動詞之後必須接 to 不定詞。

The company strives to satisfy its customers.
　　　　　　　　　動詞 strive 的受詞
公司致力於滿足客戶。

strive 努力
satisfy 使滿足；使滿意

1 「主詞＋及物動詞＋受詞」句型中的動詞＋ to 不定詞

to 不定詞扮演「主詞＋及物動詞＋受詞」句型中的受詞。

to 不定詞的型態：
to ＋原形動詞

2 將 to 不定詞作受詞使用的動詞 必背★

主要包括帶有未來、計畫、意圖、肯定、發展方向等意味的動詞。

want to V 想要	need to V 需要	wish to V 但願
題6選1	題9選1	
hope to V 希望	expect to V 期待	plan to V 計畫
題3	正1	
decide to V 決定	ask to V 要求	promise to V 答應；承諾
refuse to V 拒絕	fail to V 失敗；無法	strive to V 努力
afford to V 有足夠的時間或金錢做某事		

Mr. Baker has decided to update the training manual.
　　　　　　　　　　　　題2
貝克先生已決定更新教育訓練手冊。

應用本技巧的題目

The event coordinator wishes _____ used books that will go to the local library.
(A) to collect　　(B) had collected　　(C) is collecting　　(D) collected

event coordinator 活動統籌專員
used 二手的

活動統籌者希望能夠募集將要送至地方圖書館的二手書。
正解 (A)

opportunity 機會
participate in 參與～

技巧42 空格前的單字若為 opportunity，則 to 不定詞選項即為正解。

Successful candidates will have opportunities to participate in the annual
workshop.　　　　題6　　　　　　　　　選1　　　修飾名詞 opportunities　　題6
獲選的應徵者們將有機會參加這次的年度工作坊。

1 名詞 + to 不定詞

　to 不定詞扮演置於名詞之後修飾名詞的形容詞角色。

tip!
「in an effort to V（為了
～努力）」或「in an
attempt to V（試圖～；
企圖～）」這類慣用
片語的相關考題也常
見於多益測驗。

2 被 to 不定詞修飾的名詞　必背★

ability to V 做～的能力 　題2	opportunity to V 做～的機會
chance to V 做～的機會	effort to V 為了做～的努力
attempt to V 為了做～的嘗試	way to V 做～的方法
plan to V 做～的計畫	need to V 做～的需要
time to V 做～的時候	right to V 做～的權力
decision to V 做～的決定	

In an attempt to reduce costs, some company policies will be revised soon.
為了試圖降低成本，不久後公司將有幾項政策會做修正。

應用本技巧的題目

convert A into B 將 A 轉
換 / 轉變為 B
abandoned 被遺棄的
housing 住宅
public hearing 公聽會
conversion 轉變；改造

The renovation plan _____ an abandoned factory into affordable housing
will be discussed through a series of public hearings.
(A) converted　　(B) to convert　　(C) is converting　　(D) conversion

讓廢棄工廠搖身一變成為價格合宜住宅的改建計畫將透過一系列的公聽會
討論。
正解 (B)

技巧43 to 不定詞和虛主詞 it 是「好麻吉」。

foreign 外國的

It is difficult [to learn a foreign language].
虛主詞　　　　　真主詞
學習外語是很困難的。

1 It is + 補語 + to 不定詞（虛主詞－真主詞句型）

　若將 to 不定詞當作主詞使用，主詞會變得冗長，因此把虛主詞 it 放在
　主詞的位置，並將真主詞 to 不定詞往後挪。

It is fundamental [to cooperate with other departments].
虛主詞　　　　　　　　　真主詞
與其他部門合作是非常重要的。

2 「主詞＋及物動詞＋受詞＋受詞補語」句型中的動詞＋ it ＋補語＋ to 不定詞（虛受詞─真受詞句型）

當「主詞＋及物動詞＋受詞＋受詞補語」句型中的受詞為 to 不定詞時，由於受詞較長，難以與受詞補語做出區隔，因此使用虛受詞 it，並將真受詞 to 不定詞往後挪。

The financial advisor found it important [to save unnecessary expenses].
　　　　　　　　　　　　　　虛受詞　題2　　　真受詞
財政顧問發現節省不必要的支出是很重要的。

應用本技巧的題目

It is mandatory _____ the air pressure very closely.
(A) monitors　　　(B) monitoring　　　(C) monitored　　　(D) to monitor

監測氣壓必須十分嚴密。
正解 (D)

技巧**44** to 不定詞前面會出現的形容詞是固定的。

I was hesitant to purchase a new computer.
　　　　　hesitant + to V
我很猶豫要不要買一台新電腦。

1 形容詞＋ to 不定詞

　經常出現在形容詞之後的空格填入 to 不定詞這一類的考題。

2 和 to 不定詞一起使用的頻出形容詞 必背★

eager to V 渴望～ 題1選1	eligible to V 有資格～ 正2題2選1
pleased to V 很高興能～ 正1	hesitant to V 猶豫～
(un)able to V（不）能夠～ 題7	apt / prone to V 易於～
(un)likely to V（不）可能～	reluctant to V 不情願～
(un)willing to V（不）願意～	

All employees are eager to meet the new CEO.
全體職員都渴望與新總裁會面。

---

tip!
「虛受詞─真受詞」句式會套用在「主詞＋及物動詞＋受詞＋受詞補語」句型中，因此會與這類句型的動詞一起出題，例如：make、find、consider、think 等。

air pressure 氣壓
closely 密切地；仔細地
monitor 密切關注；監控
　正1題1

hesitant 遲疑的；躊躇的

tip!
to 不定詞除了文法相關的考題之外，也經常出現形容詞詞彙的相關考題。

PART 5

mortgage rate 房屋抵
押貸款利率
<u>negotiation</u> 談判；協商
　　題2

應用本技巧的題目

The Wisconsin Workers Fund is able _____ better mortgage rates with banks.

(A) negotiation　　(B) negotiates　　(C) negotiated　　(D) to negotiate

---

威斯康辛勞工基金能夠向銀行協商更優惠的房貸利率。
正解 (D)

技巧**45** 如果是「行為誘發動詞」，則受詞補語的位置會是 **to** 不定詞。

persuade 勸說；說服
enter 加入（競賽等）
competition 競爭；比賽

We persuaded him to enter the competition.
　　　　　　　　題3　　　　　　題2選2
　　　　　　　動詞 persuaded 的受詞補語
我們勸他去參加比賽。

1 「及物動詞＋受詞＋ **to** 不定詞」
「主詞＋及物動詞＋受詞＋受詞補語」此句型用以表受詞之行為或狀態，其中 **to** 不定詞扮演受詞補語的角色。

2 將 **to** 不定詞作受詞補語使用的動詞 必背★
主要是具有誘發受詞行為之意味的動詞。

📌 tip!
多益測驗當中相較於
主詞補語，作為受詞
補語的 to 不定詞相關
考題更常出現。

《主動語態》 及物動詞＋受詞 (A) ＋ to 不定詞	《被動語態》 受詞＋ be p.p. ＋ to 不定詞
<u>expect A to V</u> 期待 A ～；期望 A ～ 　題1	<u>be expected to V</u> 被期待～；被預期～ 　正1題4
<u>invite A to V</u> 邀請 A ～；徵求 A ～ 　正1	<u>be invited to V</u> 被邀請～；被徵求～ 　題2
<u>ask A to V</u> 要求 A ～	<u>be asked to V</u> 被要求～ 　題3
<u>require A to V</u> 要求 A ～	<u>be required to V</u> 被要求～
<u>request A to V</u> 要求 A ～	題3
<u>allow / permit A to V</u> 允許 A ～ 題3選1	<u>be requested to V</u> 被要求～
<u>advise A to V</u> 建議 A ～ 　題1選2	<u>be allowed / permitted to V</u> 被允許～ 　正1選1
<u>remind A to V</u> 提醒 A ～	<u>be advised to V</u> 被建議～ 　題2
<u>encourage A to V</u> 鼓勵 A ～ 　題2	<u>be reminded to V</u> 被提醒～ 　正1
<u>persuade A to V</u> 說服 A ～	<u>be encouraged to V</u> 被鼓勵～ 　題1
<u>enable A to V</u> 使 A 能夠～ 　正1選1	<u>be persuaded to V</u> 被說服～
	<u>be enabled to V</u> 被賦予得以～

The industry experts expect BTA Chemicals to expand into the European market. 題1選1

業界專家們期待 BTA 化學製藥拓展歐洲市場。

應用本技巧的題目

Billy's Fashion's customers are asked _____ the store's website and give feedback.
(A) visited　　(B) visiting　　(C) to visit　　(D) visitors

比力時尚要求顧客造訪該店網站並提供一些意見。
正解 (C)

feedback 反饋意見
題8

高出題率地圖
技巧 46. 動名詞若放在主詞的位置，其後應接單數動詞。1次
技巧 47. suggest 後方不能接 to 不定詞，動名詞才是正解。1次
技巧 48. 空格後方如果有補語或受詞，就選動名詞！8次
技巧 49.「be busy」的後面要接動名詞。1次
技巧 50.「look forward to」的後面不能接原形動詞，而必須接動名詞。

動名詞：
兼具動詞與名詞的功能，在動詞字尾加 -ing，使其名詞化。

技巧 46 動名詞若放在主詞的位置，其後應接單數動詞。

Inspecting assembly machines takes about two hours.
主詞（動名詞）　　　　　　　　單數動詞
檢查組裝機械約莫需要兩個小時。

1 動名詞的角色

① 作主詞使用

require 需要；要求
a lot of 許多
responsibility 責任；職責

Training new employees requires a lot of responsibilities.
主詞（動名詞）　　　　　單數動詞　　　　題4選1
訓練新進員工必須要很有責任感。

② 作及物動詞的受詞使用

The company considered opening a new branch.
　　　　　及物動詞　受詞（動名詞）
這家公司曾考慮開新的分店。

③ 作介系詞的受詞使用

join 會合；加入

You can receive a discount by joining our membership.
　　　　　　　　　　　介系詞　└→受詞　　題3
　　　　　　　　　　　　　　（動名詞）
加入我們的會員您就能夠享有折扣。

應用本技巧的題目

report 報告
daily 每天；天天
題1選2
duty 責任；義務

Reporting daily sales to the headquarters _____ one of the manager's main duties.
(A) is　　(B) are　　(C) were　　(D) have been

向總公司回報每日銷售量是經理的主要業務之一。
正解 **(A)**

技巧 47 suggest 後方不能接 to 不定詞，動名詞才是正解。

The technician suggested replacing the broken oven with a new one.

<u>suggest</u> 動名詞 題1

技師建議用新烤箱替換故障的那一台。

> broken 壞掉的

將動名詞作受詞使用的動詞 必背★

recommend ＋ V-ing 推薦～；建議～

> 題1

consider ＋ V-ing 考慮～

> 正1題2

suggest ＋ V-ing 提議～
avoid ＋ V-ing 避免～
finish ＋ V-ing 停止做～
enjoy ＋ V-ing 享受～

> 題1

> ▌tip!
> 「want、need、expect、plan」這幾個動詞會把 to 不定詞當作受詞使用，請確實區分並加以熟記。

應用本技巧的題目

Most nutritionists recommend ＿＿＿＿ a low calorie diet in addition to fruits and vegetables.
(A) eaten　　(B) to eat　　(C) ate　　(D) eating

> nutritionist 營養學家
> in addition to 除了～還～
> 　　選1
> vegetable 蔬菜

除了蔬菜水果外，大多數的營養學家還建議攝取低卡路里飲食。

正解 (D)

技巧 48 空格後方如果有補語或受詞，就選動名詞！

He is qualified for receiving a bonus.

> 動名詞　受詞

他有資格領取獎金。

> be qualified for 有資格～

1 空格後若有補語或受詞，就選動名詞。

The manager suggested (inviting / ~~invitation~~) employee's family members

> 動名詞　名詞　　　　　　　受詞

to the company picnic.

經理提議邀請員工的眷屬一同參加公司的野餐活動。

> invite 邀請；招待
> invitation 邀請；招待

2 空格前若有冠詞 (a / an / the)，就選名詞。

Johnson Bakery established an online system for the (~~delivering~~ / delivery)

> 冠詞　動名詞　名詞

of its products.

強森麵包坊為了外送產品建構了線上系統。

> establish 設立；建立

organize 組織；籌備
organization 組織；機構
題1選1

upgrade 升級
正1題4選1

③ 若用形容詞修飾的話就選名詞，若用副詞修飾則選動名詞。

Mr. Han is in charge of <u>successfully</u> (organizing / ~~organization~~) the company
retreat.　　　　　　　　　　　　　　　副詞　　　　動名詞　　　　名詞
　　選1

韓先生負責成功籌備公司員訓之旅。

應用本技巧的題目

By _____ its printers, Dawson Printing can produce larger banners than
before.
(A) upgrade　　　(B) upgrades　　　(C) upgrading　　　(D) upgraded

透過升級印刷機，道森印刷公司現在能夠製作比以往更大的橫幅。
正解 (C)

技巧**49** 「**be busy**」的後面要接動名詞。

make a plan 擬定計畫
weekly 每週的；一週
一次的

Ms. Bell <u>is busy</u> making a weekly plan.
　　　　　　be busy　動名詞
貝爾小姐正忙於擬定週計畫。

動名詞慣用片語 必背★

on / upon + V-ing 在～後立即
　　　　　　題1
be worth + V-ing 值得～
spend + 時間 / 金錢 + V-ing 花費時間 / 金錢做～
　　　　　　正1
be busy (in) + V-ing 忙於～
cannot help + V-ing 不得不～
keep + V-ing 持續～
have difficulty + V-ing 做～有困難
have a problem + V-ing 做～有問題
go + V-ing 去～
feel like + V-ing 想要～

training 訓練；培訓
題6

material 資料
題4

應用本技巧的題目

Ms. Lewis is busy _____ the training materials for employees.
(A) update　　　(B) updating　　　(C) updates　　　(D) updated

露意絲女士正忙著更新員工教育訓練的資料。
正解 (B)

技巧**50** 「**look forward to**」的後面不能接原形動詞，而必須接動名詞。

■ tip!
會出現區分介系詞 to
與不定詞 to 的考題。

We look forward to seeing you on March 30.

<u>　　　　　　　　　　動名詞</u>

我們很期待在 3 月 30 日見到你。

<u>搭配介系詞 **to** 的高頻慣用片語</u> 必背★

look forward to + V-ing 期待～
be committed to + V-ing 致力於～
　　　　　題2選1
be devoted to + V-ing 專注於～
be dedicated to + V-ing 奉獻於～
object to + V-ing 反對～
be used to + V-ing 習慣於～

應用本技巧的題目

Most residents in the public hearing objected to ＿＿＿＿＿ a new power plant in Georgetown.

(A) build　　(B) built　　(C) building　　(D) builder

public hearing 公聽會
power plant 發電廠
　　　　題2

公聽會上大部分的居民都反對在喬治城蓋一座新的發電廠。

正解 (C)

高出題率地圖

技巧 **51.** 分詞可用於修飾名詞，也可放在補語的位置。16次
技巧 **52.** 現在分詞 (-ing) 帶有主動的意味，過去分詞 (p.p.) 帶有被動的意味。22次
技巧 **53.** 放在名詞前面的分詞形容詞一定要熟悉！14次
技巧 **54.** 若名詞是情緒發生的原因，則現在分詞為正解；若名詞是感受情緒的主體，則過去分詞才是正確答案。
技巧 **55.** 與完整句子結合的分詞構句扮演副詞的角色，而非形容詞。4次

revised 修訂過的；校正過的
proposal 建議；計畫

skilled 熟練的
woodworking 木工

📑 tip!
經常出現用來修飾名詞的現在分詞與過去分詞的相關考題。

技巧 51 分詞可用於修飾名詞，也可放在補語的位置。

I will send the revised proposal to you by email.
正1題1　名詞
修飾名詞
我會把修正過的企劃書用電子郵件傳給你。

He looks skilled at woodworking.
動詞　主詞補語
他看起來對木工活很熟練。

1 分詞的角色：修飾名詞

① 前置修飾

Our flight attendant will help find your missing luggage.
分詞　　名詞
我們的空服員將協助您找回遺失的行李。

② 後置修飾

The funds [raised at a charity event] will be used to build a new hospital.
名詞　　分詞　題1
在慈善活動募得的資金將會運用在興建新的醫院。

2 分詞的角色：作為補語

①「主詞＋不及物動詞＋主詞補語」句型中動詞的主詞補語

This hiking trail is very challenging, but it has picturesque scenery.
主詞補語 正1
「主詞＋不及物動詞＋主詞補語」句型中的動詞
這條登山步道相當具有挑戰性，但沿途的風景美得像幅畫。

②「主詞＋及物動詞＋受詞＋受詞補語」句型中動詞的受詞補語

Please keep your workspace organized.
受詞補語
「主詞＋及物動詞＋受詞＋受詞補語」句型中的動詞
請將你的工作區域維持在一個整齊的狀態。

應用本技巧的題目

The simple and sleek design made the Chef's Choice's product _____ to younger people.
(A) is appealed　　(B) to appeal　　(C) appeals　　(D) appealing

sleek 光滑的；線條流暢的
appealing
　　選 1
吸引人的；有魅力的

簡約時尚的設計讓 Chef's Choice 的產品對年輕族群具有吸引力。
正解 **(D)**

技巧 **52** 現在分詞 **(-ing)** 帶有主動的意味，過去分詞 **(p.p.)** 帶有被動的意味。

Bandit Cosmetics has become a leading company.
　　　　　　　　　　　　　　　　正 1 題 1
　　　　　　　　　　　　　　公司具有領先、領導地位（主動關係）
Bandit 美妝已成為一家具有領先地位的公司。

leading 領導的；頂級的

Residents should park their cars in a designated area.
　　　　　　　　　　　　　　　　被指定的空間（被動關係）
居民應將車子停在指定區域。

resident 居民
park 停車
designated 被指定的

1 現在分詞
　① 假如分詞和被修飾的名詞是主動關係，就要用現在分詞。
　　Street vendors (selling / ~~sold~~) food or drinks will display the permit on
　　　　　　　　　　選 4
　　攤商販賣～（主動關係）
　　their stand.
　　販售食物或飲料的路邊攤將會在他們的攤子展示許可證。
　② 假如主詞和補語或受詞和補語是主動關係，就要用現在分詞。

由於不及物動詞沒有被動語態，故只能用現在分詞。

2 過去分詞
　① 假如分詞和被修飾的名詞是被動關係，就要用過去分詞。
　　The store refunded for the (damaged / ~~damaging~~) item.
　　　　　　　　　　　　　　正 1 題 2
　　　　　　　　　　　　商品被毀損（被動關係）
　　這間商店退還了毀損商品的款項。
　② 假如主詞和補語或受詞和補語是被動關係，就要用過去分詞。

應用本技巧的題目

She found all reimbursement requests _____.
(A) approve　　(B) approving　　(C) approves　　(D) approved

reimbursement
　　題 1
償還；退款；補償
approve 認可；批准

她發現所有的退款要求都被核准了。
正解 **(D)**

report 報告
existing 現存的；現行的
workforce 勞動力；（特定組織的）所有員工

▌tip!
不用透過主動或被動關係來區分，只要把這些重要詞彙背起來就能輕易解題。

技巧**53** 放在名詞前面的分詞形容詞一定要熟悉！

The manager wrote a report about the existing workforce.
分詞型態的形容詞　題1
經理寫了一份關於現有人力的報告。

1 分詞型態的形容詞：雖然是分詞型態，但是已固定作為形容詞使用的單字。

① 頻出現在分詞型態形容詞 必背★

leading 領導的	outstanding 出色的；傑出的
rewarding 有價值的；有利的 題1	題2
inviting 吸引人的	existing 現存的；現行的
encouraging 令人鼓舞的	missing 遺失的
lasting 持續的	challenging 具有挑戰性的
promising 有希望的	convincing 有說服力的
entertaining 有趣的 選1	surrounding 周圍的；附近的 選1
demanding 苛求的	emerging 新興的

The home appliance rental is an emerging industry.
題1　　題3
家電產品租借是一項新興產業。

② 頻出過去分詞型態形容詞 必背★

attached 附屬的；附加的 題2選1	renovated 翻新的；重建的 選1
damaged 受損的	experienced 經驗豐富的 正1題3
reserved 預訂的	
detailed 詳盡的 正1題1選2	limited 被限制的；限定的 正1選1
skilled 熟練的	reduced 減少的；降低的
enclosed 被圍住的 題1	preferred 偏好的
revised 修正過的	qualified 合格的 正1題1
designated 被指定的	updated 更新的 選1

For more detailed information about booking a hotel, feel free to contact
the event organizer.
正2題4
預訂飯店房間如需更詳細的資訊，請儘管與活動主辦人聯繫。

應用本技巧的題目

With the opening of the department store nearby, there is _____ parking here.
(A) limiting　　(B) limited　　(C) being limited　　(D) limit

隨著附近百貨公司開幕，這邊的停車空間有限。
正解 (B)

department store 百貨公司
nearby 在附近
limit 限制；限度
limited 被限制的；限定的

技巧 **54** 若名詞是情緒發生的原因，則現在分詞為正解；若名詞是感受情緒的主體，則過去分詞才是正確答案。

This magazine is full of <u>interesting</u> articles on mobile devices.
　　　　　　　　　　　題1
　　　　　　　　文章是讓人感到有趣的原因
這本雜誌有非常多關於手機裝置的有趣文章。

magazine 雜誌
article 文章

<u>The client</u> <u>interested</u> in investing in our business contacted the CEO.
　　題1選1
客戶是感到有趣的主體
這位有興趣投資我們公司的客戶已和執行長聯絡。

invest in 投資於～

常考由情緒動詞變化而來的現在分詞或過去分詞 必背★

satisfy 使滿意──**satisfying** 令人滿意的──**satisfied** 感到滿意的
　　　　　　　　　　　　　　　　　　　　　題1
bore 使無聊──**boring** 令人感到無聊的；無趣的──**bored** 感到無聊的
surprise 使驚訝──**surprising** 令人驚訝的──**surprised** 感到驚訝的
　　　　　　　　　題1選2　　　　　　　　選2
excite 使興奮──**exciting** 令人興奮的──**excited** 感到興奮的
　　　　　　　　題2
tire 使疲倦──**tiring** 令人疲倦的──**tired** 感到疲倦的
interest 使產生興趣──**interesting** 引起興趣的；有趣的──**interested** 感興趣的
disappoint 使失望──**disappointing** 令人失望的──**disappointed** 感到失望的
　　　　　　　　　　　　題1
annoy 使生氣──**annoying** 令人生氣的──**annoyed** 感到生氣的

tip!
作答準則：若主詞為事物，則選現在分詞；若主詞為人，就選過去分詞。

People found the new film (boring / ~~bored~~). 民眾覺得這部新電影很無趣。
　　　　　　　　　　電影是讓人感到無趣的原因

應用本技巧的題目

The director urgently called a manager meeting due to the _____ sales of the summer collection.
(A) disappoint　(B) disappointing　(C) disappointed　(D) disappointment

由於夏季系列服飾的銷售數字令人失望，因此處長緊急召集管理階層來開會。
正解 (B)

urgently 緊急地；急切地
　　正1
call 召集；召喚
collection
　　題1
系列服飾；時裝設計師的新作發表會；新商品的總稱
disappointment 失望；沮喪

flexible 可變通的；有
彈性的
allow 允許

▌tip!
在多益測驗當中為了
正確傳達分詞構句的
意思，「副詞子句連
接詞照樣放在分詞構
句前面使用」這種類
型的考題更為常見。

技巧**55** 與完整句子結合的分詞構句扮演副詞的角色，而非形容詞。

Maxx Warehouse will offer a flexible work schedule, allowing employees to
　　　　完整的句子　　　　題2　　　　　　　分詞構句（扮演副詞的角色）

work from home.
麥司物流將提供彈性工時制度，允許員工們居家辦公。

1 分詞構句

① 分詞構句是利用分詞將「連接詞＋主詞＋動詞」的副詞子句變成
副詞片語的句子。

Because I arrived late, I missed the most important part of the presentation.
= Arriving late, I missed the most important part of the presentation.
因為我遲到了，所以錯過了這場簡報當中最重要的部分。

② 如果主要子句的主詞與分詞構句是主動關係，就用現在分詞；如
果是被動關係，就用過去分詞。

Entering the building, he ran into the department head.
他進到建築物裡面（主動關係）
進入大樓之後，他撞見了部長。

Situated in the center of the town, the shopping mall attracts a lot of
　題1　　　　　　　　　　　位於～的購物中心（被動關係）

tourists. 座落於市中心鬧區，這家購物中心吸引了大批的觀光客。
題2

2 只會以現在分詞或過去分詞當中的其中一種來出題的句型

① 必定以現在分詞出現在考題中的詞彙 必背★

beginning / starting 開始～；著手～
preferring to V 偏好～
allowing A to V 允許 A ～
ensuring that 主詞＋動詞：確保～；保證～

② 必定以過去分詞出現在考題中的詞彙 必背★

compared to 與～相比　　　　　　　　unless otherwise p.p. 除非有另行～
　　　　　　　　　　　　　　　　　　　　　　　　題1選2
as p.p. 像～一樣；如同～（as discussed 如同先前所討論的、as mentioned
如同先前所提到的、as stated 如同先前所聲明的）

comment 評論；意見
題1選2
suggestion 建議；提議
題4選1
manuscript 原稿；手稿

應用本技巧的題目

Please use a red pen when _____ comments or suggestions to the
manuscripts here at Middleton Publishing.
(A) had made　　(B) to make　　(C) making　　(D) made

要在原稿上留下意見或建議時，在米道頓出版社這邊請使用紅色原子筆。
正解 (C)

對等連接詞、相關連接詞與名詞子句連接詞

對等或相關連接詞的考題出現了 16 次，名詞子句連接詞的考題出現了 8 次。

高出題率地圖

技巧 **56. either** 之後接 **or**，**both** 之後接 **and**，這樣作答就對了！4次
技巧 **57.** 對等連接詞最重要的就是並列。15次
技巧 **58. what** 之後接不完全子句，**that** 之後接完整的句子。8次
技巧 **59. to** 不定詞是名詞子句連接詞的「最佳拍檔」。
技巧 **60.** 若空格之後有 **or**，則 **whether** 即為正解。

技巧 **56** **either** 之後接 **or**，**both** 之後接 **and**，這樣作答就對了！

Emily is both a designer and a model.
艾蜜莉既是設計師，也是模特兒。
He was able to participate in either the client meeting or the orientation for new hires.
  題3選1
他能參加客戶會議或新人教育訓練當中的其中一場。

be able to 能夠～
participate in 參與～
client 客戶

具代表性的相關連接詞 必背★

both A and B：A 和 B 兩者都 題1選3	**either A or B**：A 或 B 的其中之一 正2選7
neither A nor B：既不是 A 也不是 B 題1選2	**not A but B**：不是 A 而是 B
not only A but (also) B = B as well as A：不僅是 A 還有 B 也是 正4選1	

相關連接詞：
成雙成對的連接詞，
扮演連接兩個詞性相
同之詞彙或句子的角
色。

應用本技巧的題目

Delaware Vincent Hotel will offer _____ a meal voucher and a shuttle service to the airport.
(A) both   (B) or   (C) nor   (D) either

offer 提供
meal voucher 餐券

德拉瓦文森飯店會提供餐券以及機場接送服務。
正解 (A)

技巧 **57** 對等連接詞最重要的就是並列。

This printer is designed for personal and business use.
  正1題1選1   形容詞 對等 形容詞
       題3   連接詞
這台印表機是為了個人及企業用戶所設計的。

對等連接詞：
主要用來連接兩個對
等的詞彙或句子。

並列：
兩邊的詞性或構造相
同，達成平衡之意。

1 單字對單字

This wrist watch is lightweight and cheap.
       單字 對等 單字
          連接詞
這只腕錶很輕又很便宜。

lightweight 輕（量）的
cheap 便宜的

2 片語對片語

He will visit our factory this Monday or next month.

　　　　　　　　　　　　　　　　片語　　對等　　片語
　　　　　　　　　　　　　　　　　　　連接詞

他會在這個星期一或下個月訪問我們的工廠。

3 子句對子句

represent 代表；代理
assistant 助理

Mr. Winston was representing the company at the conference, but

　　　　　　　　　選2　　　　子句　　　　　　　　　　對等連接詞

his assistant returned to the office.

　　　　題5　　　子句

溫斯頓先生代表出席會議，但他的助理回辦公室了。

對等連接詞 必背★

and	or	but	yet	for	so
正2	正1	正2			正1

spacious 寬敞的
various 各種不同的
amenities 設施
function 功能；發揮
功能；起作用
functional 實用的

應用本技巧的題目

The new office building is spacious and _____ with various amenities.
(A) function　　(B) functions　　(C) functional　　(D) functioned

新的辦公大樓很寬敞，又具備各式各樣實用的設施。
正解 (C)

不完全子句：
缺乏主詞、受詞等的
子句。

expand 擴展

技巧 **58** what 之後接不完全子句，that 之後接完整的句子。

The company announced that it will expand into Europe.

　　　　　　　　　　　　　　正1題8選1　完整的句子

該公司宣布將拓展業務進軍歐洲。

1 名詞子句連接詞 what ＋不完全子句

What you need to do to become a member is to fill out this form.

　　　　不完全子句（do 沒有受詞）

要成為會員你需要做的是填寫這份表格。

■ tip!
由於名詞子句主詞視
為單數，故須搭配使
用單數動詞。

2 名詞子句連接詞 that ＋完整的句子

interesting 有趣的
obtain 獲得

The interesting feedback is that most customers obtain product information

online.　　　　　　　　　　　　完整的句子　　　正1題3選1

題11

有趣的反饋意見是說大部分的顧客都在網路上獲取產品資訊。

3 疑問代名詞＋不完全子句

decide 決定
affordable（價格）負
擔得起的

We had a meeting to decide which is the most affordable.

　　　　　　　　　　　　　疑問代名詞　　　不完全子句（沒有主詞）

我們召開了會議來決定哪個價格最實惠。

4 疑問副詞＋完整的句子

Ms. Young explained how we prepare the annual company dinner.
　　　　　　　　　　　　疑問副詞　　選 4　　完整的句子

楊恩小姐解釋了我們如何準備公司年度晚宴。

annual 一年一次的；每年的

疑問代名詞、疑問形容詞與疑問副詞 必背★

疑問代名詞	who(m)	what	which	whose
		題 3 選 6		
疑問形容詞	what	which	whose	
疑問副詞	when	where	how	why

疑問詞也可當作名詞子句的連接詞使用。

應用本技巧的題目

The document clarifies _____ a junior accountant is responsible for.
(A) that　　　(B) what　　　(C) where　　　(D) when

這份文件闡明新進會計師負責的業務。
正解 (B)

clarify 澄清；說明清楚
junior 資淺的；地位或等級較低的
accountant 會計師
　　　　　題 2
be responsible for 負責～

技巧 **59** **to** 不定詞是名詞子句連接詞的「最佳拍檔」。

You will be sent a text message explaining how to get to our building.
　　　　　　　　　　　　　　　　　　疑問副詞　　→ to 不定詞
　　　　　　　　　　　　　　　　　　　題 4 選 1

你會收到一則說明如何抵達我們大樓的文字訊息。

1 疑問代名詞＋ to 不定詞

You have to know what to do at the conference.
　　　　　　　　疑問代名詞　　└→ to 不定詞

你必須知道在會議上要做些什麼。

tip!
在「疑問詞＋ **to** 不定詞」的題型中，以「how ＋ **to** 不定詞」的出題比重最高。

2 疑問形容詞＋名詞＋ to 不定詞 正 1 題 2

We discussed which samples to display at the trade fair.
　　　　　　疑問形容詞　　名詞　　to 不定詞

我們討論過要在展銷會上展示哪些樣品。

display 展示；陳列
trade fair 貿易展覽會

3 疑問副詞＋ to 不定詞

Employees will learn how to operate this system.
　　　　　　　　　疑問副詞　 to 不定詞
　　　　　　　　　　　　　正 1 題 1 選 1

員工們將學習如何操作這套系統。

無「why ＋ **to** 不定詞」用法。
operate 操作；營運

tutorial 個別指導；使用教學
accounting 會計

應用本技巧的題目

With a free online tutorial, you can learn _____ to use the new accounting software program.
(A) and　　(B) other　　(C) how　　(D) while

透過免費的線上使用說明，你可以學習到如何使用新的會計軟體程式。
正解 (C)

技巧**60** 若空格之後有 **or**，則 **whether** 即為正解。

be concerned about
對～有所疑慮／感到擔心
reorganize 改組；重新整理

Mr. Miller is concerned about whether his department will be reorganized or not.
　　　　　　　　　　選2　　　　　　　　　題4選1
米勒先生對於他的部門是否會改組感到很擔憂。

1 whether + or not

I will decide whether to purchase it or not.
　　　　　　　　　　選1
我會決定是否要購買這項物品。

2 whether + A or B

renew 更新
rental contract 租賃契約

They need to decide whether they will renew the rental contract or move to a larger office.
　　　　　　　　　　　　　　　　　　　A　　　　　　　B
他們需要決定是否要更新租賃合約，或者是搬到更大的辦公室。

3 名詞子句連接詞 **if** 不能放在主詞的位置，也不能放在介系詞的後面，只能放在及物動詞的受詞位置。

📝 tip!
當 whether 作為名詞子句連接詞使用時，之後的 or not／[A or B] 可省略，但當 whether 作副詞子句連接詞用時，就不能省略。

應用本技巧的題目

During the job fair, you can figure out _____ job seekers prefer your company or not.
(A) both　　(B) that　　(C) after　　(D) whether

求職者是否中意貴公司，您可以在就業博覽會期間問清楚。
正解 (D)

fair 商品展覽會
　題2
figure out 弄清楚；想出；理解
job seeker 求職者
　題2
prefer 偏好
　題4

形容詞子句連接詞

相關考題在 Part 5 出現了 9 次，在 Part 6 出現了 4 次。

高出題率地圖

技巧 **61.** 主格關係代名詞之後要放動詞。8 次
技巧 **62.** 受格關係代名詞之後應接「主詞＋動詞」。1 次
技巧 **63.** 所有格關係代名詞 **whose** 的後面必須接名詞。1 次
技巧 **64.** 關係代名詞 **that** 的前面不能有逗點或介系詞。1 次
技巧 **65.** 關係副詞之後必須為完整的句子。2 次

技巧**61** 主格關係代名詞之後要放動詞。

A new turbine [that generates energy more efficiently] is being developed.
　　　　　　　主格關係代名詞＋動詞　　　　　　　正1　　　　　正2題2選2

一種讓能量產生更有效率的新型渦輪機正被開發中。

generate 產生；造成
efficiently 有效率地

1 主格關係代名詞的種類 必背 ★

先行詞 ＼ 語法格	主格
人	who 正3
事物	which 正4
人 / 事物	that 正1

tip!
在多益測驗中空格後緊接動詞的題型，亦即選出關係代名詞主格之考題的出題率是最高的。

2 主格關係代名詞後接無主詞的不完全子句（接續緊接著就是動詞）

Ms. Baker is a new manager [who is responsible for maintaining the budgets].
　　　　　　　　　　　　　　　　主格關係代名詞＋動詞（無主詞）
　題5

貝克女士是一位負責管理預算的新任經理。

3 主格關係代名詞子句的動詞須配合先行詞的單複數來做變化

Cathy Morton attended the job fair [which was held on May 5].
　　　　　　　　　　　　　　　　單數先行詞　　單數動詞 題2

凱希·莫爾頓參加了 5 月 5 日舉辦的就業博覽會。

先行詞：
後接關係代名詞子句加以修飾的名詞。

應用本技巧的題目

Several employees ＿＿＿＿＿ went to the seminar will give a presentation to summarize it.

(A) if　　(B) who　　(C) them　　(D) what

several 好幾個的
summarize 總結；概括

參加了那場研討會的幾名職員將做簡報概述該研討會的內容。
正解 **(B)**

PART 5

reschedule 重新安排時
間;改期
quarter 季度

技巧**62** 受格關係代名詞之後應接「主詞＋動詞」。

The company dinner [which Mr. Cooper has organized] was rescheduled for the
next quarter.　　　　　　受格關係代名詞＋主詞＋動詞
庫柏先生已籌備的公司晚宴被改期到下一季了。

1 受格關係代名詞的種類 必背★

語法格 先行詞	受格
人	whom / who 選1
事物	which
人 / 事物	that 正1

2 受格關係代名詞後接無受詞的不完全子句

Mr. Hampton is one of the clients [whom I met in Tokyo last month].
　　　　　　題3　　　　　　受格關係代名詞＋主詞＋動詞（無受詞）
漢普頓先生是我上個月在東京會見的其中一位客戶。

🔖 tip!
為了判斷空格後所接
的子句是否為無受詞
的不完全子句,必須
判斷動詞是及物動詞
或不及物動詞。

受格關係代名詞可省
略。

應用本技巧的題目

The 12 digit code _____ you can use to track your order will be sent to your
email.
(A) though　　(B) even　　(C) for　　(D) that

這組十二位的數字代碼可用來追蹤訂單,我們會把它寄到您的電子郵件信
箱。
正解 (D)

digit 數字
code 密碼;代號;代碼
　題3
track 追蹤
　題3

技巧**63** 所有格關係代名詞 whose 的後面必須接名詞。

This car insurance is suitable for people [whose cars are used just for
commuting].　　　　　　　　　　所有格關係代名詞＋名詞
這份汽車保險適合車子只用來通勤的人。

insurance 保險
be suitable for 適合～;
適用於～
commuting 通勤

1 所有格關係代名詞的種類 必背★

語法格 先行詞	所有格
人	whose
事物	whose 正1

2 所有格關係代名詞後接完整的句子（之後緊接著就是動詞）

All reimbursement requests will be <u>directed</u> to the chief accountant [whose duties <u>include</u> reviewing them].　正1選1

所有格關係代名詞＋完整的句子
所有的報銷單將會全數交給會計主任，其職責包含審核這些申請。

所有格關係代名詞與其後所接的名詞之間不能放冠詞。

應用本技巧的題目

Calhoun Law Firm wants to recruit a receptionist _____ main responsibility would be answering phone calls.
(A) who　　(B) that　　(C) whose　　(D) which

卡爾霍恩律師事務所想要招募一名櫃檯接待員，其主要職務為接聽來電。
正解 (C)

recruit 徵募；招收
receptionist 櫃檯接待員；服務台人員
main 主要的；最重要的
　題5
responsibility 責任；職責
answer 回答；接聽電話
　題2選1

技巧 **64** 關係代名詞 that 的前面不能有逗點或介系詞。

Mr. Harris is one of my <u>former</u> <u>colleagues</u>, ~~that~~ is working in the New York branch.　題2選1　　題4選2　　逗點後不能放 that (→ who)
哈里斯先生是我的一位前同事，目前在紐約分公司上班。

former 以前的；前任的

1 關係代名詞 that 的特徵

① 不可置於逗點之後

I worked as a <u>server</u> at a café, (~~that~~ / which) was newly opened.
　　題2
我在一家新開幕的咖啡館做服務生。

② 不可置於介系詞之後

The restaurant at (~~that~~ / which) all dishes are served with free dessert is always <u>crowded</u>.
　題5選2
所有餐點皆附贈免費甜點的那間餐廳總是高朋滿座。

③ that 可取代 who、whom 或 which，但不能替換 whose。

應用本技巧的題目

Ms. Phelps, _____ was originally hired as an intern, has now become a permanent staff member.
(A) she　　(B) who　　(C) that　　(D) how

原本以實習生身分被雇用的菲爾普斯小姐現在已經成為正職員工了。
正解 (B)

originally 原本
　選2
hire 雇用
permanent staff member
　題2
固定編制工作人員

技巧 **65** 關係副詞之後必須為完整的句子。

This is the office building [where I used to work].
　　　　　　　　　　　　　關係副詞＋完整的句子
這是我以前上班的辦公大樓。

1 關係副詞的種類 必背★

先行詞	關係副詞
表場所的名詞（the place、the building 等）	where
表時間的名詞（the time、the day 等）	when
表原因的名詞（the reason）	why
表方法的名詞（the way）	how

2 關係代名詞與關係副詞

① 關係代名詞後接無主詞、受詞或補語的不完全子句，而關係副詞之後必須接完整的句子。

Laura wanted to know the reason [(which / why) her supervisor was upset].
　　　　　　　　　　　　　　　　選 2　　　　　　　　　　　　　完整的句子
蘿拉想知道她的主管之所以生氣的原因。

② 關係副詞可作「介系詞＋關係代名詞」使用。
　　　　　　　　　　　　　　　題 3

表場所的名詞＋ where ＝ in / at / on / to which
表時間的名詞＋ when ＝ in / on / at which
表原因的名詞＋ why ＝ for which
表方法的名詞＋ how ＝ in which

應用本技巧的題目

The library has study rooms on every floor _____ doctoral students are working on their theses.
(A) why　　　(B) where　　　(C) unless　　　(D) those

這間圖書館的每一個樓層都有自修閱覽室，博士生們正在裡頭撰寫他們的論文。
正解 (B)

關係副詞 how 不能與先行詞 the way 一同使用。

「介系詞＋關係代名詞」之後應接完整的句子。

doctoral 博士學位的
work on 從事；做
thesis 論文（複數形為 theses）

副詞子句連接詞

相關考題在 Part 5 出現了 31 次，在 Part 6 出現了 2 次。

高出題率地圖

技巧 66. 副詞子句連接詞必須接完整的句子。
技巧 67. 關於「介系詞、連接詞、（連接）副詞」的題目必考！28次
技巧 68. 副詞子句連接詞的相關考題必須理解文意。5次
技巧 69. 副詞子句連接詞之後也可能會接分詞。4次
技巧 70. 複合關係副詞也是副詞子句連接詞。2次

技巧 **66** 副詞子句連接詞必須接完整的句子。

I lost my umbrella when I was on the subway yesterday.
　　完整的句子　　　　　　　　　完整的句子
　　　　　　　└→ 副詞子句連接詞
我昨天在地鐵上搞丟了雨傘。

1 副詞子句會放在主要子句的前面或之後

Before you review loan applications, please meet Ms. Han.
　　　副詞子句　　題3　　　　　題24　　主要子句
在審查貸款申請書之前，請去找一下韓女士。

2 副詞子句 vs 形容詞子句 vs 名詞子句

① 副詞子句：扮演副詞的角色，後接完整的句子。

② 形容詞子句：扮演形容詞的角色，修飾前面的名詞。

There is a girl who is reading a book.
　　題4　　　名詞　形容詞子句（修飾名詞）
有個正在看書的女孩。

③ 名詞子句：扮演名詞的角色，擔任主詞或受詞。

She doesn't know what she has to do.
　　　　　　動詞　　名詞子句（擔任受詞）
她不知道她必須做什麼。

應用本技巧的題目

_____ Ms. Lawrence is a long-time customer, she qualifies for this special offer.
(A) Because　　(B) By then　　(C) Only　　(D) Despite

由於勞倫斯女士是老客戶，因此有資格拿到特惠價格。
正解 (A)

副詞子句連接詞：
引導出一個句子，使其成為副詞子句的連接詞。

lose 失去；遺失

loan 貸款

PART 5

qualify for 具備～的資格

earn 賺得；應獲得；
贏得
certificate 證明；證書
apply for 申請；請求
得到
position 位置；職位

N：名詞
S：主詞
V：動詞

技巧**67** 關於「介系詞、連接詞、（連接）副詞」的題目必考！

Because he earned the certificate, he was able to apply for the position.
連接詞（介系詞 Due to 為誤）　正1
因為取得了證照，所以他能應徵這個職位。

1 介系詞、連接詞、連接副詞的句構比較
　① 介系詞＋ N
　②「連接詞＋ S ＋ V, S ＋ V」／「S ＋ V, 連接詞＋ S ＋ V」
　③ S ＋ V. 連接副詞, S ＋ V

2 意思相近的連接詞與介系詞

	連接詞	介系詞
時間	**when** 當～的時候 正3題19選5 **as / while** 在～期間 　正3題8選5 **as soon as** 一～就～ 正3題1選1 **once** 一旦～ 正1題5選2 **by the time** 到～的時候	**during** 在～期間 **by** 在～之前 **following** 在～之後 **prior to** 在～之前
原因	**because / since / now that / as** 　正4　　　正1　　　題1選1 因為～；由於～	**because of / due to / owing to /** 　正2題6選3 **on account of** 因為～；由於～ **thanks to** 由於～；感謝～；多虧～ 　題3
條件	**provided[providing] (that) /** 　選1 **assuming (that) / supposing (that) /** **if** 假如～；如果～ 正2題7選2 **unless** 除非～ 正4題1選4 **as long as** 只要～ **only if** 唯有～ 　選2	**without** 沒有～ **in case of** 如果發生～；萬一～ **in the event of** 如果發生～；萬一～
讓步	**although / though / even if /** 　正2題6 **even though** 雖然～；即使～ 　正1題1 **while / whereas** 反之；卻 　　選5	**despite / in spite of /** 　　　選4 **notwithstanding** 儘管～；即使～；雖然～

應用本技巧的題目

_____ mobile phones feature new and innovative functions, people tend to use only the ones familiar to them.
(A) Since　　(B) Although　　(C) Despite　　(D) Then

儘管手機的特色是具有新穎且富創意的功能，但民眾還是傾向於使用他們所熟悉的物品。

正解 **(B)**

技巧 **68** 副詞子句連接詞的相關考題必須理解文意。

Although this product is newly **introduced**, it is quite similar with the old version.
雖然～　　　　　　　　　　　　　　　　題3
雖然這項產品是新上市的，但它跟舊版本頗為相似。

1 時間連接詞

when 當～的時候	**after** 在～之後 正1題4選3	**before** 在～之前 題2
as soon as 一～就～	**once** 一旦～	**while** 在～期間
until 直到～ 正1題2選2	**as** 當～時；如同～	**since** 自～以後
by the time 到～的時候		

2 原因連接詞

because 因為～；由於～	**as** 因為～；由於～
since 因為～；由於～	**now that** 既然～；因為～

3 條件連接詞

if 如果～	**as long as** 只要～
assuming (that) 假如～	**supposing (that)** 假如～
providing / provided (that) 假如～	**unless** 除非～

4 讓步連接詞

although 雖然～	**even though** 儘管～；即使～
though 雖然～	**whereas** 反之；卻
even if 儘管～；即使～	**while** 反之；卻

5 目的連接詞

so that 為了～；以便～ 正1題5	**in order that** 為了～；以便～ 選1

---

innovative 創新的；有創意的
function 功能
　題1選1
tend to 傾向～；易於～
familiar to 對～熟悉的
　正1選1

📑 tip!
必須先了解文意，再從選項中選出語意最自然的連接詞。

similar 相似的

當表條件的副詞子句與主要子句皆描述未來事物時，副詞子句使用現在式，而主要子句使用未來式。

📑 tip!
表讓步的副詞子句內容與主要子句內容總會呈現相反或對立的情形。

PART 5

remaining 剩餘的；其餘的
trade fair 貿易展覽會

_____ Ms. Barkley brought all remaining brochures to the trade fair, the purchase department ordered 500 more copies.
(A) Since　　(B) Until　　(C) Unless　　(D) While

因為巴克利女士把所有剩下的小冊子都帶到展銷會了，所以採購部就又訂了五百份。
正解 (A)

分詞：
現在分詞 (V-ing)
過去分詞 (p.p.)

book 預訂
be sure to 一定要～
compare 比較
rate 費用

seem to be 看似～；似乎～
hurt 受傷的；使受傷

技巧 **69** 副詞子句連接詞之後也可能會接分詞。

When booking a flight, be sure to compare the rates.
副詞子句　分詞　　　　　　　題2
連接詞
預訂班機時，務必先比較價格。

1 副詞子句的縮減
　　　　　　　　　　　　　　　┌ 主詞
He seemed to be hurt while he was working.
　　　　題2　　　　　　　　副詞子句　be動詞　分詞
　　　　　　　　　　　　　連接詞

省略主詞 (he) 與 be 動詞 (was) ─┐
He seemed to be hurt while working.
　　　　　　　　　副詞子句連接詞　　分詞
他似乎在工作的時候受傷了。

2 經常在分詞構句前出現的副詞子句連接詞

When + V-ing / p.p. 當～的時候
　　　　　　題5
While + V-ing / p.p. 在～期間
　　　　正1題2
Before / After / Since + V-ing / being p.p. 在～之前 / 在～之後 / 自～以來
as / if / once / unless / though (although, even though, even if) + p.p.
　　　　　　　　　　　　　　　　　　　　　　正1
如同～；如果～；一旦～；除非～ / 儘管～

_____ booking a flight and hotel room for business trips, please contact Jade Travel Company.
(A) When　　(B) In order to　　(C) Nor　　(D) Such

當你需要預訂出差機票和飯店房間時，請與捷得旅行社聯繫。
正解 (A)

tip!
如何判斷副詞子句連接詞之後要接 V-ing 還是 p.p.：
(1) 透過句意來判斷
(2) 其後若有受詞，選 V-ing；若無受詞，就選 p.p.。

contact 聯絡

技巧**70** 複合關係副詞也是副詞子句連接詞。

Whenever you need my help, feel free to call me.
複合關係副詞—副詞子句
無論什麼時候，只要你需要我的幫忙，歡迎隨時與我聯絡。

1 複合關係副詞

whenever (= no matter when) 無論何時
正 2 題 1 選 1
wherever (= no matter where) 無論何地
　　選 1
however (= no matter how) 無論如何；不管怎麼樣
　　選 5

The audience can ask questions whenever they want.
觀眾可以隨時在想要發問的時候提問。

audience 觀眾

We will find a solution however long it will take.
無論要花多久的時間，我們會找出解決方案的。

solution 解決辦法

2 複合關係代名詞也可以導出副詞子句

whoever (= no matter who) 無論誰
　　選 4
whatever (= no matter what) 無論什麼事
whichever (= no matter which) 無論哪個
　　正 1 選 2

複合關係代名詞既能
導出副詞子句，也能
導出名詞子句。

Whoever comes in, don't open that window.
無論誰進來，都不要開那扇窗戶。

Whatever happens, don't press the red button.
無論發生什麼事，都不要按下紅色的按鈕。

happen 發生
press 按；壓

應用本技巧的題目

_____ you stay at our hotel chain, the reward points will be accumulated in your account.
(A) Always　　(B) So that　　(C) During　　(D) Whenever

stay 停留；留宿
reward 酬謝；獎賞
　　題 2

無論任何時候，只要您投宿於我們旗下的連鎖飯店，就能在您的帳號累積
回饋點數。
正解 **(D)**

PART 5

Unit 15 比較句型

相關考題在 Part 5 出現了 14 次。

高出題率地圖

技巧 71. as ... as 之間必須是形容詞或副詞的原級。
技巧 72. 只要看到 than，就選比較級！7 次
技巧 73. 空格後如果是比較級，則強調比較級的副詞「emfas」即為正解。
技巧 74. 空格前若出現定冠詞 the，或者題目中有 among 一字，則答案應選最高級選項。6 次
技巧 75. at least 之後接數字，no later than 之後接時間。1 次

原級的比較用法：
以原級表達兩者是一樣的。

produce 生產；製造

expensive 昂貴的
suitcase 手提行李箱

brief 短暫的；簡短的
advertise 登廣告；宣傳

transition 轉變
accounting 會計
proceed（繼續）進行
smoothly 順暢地；順利地
plan 計畫

museum 博物館
regulate 調節；控制
　選 3
display room 展出室
temperature 溫度
　選 1
careful 小心的
正 1 選 2
carefully 小心地

技巧 71 as ... as 之間必須是形容詞或副詞的原級。

This color printer can produce as fast as the black-and-white one.
　　　　　　　　　　　　　題 1 選 3　副詞原級
這台彩色印表機可以列印得跟黑白印表機一樣快。

1 A ＋ as ＋原級＋ as ＋ B：A 跟 B 一樣～

This bag is as expensive as that suitcase.
　　　　A　　　　　原級　　　　　B
這個包包跟那個行李箱一樣貴。

2 形容詞 vs 副詞 必背★

① 形容詞：當前面有缺乏補語的不完整句子時

The Q&A session was as brief as it was advertised.
　　　　缺乏補語的不完整句子　　形容詞作 was 的補語
　　　　　　　　　　　　　　　　正 1 選 2
QA 環節跟當初宣傳的時間一樣短。

② 副詞：當前面有完整的句子時

The transition to the new accounting system proceeded as smoothly as planned.　　完整的句子　　　　　　　　副詞
　　題 1
新會計系統的轉換作業如原先的計畫進行得很流暢。

應用本技巧的題目

The museum employees should regulate the display room temperature as _____ as they can.
(A) cared　　(B) careful　　(C) cares　　(D) carefully

博物館的職員們應儘可能小心調控展示廳的溫度。
正解 (D)

技巧**72** 只要看到 than，就選比較級！

The newly released couch is wider than the old one.
　　　　　　　　　　　　wide 的比較級
　　　　　　　　　　　　正 2 題 3 選 2

這款新上市的沙發比舊款來得寬。

1 比較級的型態

〔單音節的單字〕形容詞 / 副詞 **-er** ＋ **than**：比～更～
　　　　　　　　　　　　　　　　　　題 7 選 2

〔雙音節或多音節的單字〕**more** 形容詞 / 副詞 **than**：比～更～
　　　　　　　　　　　正 1 題 13 選 3

　　　　　　　　　less 形容詞 **than**：比～更少
　　　　　　　　　　題 1

2 形容詞 **vs** 副詞 必背★

① 形容詞：當前面有缺乏補語的不完整句子時

The prices of lunch specials at Fast Dinners are more reasonable than
Vincent Seafood.　　　缺乏補語的不完整句子　　　形容詞作 are 的補語
　　　　　　　　　　　　　　　　　　　　　　　　　　選 1

Fast Dinners 餐廳的午間特餐價格比 Vincent Seafood 餐廳來得合理。

② 副詞：當前面有完整的句子時

This computer runs more efficiently than any other system.
　　　完整的句子　　　　　　　副詞

這台電腦運作起來比其他任何系統都要來得有效率。

應用本技巧的題目

The weight of the new keyboard was _____ than the previous models.
(A) heavy　　**(B) heavier**　　**(C) heaviest**　　**(D) heavily**

這個新鍵盤的重量比以往的型號還要重。
正解 (B)

技巧**73** 空格後如果是比較級，則強調比較級的副詞「**emfas**」即為正解。

The new design is much more sophisticated than our competitor's.
　　　　　　　強調比較級的副詞　　　比較級

比起我們的競爭對手，這款新設計精緻多了。

1 強調比較級的副詞：**even**、**much**、**far**、**a lot**、**still** 必背★

2 增減副詞也可修飾比較級：如 **considerably**、**significantly**、
substantially、**markedly** 等　　　正 3
　　正 1 選 1

比較級：
以形容詞或副詞的比較級來比較兩者的句型。

release 釋出；發表
couch 長椅；沙發
wide 寬的

不規則變化：
good / well—**better**
bad / badly—**worse**
many / much—**more**
little—**less**

price 價格
reasonable 合理的

efficiently 有效率地

weight 重量
previous
正 1 題 3 選 2
先前的；以前的

emfas：
在此為強調比較級之副詞 **even**、**much**、**far**、**a lot**、**still** 等的第一個字母所組成的簡稱。

sophisticated 精密的；老練的
competitor 競爭者；對手

PART 5

spacious 寬敞的
　　　題1
appear 出現;看起來～

最高級:
以形容詞或副詞的最
高級來比較三者以上
的句型。

competent 有能力的

contribute 捐贈;貢獻
significantly 顯著地
success 成功

well known for
　　題1選1
以～著稱
collection 收藏品;搜
集的物品
discounted 折扣的
　　正3選2

應用本技巧的題目

The standard room was _____ more spacious than it appears on the website.
(A) even　　(B) nearly　　(C) very　　(D) ever

標準房甚至比網站上看起來的還要更加寬敞。
正解 (A)

技巧 **74** 空格前若出現定冠詞 the,或者題目中有 among 一字,則答案應選最高級選項。

Billy Johnson was <u>the</u> <u>most competent</u> of the new interns.
　　　　　　　　　　　　最高級
比利·強森是這批新進實習生當中最能幹的。

① 最高級的型態
〔單音節的單字〕the / 所有格 + (形容詞 / 副詞) -est:
　　　　　　　　　　最～的 / 最～地
〔雙音節或多音節的單字〕the / 所有格 + most + (形容詞 / 副詞):
　　　　　　　　　　　　最～的 / 最～地
　　　　　　　　　the / 所有格 + least + (形容詞 / 副詞):
　　　　　　　　　最小的;最少的;最不～的 / 最小;最少;
　　　　　　　　　最不～地

② 與範圍或類型一同使用 必背★

among 在～之間	out of 在～當中	of all 在所有的～之中
正4選8		題3
in 在～	ever 至今最～的	

Mr. Cooper contributed <u>most significantly</u> to the success of the new product
　　　　　　　　　　　　　　最高級
<u>among</u> the managers.
範圍
在經理人當中,庫柏先生對這項新產品的成功貢獻最大。

應用本技巧的題目

Marvin Footwear is well known for having the _____ collection of discounted shoes in Mayfair Mall.
(A) wide　　(B) wider　　(C) widest　　(D) width

瑪紋鞋履以在梅費爾購物中心擁有最多樣化折扣鞋款系列商品而聞名。
正解 (C)

技巧**75** **at least** 之後接數字，**no later than** 之後接時間。

Your application must be received <u>no later than</u> <u>July 25.</u>
　　　　　　　　　　　　　　　　　　　　　　　　　日期

你的申請書最晚必須在 7 月 25 日送達。

⬚1 比較級慣用語

「<u>no later than</u> 最晚要在～」= **by** ＋日期或時間 _{題1}	**than ever** 比起過去
「<u>more than</u> ＋數字／時間用語」多於～；～以上 _{題4}	**other than** ～以外
A rather than B 不是／沒有 B，而是 A _{選2}	<u>no longer</u> 不再～ _{題2}
no sooner A than B 一 A 就 B	

She is <u>no longer a senior accountant.</u>

她已經不是資深會計師了。

senior 資深的；級別高的
accountant 會計師

⬚2 最高級慣用語

<u>at least</u> 至少 _{正1題8}	**at the latest** 最晚；至遲
<u>at your earliest convenience</u> 盡早	**at the earliest** 最早

Please email me <u>at your earliest convenience.</u>

方便的話請盡早傳電子郵件給我。

應用本技巧的題目

Please allow ＿＿＿＿＿ three business days to complete your special request.
(A) much too　　　(B) even as　　　(C) as though　　　(D) at least

allow 允許
business day 營業日
_{題2}
request 要求；請求

請給我至少三個工作天的時間來完成您的特殊要求。

正解 **(D)**

高出題率地圖

技巧 **76.** 名詞或動詞詞彙的考題，前後文就是線索。81次
技巧 **77.** 人稱代名詞或指示形容詞所指稱的名詞要從前文裡面找。10次
技巧 **78.** 指示代名詞可概述前文的內容。1次
技巧 **79.** 時態考題會以前後文的時態和寫文的時間點為基準。39次
技巧 **80.** 一般的事實會用現在式來表達。2次

advice 建議；勸告
attract 吸引；引起
（注意或興趣等）
a series of 一系列的；
一連串的

技巧 **76** 名詞或動詞詞彙的考題，前後文就是線索。

Dear Ms. Quinn,

Thank you for your advice on attracting customers. Our store will hold a series
與顧客相關的建議　　　　　　　　　　　正3試1選1
of _____ over the next quarter as you recommended.
名詞　　　　　　　　　　　　　　　　正1試4

(A) promotions　　　(B) interviews

親愛的葵茵女士：

感謝您建議我們如何吸引顧客，敝店將依照您的建言，在下一季舉辦一系
列的宣傳活動。

(A) 宣傳活動　　　(B) 面試

應用本技巧的題目

Pirelli's Pizza & Pie attracts scores of tourists and is marked on almost
every local map. Located downtown on Main Street here in Decatur, it has
been a _____ here since 2005.

(A) cafeteria　　　(B) preference　　　(C) history　　　(D) landmark

「裴瑞立披薩＆派」吸引眾多觀光客，幾乎每一區的當地地圖上都有標示這
間餐廳。座落於迪凱特城市中心鬧區的主街上，此餐廳自 2005 年以來就是
在地的地標。

(A) 自助餐廳　　　(B) 偏愛　　　(C) 歷史　　　(D) 地標
正解 (D)

scores of 許多
mark 做記號；標記
正1試1
local 當地的；地方的
試6選4

技巧**77** 人稱代名詞或指示形容詞所指稱的名詞要從前文裡面找。

Come see our new cars!

Valance Auto Dealers offers the best <u>trade-in values</u> on all vehicles when
　　　　　　　　　　　　　　　　　　　　試 3　　　　　試 2 選 2
　　　　　　　　　　　　　　舊換新折扣價

<u>purchasing a new one.</u> Come in to find out how much ＿＿＿＿ is worth!
　　購買新車時　　　試 1　　　　　　　　　　　人稱代名詞　　　試 1

(A) theirs　　(B) yours

歡迎賞車！

瓦倫斯汽車經銷商在您購買新車時，提供最優惠的舊換新折扣價給所有車款。現在就請蒞臨門市確認您的愛車價值多少吧！

1 頻出人稱代名詞：me、my、us、our、your、his、her、its、their、
　　　　　　　　　　you、him、it、them

2 頻出指示形容詞：this、these、that、those
　　　　　　　　　選 26　試 15 選 8　　正 1 試 1 選 1

應用本技巧的題目

> This email is to thank you for your giving a review of our EverBrite tablet device. Our company relies on customers like ＿＿＿＿ who help us figure out what we are doing wrong and how we can improve our products and services.

(A) me　　(B) you　　(C) them　　(D) us

這封電子郵件是為了感謝您對我們的 EverBrite 平板裝置留下評論，本公司仰賴像您這樣的顧客幫助我們明白公司哪裡做得不好以及如何改善產品與服務。

正解 (B)

trade-in 折舊交易
value 價格；價值
vehicle 車輛；（陸上）
交通工具

review 評論；審核
正 1 試 10 選 3
device 裝置
rely on 依靠～
試 2
figure out 弄清楚；想
出；理解
improve 改善
試 3

PART 6

技巧**78** 指示代名詞可概述前文的内容。

Santa Clara Steakhouse—Employee Guidelines (p. 7)

試4

Every employee should wash their hands after handling raw meats. In addition,

洗手

正4試2選5

you have to use designated knives and cutting boards for preparing them.

使用指定的刀具及砧板

試2選1

_____ must be strictly adhered to.

指示代名詞

試1

(A) These   (B) You

聖塔克拉拉牛排館——員工手冊（第7頁）

所有員工在處理過生肉之後都必須洗手。此外，在料理生肉食材時必須使用指定的刀具及砧板。上述事項務必嚴格遵守。

指示代名詞的種類：**this**、**these**、**that**、**those**

應用本技巧的題目

Please keep in mind that we operate on a strong feedback exchange system. _____ relies on the integrity of all involved in a transaction.

(A) Either   (B) Some   (C) This   (D) Both

請記住，我們是靠著強大的意見回饋交流系統在運作。這仰賴的是所有交易相關人士的誠信。

正解 **(C)**

左欄詞彙

raw meat 生肉
in addition 此外
designated 被指定的
cutting board 砧板
strictly 嚴格地；嚴厲地
adhere to 忠於～；堅持～

keep in mind 牢記
operate 操作；營運

試3選1

exchange 交換
integrity 正直；真實性
involved in 涉及～的；與～相關的
transaction 交易

技巧79 時態考題會以前後文的時態和寫文的時間點為基準。

Dear Ms. Carbone,

Thank you for renewing your subscription to *Monthly Mechanics Magazine*.
　　　感謝您的續訂（續訂—過去）　　　　試1選2

We are glad to let you know that in five business days, you will receive the
gift that you _____ at the renewal.
試4選1　　　　　　動詞　　　　　試1
　　　　　　　　　　　　　在續訂時（過去）

(A) will select　　　**(B)** selected

親愛的卡夢女士：

感謝您續訂《Monthly Mechanics Magazine》。很開心通知您，您將會在五個工作天之後收到您在續訂時所選擇的贈品。

1 文章：以試題內容最上方所標的刊出日為基準來決定要使用過去式或未來式

2 電子郵件或信件：以寫信日期為基準來決定要使用過去式或未來式

renew 更新
subscription 訂閱；訂購服務
renewal 更新

應用本技巧的題目

HARTFORD (17 March)—Designs by Diaz has announced at a press conference that it _____ into the international market. Their first overseas branch will open later this year.

(A) has been expanding　　　**(B)** will be expanding
(C) has expanded　　　　　　**(D)** is expanded

哈特佛（3 月 17 日）——迪亞茲設計在記者會上宣布將進軍國際市場，他們在海外的第一間分店將於今年的下半年開幕。

正解 **(B)**

announce 公告；宣布
正2試23選3
press conference 記者會
international 國際的
試4
overseas 海外的
試2
branch
正2試2
分公司；分店；分行

技巧**80** 一般的事實會用現在式來表達。

Bartlett Law Firm is currently looking for legal research assistants. This position
試2　　　　　　試1選1　試5　　　試1　　　試11選5
此職位

_____ a BA degree or higher in a legal related major. Successful candidates
試11選5　　　　　　　　　試1選1　試4選1　試4選1　試2
須具備（一般的事實）　　法律相關科系學士以上的學歷

are responsible for the tasks listed below.
正1試1

(A) requires　　　(B) had required
正1試5選2

> 巴特利律師事務所現正徵聘數名法律研究助理，此職位必須具備法律相關
> 科系學士學位以上的學歷，獲錄取之應徵者負責的業務內容如下所述。

應用本技巧的題目

> Congratulations on joining the VIP Sky Club! There are many benefits that
> come along with your membership. You now have access to our airport
> lounges, which _____ high-speed Internet access, comfortable lounge
> chairs, and a shower room.

(A) to feature　　　(B) featuring　　　(C) have featured　　　(D) feature

> 恭喜您加入 VIP Sky Club！成為會員之後將有許多優惠隨之而來，您現在可
> 進入我們的機場貴賓室，使用當中備有的高速網路、舒適座椅以及淋浴間。
> 正解 (D)

Sidebar (left margin):

currently 目前
legal 法律上的；法律
方面的
BA degree 學士學位
(= Bachelor of Arts
degree)
related 相關的

benefit 利益；好處
試2選2
come along with
伴隨～而來
have access to
可進入／接近～
comfortable 舒適的
正1試1選2

高出題率地圖

技巧 **81.** 連接副詞的考題首先要理解空格前後句的文意。28次
技巧 **82.** 連接副詞考題的決定性線索就是選出適切的句子。11次
技巧 **83.** 選擇適切的句子時，代名詞及指示詞要 **100%** 活用！46次
技巧 **84.** 當 **Enclosed** 或 **Attached** 出現在句子前面時，主詞和動詞須倒裝。
技巧 **85.** 空格附近若有 **if**，就從確認主要子句與 **if** 子句的動詞時態是否相對應著手。

技巧 **81** 連接副詞的考題首先要理解空格前後句的文意。

The international film festival has drawn more global attention this year than

試3　　　　試3選1
在全球引起了更多的矚目

ever before. _____ we highly recommend you book a hotel room in our city

連接副詞　　試4選1　強烈建議預訂

in advance.

試2選1

(A) Therefore　　(B) However

相較於往年任何一屆，本年度的國際電影節在全球已引起了更多的矚目。
因此，我們強烈建議預先向位於我們城市的飯店訂房。

(A) 因此　　**(B)** 然而

draw attention 引起注意
highly recommend (that) 強烈建議～

補充	**besides / moreover / in addition** 此外；再者 選3　　正2試1選3　正4試1選5 **also** 也；而且 正5試17選7	**furthermore** 而且；此外 正1試2選1
因果	**hence / therefore / thus** 因此；所以 正5試17選7　試1選1 **accordingly** 於是 試1選2	**consequently** 結果；因此 選3
轉折	**nevertheless / nonetheless** 不過；仍然 正1選4 **otherwise** 否則；不然 正4試5選3	**however** 然而 正4試5選3

應用本技巧的題目

As a company that truly cares about its customers, Donut Delight will now offer healthy foods such as whole grain muffins. _____ we have changed our original recipe to reduce the amount of fat and sugar in our donuts by 10%. Now you can feel better about enjoying our products.

care about 在乎～
whole grain 全穀物
recipe 食譜；料理方法
reduce 減少；降低
fat 脂肪
flavor 味道

PART 6

(A) Moreover   (B) Instead   (C) Unless   (D) Despite

作為一家真正關心顧客的公司，樂事甜甜圈現在即將開始供應像全麥瑪芬這類的健康食品。_____，我們已更改甜甜圈原先的配方，減少了 10% 的脂肪及糖分含量。今後您在享用我們的糕點時，心理負擔就不會那麼大了。

(A) 而且   (B) 反而   (C) 除非   (D) 儘管

正解 (A)

技巧 **82** 連接副詞考題的決定性線索就是選出適切的句子。

name A B 將 A 指定為 B
試 4

sole 唯一的；單獨的
office supply provider
辦公用品供應商
sales 銷售量

My business would like to know if you have any interest in naming us your sole office supply provider. You could get discounted supplies while my sales would
  試 1 選 1   試 4 選 1   折扣的   正 1 試 8 選 5
increase. _____. Please let me know what you think.
正 1 試 3 選 3

(A) Consequently, our shipping partner is both reliable and punctual.
   結果；因此   試 7 選 5

(B) In addition, we offer you same-day delivery.
   此外   提供當日配送服務   試 4 選 1

本公司想了解您是否有興趣指定我們成為貴公司的獨家辦公用品供應商，您可以折扣價購入辦公用品，同時本公司的銷售量也會增加。_____。不知您意下如何？

(A) 結果和我們配合的物流公司不僅值得信賴，還十分守時。
(B) 此外，我們還提供當日配送服務。

應用本技巧的題目

security 保安
ensure 確保；保證
safety 安全
privacy 隱私；私生活
account 帳戶；帳號
prevent 阻止；防止
intrude 入侵；闖入
secure 安全的
proper 適當的；正確的
threat 威脅；恐嚇
serious 嚴重的
immediate supervisor
直屬上司
measure 措施；方法

Only thanks to our network security team we are able to ensure the safety and privacy of our client accounts. They do an excellent job of preventing our network from being intruded into. _____. For example, you are all required to use a secure password that is to be changed every other month.

(A) Therefore, be sure to use the proper format.
(B) Besides, cyber threats are more serious than ever these days.
(C) If you have a question, ask your immediate supervisor right away.
(D) Nonetheless, some security measures must be followed by all employees.

多虧了網路安全組，我們才能確保顧客帳戶的安全及隱私。他們在防止我們的網路遭到入侵這方面做得非常出色。_____。例如，大家都必須使用每隔一個月變更一次的安全密碼。

(A) 因此，請務必使用正確的格式。
(B) 此外，近期的網路威脅比起以往還要嚴重。
(C) 如果有任何疑問，請立即詢問直屬上司。
(D) 儘管如此，全體職員仍須遵守幾項安全措施。

正解 **(D)**

技巧 **83** 選擇適切的句子時，代名詞及指示詞要 **100**％ 活用！

The Mix o' Matic is a great kitchen tool. It is easier to use than a regular blender.
　　　　　　　　　　　　　　試 4　　　試 1 選 2　　　　　　　試 4 選 2
It just has a single dial for speed! Despite that, it also has special features that
　　　　　　　　　　　　　　　　　　　　　　　　　　　　　　試 2
make it safe even for a child to handle. For example, there is a sensor that stops
the blade if your fingers get too close to them. _____ . That is probably my
　　　　　　　　　　　　　　　　　　　　　　　　　代名詞
favorite thing about the Mix o' Matic.
最中意的一點

regular 固定的；經常性的
blender 食物調理機
feature 特色；特點
blade 刀片；刀身

(A) Many other customers have left reviews.
(B) Most of all, it makes cleanup much easier.

Mix o' Matic 是一款優秀的廚房用具，它在使用上比一般的食物調理機更簡便，調整速度只需要一個旋鈕！此外它還具備特殊的功能，即使讓小朋友操作也同樣安全無虞。比方說，假如手指頭太靠近刀片，感應器就會讓刀片停止運轉。_____。這大概是我對 Mix o' Matic 最中意的一點了。

(A) 許多其他顧客也都留下了評論。　　**(B)** 最重要的是，清洗機身簡便許多。

應用本技巧的題目

The city of New Rochelle will be celebrating the New Year with the Festival of Light. This annual event has attracted tourists from all around the region ever since it first started nearly 20 years ago. This year, Central Park will be adorned with strings of colorful lights. _____ . With this new feature, more people are expected to visit after sundown.

adorn A with B 用 B 裝飾 A
string 細繩；帶子

(A) Information about the festival will be distributed by the Department of Tourism.
(B) Photos of last year's event have been posted on the city's website.
(C) They will be turned on at sundown and remain lit until midnight.
(D) Parking passes can be obtained from City Hall.

PART 6

新羅謝爾市將以燈火節來慶祝新年。這場年度盛會打從將近二十年前開始舉辦以來，就不斷吸引本區各地的觀光客到訪。今年中央公園將以彩燈串裝飾。_____。有了這個奪目的新特色，預計日落後會有更多人來參觀。

(A) 燈火節的相關資訊將由觀光部發布。
(B) 去年的活動照片已張貼在本市網站上。
(C) 燈飾會在日落時分被點亮，並且一直亮到午夜。
(D) 停車券可至市政府領取。

正解 **(C)**

倒裝：
在句子當中變換語順，比方說動詞在主詞前面出現，或否定副詞片語在句子前面出現等。

approved 被認可的；經批准的
floor plan 建築物的平面圖
renovation 翻修；革新

技巧 **84** 當 Enclosed 或 Attached 出現在句子前面時，主詞和動詞須倒裝。

_____ are an approved floor plan and a renovation schedule.
be 動詞　　　　　　　　　　　　主詞

(A) Attached　　　(B) Promoted
試 1 選 1

附件是已經批准的平面圖和整修日程表。
(A) 附上　　(B) 宣傳

1 若是為了強調 be 動詞後的主詞補語而將其放在句首，則之後主詞、動詞的順序就會有變動。

2 若考題空格位於句首，尤其是在 PART 6，則正確答案是 Enclosed 或 Attached 的機率很高。

應用本技巧的題目

_____ you will find the current schedule. Please let me know if you are available to assist with this event.

(A) Attached　　(B) Impressed　　(C) Informed　　(D) Experienced

附件為目前的行程表，請告知您是否有空協助這次的活動。
(A) 附上　　(B) 使印象深刻　　(C) 通知　　(D) 經歷

正解 **(A)**

---

current 目前的；當今的
available 可利用的；可獲得的；有空的

技巧 **85** 空格附近若有 if，就從確認主要子句與 if 子句的動詞時態是否相對應著手。

If Ms. Evans _____ the office 10 minutes earlier, she would have arrived on time.

假設語氣
on time.
　　選 3

would have p.p.—使用過去完成式的假設語氣（與過去事實相反）

(A) leaves　　(B) will leave　　(C) left　　(D) had left

如果伊凡斯女士當時提早十分鐘離開辦公室，她應該就能準時抵達了。

1 if 條件句和假設語氣

if 條件句 （如果～，就～。）	If＋主詞＋現在式動詞, 主詞＋will＋原形動詞.
使用過去式的假設語氣 （與現在事實相反）	If＋主詞＋過去式動詞, 主詞＋would / could / should / might＋原形動詞.
使用過去完成式的假設語氣 （與過去事實相反）	If＋主詞＋had p.p., 主詞＋would / could / should / might＋have p.p.
動詞用原形前加 should （未來發生的可能性較低）	If＋主詞＋should 原形動詞, 主詞＋will / can / may / should＋原形動詞.

2 倒裝：如果 If 在「未來假設語氣」當中被省略了，則 Should 須移至句首。

〔未來假設〕

If you should need any assistance, you can visit our information desk.

主詞　should　動詞　　　試 1 選 2

〔倒裝句〕

Should you need any assistance, you can visit our information desk.

should　主詞　動詞
萬一您需要任何協助，可以到我們的服務台洽詢。

應用本技巧的題目

If she _____ the contract, she would have hired a personal assistant.

(A) will win　　(B) had won　　(C) wins　　(D) will have won

假如當初她贏得了合約，她早就雇用一名私人助理了。
正解 (B)

tip!
在使用過去式的假設語氣中，如果 if 子句的動詞是 be 動詞，則必須改成 were。

PART 6

personal assistant
私人助理

高出題率地圖

技巧 86. 若是詢問主題或目的的考題請直攻短文開頭！126次
技巧 87. 若是詢問細節的考題就用五大關鍵字來解決。458次
技巧 88. 若是詢問問題點的考題，就先從短文開頭出現的否定或負面詞彙找起。8次
技巧 89. 若是詢問要求或叮嚀事項的考題，則短文後半段的祈使句為決定性的線索。36次
技巧 90. 若題目中含有 indicate、mention、state、true 等字，則 about 之後出現的名詞就是關鍵字。230次
技巧 91. 若是 "NOT" 類的考題，請對照各選項與短文當中的線索，先刪去錯誤選項。

技巧 **86** 若是詢問主題或目的的考題請直攻短文開頭！

tip!
電子郵件或信件主要想表達的內容也可能會在後半段出現。

attach 貼上；附上
unforeseen 預料之外的

Dear Ms. Warren,

I have attached the travel itinerary for your upcoming trip from November 14-
22次　已將旅遊行程表添加於附件　　32次
17. Your flight ticket, hotel, and rental car reservation details are all included.
28次　12次
詳細資訊包含在內

Also, it's not too late to purchase trip insurance if you decide you would like to
18次

do so. We highly recommend it just in case any unforeseen problems come up
4次　12次　　10次

during your vacation.

Q. What is the purpose of the email?
詢問目的

(A) To provide travel arrangement details
14次

(B) To announce a travel policy change
38次

華倫女士您好：

您 11 月 14 日到 17 日的旅遊即將成行，隨信附上行程表，您的機票、飯店和租賃車輛預約等詳細資訊都包含在內。另外，假如您有意願的話，現在購買旅遊險也還來得及。我們強烈建議您購買旅遊險，以防萬一您在度假期間發生意想不到的問題。

Q. 這封電子郵件的目的是什麼？
(A) 為了提供旅程安排的詳細資訊
(B) 為了告知旅遊政策有所變動

[1] 多益常考的問主題或目的之類型

What is the memo mainly about?
這則備忘錄主要與什麼有關？

What is the purpose of the letter?
這封信的目的是什麼？

2 線索在文章的前半段

線索會出現在 <u>announce</u>、<u>inform</u>、tell、let you know、<u>I'm writing to V</u>、
　　　　　　　　72次　　　　194次　　　　　　　　　　　　　　　　6次
I'd like to V 等用語之後。

應用本技巧的題目

EVANSVILLE (March 5) — After months of negotiations, the city council has finally approved a proposal to construct a 15,000-seat stadium at the northern end of town. The facility will be used for a variety of sports games. Construction will begin on May 20, and the completed structure will be open for use in approximately three years. Taxpayers are overwhelmingly in favor of the change, as it will attract more visitors to Evansville as well as provide a space for numerous events. For more information, visit www.evansville.gov/news.

Q. What is the article mainly about?
(A) A building project
(B) A sports competition
(C) A construction company
(D) A local store

negotiation 談判；協商
proposal 建議；計畫
facility 設備；設施
taxpayer 納稅人
overwhelmingly 壓倒性地
in favor of 支持～；贊成～

伊凡斯維爾市（3 月 5 日）——歷經數月的協商，市議會終於通過了提案，將於市鎮北端興建一座擁有 15,000 個座位的體育場館。該設施將用於各種運動賽事。建設工程將於 5 月 20 日開始進行，預計約於三年後完工並開放使用。納稅人們壓倒性地支持此變革，因為這座體育館將吸引更多人到訪伊凡斯維爾市，同時也能提供空間來舉辦許多活動。如需更多資訊，請上網 www.evansville.gov/news。

Q. 這篇文章主要與什麼有關？
(A) 一項建設計畫
(B) 一場運動賽事
(C) 一家建設公司
(D) 一間在地商店

正解 (A)

culinary 烹飪的；廚房的
notable 值得注意的；顯著的
hands-on 實際動手做的
instruction 指導
cuisine 菜餚；烹飪
certification 證明；證書

技巧87 若是詢問細節的考題就用五大關鍵字來解決。

Tucson Culinary School (TCS) has been training professional chefs for over a
（44次）　（20次）
decade. Some notable points about our academy include:
（12次）　　　　　　　　　（4次）

— Hands-on instruction in any of 20 different cuisines
（2次）　　　　　　　　　　（6次）
— Official certification after 5 weeks
（6次）

Those who register on or before May 31 can get a savings of 15%. Call at 555-
（5月31日之前）　　　（2次）
6245 or visit us directly at 3520 Elk Road here in Tucson.
（12次）

Q. What will happen in June?
（時間關鍵字）
(A) A new course will be available.
(B) An enrollment discount will expire.
（2次）　　　　　　（4次）

塔森廚藝學院 (TCS) 十餘年來持續不斷在培育專業廚師。我們學院值得注意的幾項特點包括：
— 講師親身指導任二十道不同的料理
— 五週後頒發官方研習證書

5月31日或更早之前報名的學員可享有八五折的優惠。請致電 555-6245 或親洽艾爾路 3520 號塔森學院辦理。

Q. 六月會發生什麼事？
(A) 一門新課程會開課。
(B) 報名折扣優惠會截止。

1 五大關鍵字：時間、場所、專有名詞、數字、身分名詞
Who is Ms. White? 懷特女士是誰？
（專有名詞）
Why did Ms. Mills go to the factory? 米爾斯小姐為何去了工廠？
（場所）

2 解題策略
確認關鍵字→掃視短文內容（確認關鍵字出現的位置）→對照該部分與選項並選出正確解答

應用本技巧的題目

Yoga Connect
Tuesdays and Thursdays, 7 A.M. – 8 A.M. Free yoga lesson near the tennis courts at Saginaw Park (moved to the covered picnic area in case of rain). All levels welcome. Just show up on the mornings that you want to participate.

Costello Dance Studio (CDS)
Open Tuesday to Sunday, 10 A.M. – 9 P.M. Rushford's newly opened dance facility, CDS offers a variety of classes for all ages and abilities. Fees apply.

Q. What is true about Yoga Connect?
(A) It has different levels on different days.
(B) It will be canceled in bad weather.
(C) It does not require registration.
(D) It is collecting optional donations.

covered 有頂棚的
in case of 如果發生～；萬一～
show up 出現；露臉

ability 能力；才能
fee 費用

瑜珈連結
每週二及每週四的上午七點到八點，薩吉諾公園的網球場附近免費的瑜珈課程（如下雨則移至設有頂棚的野餐區進行）。歡迎任何程度的朋友參加，只要在你想參加的課程當天早晨出席即可。

卡斯提洛舞蹈教室 (CDS)
開放時間為週二至週日的上午十點到晚上九點，地點在拉什福德市新開幕的舞蹈空間，CDS 提供多樣化的課程給所有年齡層的朋友，程度不拘，須付費。

Q. 關於瑜珈連結的敘述，下列何者為真？
(A) 在不同日期會有不同程度的課程。
(B) 天候不佳時會取消課程。
(C) 課程不需要報名。
(D) 目前正在募集自由捐款中。

正解 (C)

技巧**88** 若是詢問問題點的考題，就先從短文開頭出現的否定或負面詞彙找起。

From: Doreen Eichel

I'm afraid there is a scheduling conflict with the budget committee meeting
負面詞彙　　　　　　　行程衝突 2次　　　　　　　　8次
planned for tomorrow morning. I just realized that four of our committee members
　　　　　　　　　　　　　　　　　　　2次
have already been scheduled to attend the professional development seminar,
so they'll be gone all day. We'll need to reschedule the meeting for later this
　　　　整天都不在　　4次　　　　　　　　8次
week.

Q. What problem does Ms. Eichel mention?
　　　　詢問問題點
　(A) A budget report contains an error.
　　　　　　　　　　　20次　　14次
　(B) Some coworkers will be away from the office.
　　　　　12次　　　　　　18次

scheduling conflict
行程排定衝突
budget 預算
committee 委員會
realize 領悟；意識到
professional
development 專業發展

寄件者：朵琳・艾秋
原定於明天上午舉行的預算委員會會議恐怕與其他行程有所衝突。我剛才才發現我們有四位委員已經預定要出席專業職能發展研討會而整天都會不在，因此會議需要改到本週稍晚的時間。

Q. 艾秋小姐提及什麼問題？
　(A) 預算報告中含有一項錯誤。
　(B) 有幾位同事將不在辦公室。

---

1 詢問問題點的題型：problem、concerned、issue 52次
What is the problem with an item?
產品有什麼問題？
What is Mr. McRae concerned about?
麥克雷先生在擔心什麼？

2 短文中出現的否定或負面詞彙就是線索
I'm afraid there is a scheduling conflict.
恐怕行程會撞期。
Unfortunately, the book is out of stock.
　　12次　　　　　　　2次
很遺憾這本書目前沒有現貨。

▌tip!
否定或負面詞彙如
not、unfortunately、
afraid、trouble 等字
經常出現在考題中。

應用本技巧的題目

To: Arroyo Fashions <info@arroyofashions.com>
From: Lauren Keith <laurenk@wonder1mail.com>

I ordered some clothing on your website a few days ago (order #58295), and I just received the delivery of goods today. Unfortunately, there was a problem with one of the items. When I tried on the button-up silk blouse that I ordered in navy blue, I realized that it did not fit me at all. I checked the tag and saw that I was sent a petite instead of the medium that I ordered. Please send me the correct item that I had ordered. I would like this issue to be resolved as soon as possible.

fit 合身
petite 小號尺寸的衣服
resolve 解決

Q. What is the problem with an item in Ms. Keith's order?
    (A) It was missing a button.
    (B) It was the wrong size.
    (C) It was in damaged condition.
    (D) It was the wrong color.

收件者：Arroyo Fashions <info@arroyofashions.com>
寄件者：Lauren Keith <laurenk@wonder1mail.com>

前幾天我在貴公司網站上買了幾款衣服（訂單編號 58295），而今天剛收到貨。很遺憾的是其中一款有問題。當我試穿深藍色的那件開釦絲質上衣時，才意識到這件衣服一點都不合身。確認過衣服標籤後，發現我收到的是小號尺寸，但我訂的是中號。請將我訂購的正確尺寸寄給我，我希望盡快解決這件事。

Q. 凱斯小姐訂購的其中一件商品有什麼問題？
    (A) 衣服缺一顆釦子。
    (B) 衣服尺寸不對。
    (C) 衣服狀況破損。
    (D) 衣服顏色不對。

正解 (B)

技巧**89** 若是詢問要求或叮嚀事項的考題，則短文後半段的祈使句為決定性的線索。

To: Harlington Inc. Employees

I would like to inform you of a change regarding the coffee offered in the break
　　46次　　　　　　　　　　　　18次
room. We are looking for ways to cut costs. Therefore, we will no longer be
　　2次　　30次　　　　　　　　　　　　　　　　　　　　14次
supplying paper cups for coffee. Instead, just bring a cup from your home for
　　　　　　　　　　　　　　　祈使句（從家裡帶杯子來）
your own use. By doing so, you will help us to create less waste as well as save
　　　　　　　　　　　　　　　44次　　　　　16次　　　12次
money.

Q. What are staff members asked to do?
　　　　　　　　　　　要求
(A) Help to pay for coffee
　　　　4次
(B) Bring their own cups to work

inform A of B 將 B（事）
通知 A
regarding 關於～；就～
而言
supply 供給；供應

收件者：哈靈頓公司的職員們

我有一項變動要通知大家，是關於在休息室所提供的咖啡。我們正在尋求削減支出的辦法，因此我們將不再提供喝咖啡用的紙杯，請各位從家裡帶個自用的杯子過來取代紙杯，如此一來不僅有助於減少垃圾量，還能節省開銷。

Q. 職員們被要求做什麼？
(A) 協助支付咖啡的費用
(B) 自備杯子來上班

---

1 經常出題的要求或叮嚀類型

What are the managers asked to do?
經理們被要求做什麼？
What is Ms. Yee encouraged to do?
易小姐被鼓勵做什麼？

2 作答線索會在文章後半段出現

Could you email me the report?
可以請你用電子郵件把報告寄給我嗎？
Please go to our website and leave a comment.
　　　　　　　　　　　　　　　　14次
請到我們的網站留下評論。

🔖 tip!
如果是祈使句（命令句），考題中經常會出現 Please、You
　　　　　　194次
should、Could you 等關鍵詞彙。

應用本技巧的題目

Irving Garage
Oil Change: $19.99 with coupon

Receive up to 5 quarts of oil and a new oil filter.

Courtesy vehicle inspection: we will refill window washer fluids and engine coolant, check that the battery charge is high enough, test the tires' air pressure, and inspect the turn signals and brake lights.

Please be sure to tell an employee that you are using this coupon prior to the oil change and inspection.

Q. What are customers asked to do?
   (A) Choose an oil brand at the start of the work
   (B) Inform staff about the coupon before the service begins
   (C) Leave their car at the business overnight
   (D) Approve further repairs by filling out a request form

quart 夸脫（容量或液量的單位）
courtesy 免費的
inspection 檢查；檢驗
refill 裝滿；補滿
window washer fluid 窗戶清潔劑
coolant 冷卻液
air pressure 氣壓
turn signal 方向燈
brake light 煞車燈

厄文修車廠
換機油：使用折價券享 **19.99** 美元優惠價

最多可獲得 5 夸脫機油並更換機油濾芯。

免費車輛檢驗：我們會幫您把車窗玻璃清潔劑和引擎冷卻液裝滿、確認電瓶的電量是否充足、測試輪胎胎壓，並檢查方向燈與煞車燈是否正常。

請務必在更換機油及驗車前先告知工作人員欲使用折價券。

Q. 顧客被要求做什麼？
   (A) 在準備開始換機油時選擇機油廠牌
   (B) 在服務開始前先告知工作人員有關折價券的事
   (C) 讓車子在該營業場所停一晚
   (D) 填寫服務申請表以同意更進一步的修理作業

正解 (B)

技巧**90** 若題目中含有 indice、mention、state、true 等字，則 about 之後
出現的名詞就是關鍵字。

---

located at 位於～的
apply 適用；起作用
per 每個
complimentary 免費贈
送的
beverage 飲料

Fletcher Ripley's will be opening a new branch here in Woodbury. Bring this

14次

coupon to the new branch, located at 4310 Ferguson Street to receive a free soft

關鍵字　　　　　　　　　56次　　　　　　　　　　　獲得一杯免費飲料

drink with the purchase of any sandwich. Only one coupon can be applied per

54次

order.

Q. What is true about the coupon?

關鍵字（折價券）

(A) It is good for a complimentary beverage.

2次　　　　　26次　　　　18次

(B) Customer service managers have to approve it.

Fletcher Ripley's 將要在本地伍德伯里開一間新分店，持優惠券至位於佛格
森街 4310 號的新分店購買任一款三明治，即可免費獲得一杯無酒精飲料。
每次消費限用一張優惠券。

Q. 關於優惠券的敘述，下列何者為真？
(A) 它可以用來兌換一杯免費飲料。
(B) 客服經理們必須批准它。

---

1 頻出考題類型

What is true about the new policy?
關於新政策的敘述，下列何者為真？
What does the article indicate about Ms. Bravo?
關於布拉沃女士，文中指出了什麼訊息？

2 解題策略

確認 about 之後的名詞→掃視短文內容（確認關鍵字出現的位置）→
對照該部分與選項並選出正確解答

應用本技巧的題目

Dear Ms. Bloomfield,

Due to a computer error, your order #9561 was not dispatched on September 30 as planned. It will be sent today using our three-day delivery service.

Order Summary: Hennisaw leather hiking boots, size 9, green and tan

By way of apology, we will return the shipping fee of $6.95 that you were charged. It will appear in your account within three business days.

Q. What is indicated about Ms. Bloomfield's account?
   (A) It will be automatically renewed.
   (B) It will receive a refund payment.
   (C) It can be accessed by phone.
   (D) It can be activated after three days.

---

dispatch 發送；派遣
summary 概要；總結
tan 棕褐色
charge 收費；索價
appear 出現；看起來～

布蓉菲爾德女士您好：

由於系統發生錯誤，您編號 9561 的訂單未能如期在 9 月 30 日出貨，而將會在今天採用我們的三日配服務發送。

訂單摘要：軒尼索皮革登山靴、尺寸 9 號、綠色和棕褐色

為了表示歉意，我們會將已扣款的 6.95 美元運費退還給您，這筆款項將會在三個營業日內退至您的帳戶。

Q. 關於布蓉菲爾德女士的帳戶，文中指出了什麼訊息？
   (A) 該帳戶將自動更新。
   (B) 將有一筆退款入帳。
   (C) 可用電話讀取該帳戶。
   (D) 三天後可啟動該帳戶。

正解 **(B)**

技巧 **91** 若是 "**NOT**" 類的考題,請對照各選項與短文當中的線索,先刪去錯誤選項。

---

competition 競爭;比賽
amateur 業餘的
spread the word 散布消息;廣為宣傳
charge 收取的費用
registration 註冊;報名
winning entry 得獎的參賽作品

April 2 — The Burlington Library will hold an art competition for <u>amateur artists</u>
(2次)
of all ability levels. <u>A contest such as this has never been held in Burlington</u>
(20次) 沒有舉辦過(初次舉辦)──刪去 (A) 選項
<u>before</u>, so event <u>planners</u> are working hard to <u>spread</u> the word. There is no
(4次) (2次)
charge to enter the contest, but a registration form must be completed. These
are available at the library's information desk. The <u>winning</u> entries will be
(10次)
selected on May 30 and will be displayed in the library's <u>lobby</u> for three weeks.
(20次)

Q. What is <u>NOT</u> true about the event?
(A) It is being held <u>for the first time.</u>
(4次)
Ⓑ It requires a participation fee.

4 月 2 日──伯靈頓圖書館將舉辦一場程度不拘的業餘藝術家美術大賽。由於伯靈頓從未舉辦過這一類的賽事,因此活動企劃人員正在努力宣傳。參加比賽不需要繳交報名費,但一定要填寫報名表,報名表單可向圖書館服務台索取。獲獎作品將於 5 月 30 日選出,並將於圖書館大廳展出三個星期。

Q. 關於活動的敘述,下列何者「有誤」?
(A) 此活動是初次舉辦。
(B) 此活動須繳交報名費。

① NOT 題型

What is <u>NOT</u> mentioned in the advertisement?
下列何者在廣告中「未」被提及?
What is <u>NOT</u> true about Star Inc.?
關於繁星公司的敘述,下列何者「有誤」?

② 解題策略(刪去法)
確認選項→對照短文內容→刪去內容有提及的錯誤選項並選擇剩下的選項

應用本技巧的題目

Item: 10-speed Bicycle—Blue
Same brand as used by Olympian Brenda Foster!

Asking Price: $125
Location: Worcester, MA
Description:
— Purchased lightly used 2 years ago. Paid $215.
— Chain is rusted and should be replaced.
— Wheels/frame/brakes etc. all in good condition.
— $125 or best offer.
Contact Information: Mobile phone 555-1234, ask for Eddy.

Q. What is NOT stated about the bicycle?
    (A) Its brand was used by a professional athlete.
    (B) It needs to have a part fixed.
    (C) It was bought two years ago.
    (D) It should be repainted.

location 地點；位置
description 描述；形容
replace 替換
rusted 生鏽的
wheel 輪胎
frame 骨架
in good condition 狀況
良好

professional athlete
職業運動員
fix 修理

商品：10 段變速腳踏車（藍色）
奧運選手布蘭達・福斯特同款品牌！

賣方報價：125 美元
所在位置：伍斯特（麻薩諸塞州）
商品描述：
— 兩年前以 215 美元購入，很少騎。
— 鏈條生鏽了，須更換。
— 輪胎、車架、煞車等狀況良好。
— 125 美元或最高出價者得。
聯絡方式：手機 555-1234，找艾迪。

Q. 關於腳踏車的敘述，下列何者「有誤」？
    (A) 職業運動員曾使用過該品牌。
    (B) 該腳踏車的一項零件須修理。
    (C) 該腳踏車是兩年前購入的。
    (D) 該腳踏車須重新烤漆。

正解 (D)

PART 7

高出題率地圖

技巧 **92.** 如果是考插入句，則連接詞、指示詞或代名詞為決定性的提示。
技巧 **93.** 如果是考理解文章 / 對話的意圖，就要掌握前後文的脈絡。24次
技巧 **94.** 若試題內容中出現星號、斜體字或 **Note**，則該處即為出題重點。
技巧 **95.** 若圖表或表格中的資訊出現在選項當中，十之八九為關聯題。6次
技巧 **96.** 如果是詢問廣告標的物的考題，請進攻短文的開頭。50次
技巧 **97.** 若是折扣、宣傳、補充資訊或申請方法等相關考題，請進攻短文後半段。24次

技巧 **92** 如果是考插入句，則連接詞、指示詞或代名詞為決定性的提示。

連接詞：
however、therefore、
also 等

指示詞 / 代名詞：
he、his、her、this、
those、it、they 等

award-winning 獲獎的
self-help 自我啟發的

— [1] —. As part of a national book tour, award-winning author Yolanda Reeves
will hold a book-signing event at Hillcrest Books on October 5 from 10 A.M. to
3 P.M. Ms. Reeves worked as a professional dancer for twelve years with the
Toronto Ballet Troupe. — [2] —. The book was called "a self-help guide that
speaks to the soul" by the Toronto Herald.

Q. In which of the positions marked [1] and [2] does the following sentence
best belong?

"Now she operates her own dance studio for underprivileged youth."

(A) [1]　　(B) [2]

— [1] — 作為全國圖書巡展的其中一個環節，獲獎作家約蘭達‧李維女士
的簽書會將於 10 月 5 日上午十點至下午三點在希爾克雷斯特書店舉行。李
維女士曾在多倫多芭蕾舞團擔任專業舞者長達十二年。— [2] — 本書被《多
倫多先驅報》稱為「與靈魂對話的自我啟發指南」。

Q. 下面這個句子插入文中標示的 [1]、[2] 二處當中的何處最符合文意？

「現在她為弱勢的年輕人經營著自己的舞蹈工作室。」

(A) [1]　　(B) [2]

---

① 注意考題中的指定句及短文中編號所在處附近的連接詞
② 確認考題中的指定句及短文中編號所在處附近的指示詞或代名詞

應用本技巧的題目

Oswego Harbor (12 November) — Castaneda Industries is honored to have won the bid for the construction of five new cruise ships for Silver Sail Cruises. — [1] —. This will bring the number of ships in the cruise company's fleet to 30.

Each cruise ship will feature both a deck pool and indoor pool for guests to relax and swim in regardless of the weather. The rooms will be equipped with luxury beds and entertainment systems. Also, there will be multiple ballrooms for different types of music. — [2] —. Game and arcade areas will also be included for children to enjoy.

Silver Sail Cruises has been the best-rated cruise company in the world for three years running. — [3] —. It is known for providing luxurious resort experiences at affordable prices. The new cruise ships are scheduled to set sail from their home ports sometime next summer. — [4] —.

Q. In which of the positions marked [1], [2], [3], and [4] does the following sentence best belong?

"All of those ports are situated on the east coast."

(A) [1]　　(B) [2]　　(C) [3]　　(D) [4]

be honored to 感到榮幸做～
win the bid 得標
fleet 艦隊；擁有的船隻
deck 甲板
ballroom 舞廳
port 港

奧斯維戈港（11 月 12 日）——卡斯塔尼達實業很榮幸能夠標到銀帆郵輪公司的五艘全新郵輪建造案，— [1] — 這將使該郵輪公司旗下的船隊數量來到三十艘。

為了讓旅客無論天候好壞都能夠休息或游泳，未來每艘郵輪都將設有甲板游泳池及室內游泳池，而艙房中則將配有豪華寢具及各項娛樂設施。此外，還有多個播放不同風格音樂的舞廳，— [2] — 供孩子玩樂的遊戲區及大型電玩區也包含其中。

銀帆郵輪公司連續三年穩坐全球評價最高的郵輪公司寶座。— [3] — 該公司之所以為人所熟知，是因為他們以合理的價格提供遊客豪華度假村的體驗。新郵輪預計明年夏天將從他們的母港啟航。— [4] —

Q. 下面這個句子插入文中標示的 [1]、[2]、[3]、[4] 四處當中的何處最符合文意？

「那些港口皆位於東海岸。」

(A) [1]　　(B) [2]　　(C) [3]　　(D) [4]

正解 (D)

PART 7

技巧 **93** 如果是考理解文章／對話的意圖，就要掌握前後文的脈絡。

on short notice 臨時通知

motivational 賦予動機的；激勵人心的

Shinu Barigai [1:43 P.M.]
We've got a problem. Samantha Denson cannot host the awards show tonight.

Klaudia Schulz [1:44 P.M.]
It'll be nearly impossible to find someone on such short notice.
　　　　　　　　　　　　　　　　26次　　　　4次

Shinu Barigai [1:45 P.M.]
I was thinking that your brother might be a good choice, since he's a
　　　　　　　　　　　兄弟　　　　　　　　　20次
professional motivational speaker. Could you find out if he'd be willing to do it?
　　　　　　　6次　　　　請求詢問兄弟的意願　　　　14次

Klaudia Schulz [1:46 P.M.] 考題中提及的部分
Of course. 出現的詞句（接受）
12次

Q. At 1:46 P.M., what does Ms. Schulz mean when she writes, "Of course"?
確認在試題中的哪個地方　　　　　　　　　　　　　　確認出現的詞句
(A) She will bring her brother to an event.
(B) She will speak to her relative.
　　　　　　　　　4次

Shinu Barigai〔下午 1:43〕
我們遇到了困難。莎曼莎・鄧森女士無法主持今晚的頒獎典禮。

Klaudia Schulz〔下午 1:44〕
這麼臨時才通知，要找到替代人選幾乎是不可能的。

Shinu Barigai〔下午 1:45〕
我剛在想妳弟或許是個不錯的選擇，畢竟他是個專業的激勵講師。妳可以問問看他有沒有意願嗎？

Klaudia Schulz〔下午 1:46〕
當然可以。

Q. 一點四十六分時，舒茲女士打的 "Of course." 是什麼意思？
(A) 她會把弟弟帶到活動現場。
(B) 她會和她的親屬談談。

---

1 線索出現的頻率
　　該指定詞句的前文→後文→整體脈絡

2 經常出題的情境
　　工作等方面請求和接受幫助的情境
　　確認事情是否有所進展的情境
　　同意對方意見或提議的情境

應用本技巧的題目

Karen Shaw [8:54 A.M.] Lucy, did you get to the office already?
Lucy Sutton [8:55 A.M.] Yes, I got in a few minutes ago. Why?
Karen Shaw [8:56 A.M.] I'm running late, but I'm supposed to host a client meeting at 9:15 and I haven't made copies of the handout yet. Could you do that for me?
Lucy Sutton [8:57 A.M.] Where is the original copy?
Karen Shaw [8:58 A.M.] It should be on my desk.
Lucy Sutton [8:59 A.M.] There are several folders on your desk.
Karen Shaw [9:00 A.M.] There's one with today's date. It should be in there.
Lucy Sutton [9:01 A.M.] This must be it. How many copies do you need?
Karen Shaw [9:02 A.M.] Ten, please. Thanks. I really appreciate this.

> be supposed to 應該～；預期～
> host 主辦；主持
> handout 印刷的文件資料；講義
> original 原來的

Q. At 8:59 A.M., what does Ms. Sutton most likely mean when she writes, "There are several folders on your desk"?
(A) She has to prepare for a meeting.
(B) She needs some specific details.
(C) Ms. Shaw locked a file cabinet.
(D) Ms. Shaw is in another office.

> specific 具體的；明確的
> lock 上鎖

Karen Shaw 〔上午 8:54〕露西，妳已經進辦公室了嗎？
Lucy Sutton 〔上午 8:55〕對，我幾分鐘前到了。怎麼了嗎？
Karen Shaw 〔上午 8:56〕我好像要遲到了，可是 9 點 15 分我得主持一場客戶會議，會議文件我還沒影印好，妳可以幫我印嗎？
Lucy Sutton 〔上午 8:57〕原稿在哪裡？
Karen Shaw 〔上午 8:58〕應該在我的桌上。
Lucy Sutton 〔上午 8:59〕妳桌上有好幾個資料夾。
Karen Shaw 〔上午 9:00〕其中一個資料夾有標今天的日期，文件應該就在裡面。
Lucy Sutton 〔上午 9:01〕應該是這個吧。妳需要幾份？
Karen Shaw 〔上午 9:02〕麻煩幫我印十份，謝謝。真的很感激妳的幫忙。

Q. 八點五十九分時，薩頓小姐打的 "There are several folders on your desk." 最有可能是什麼意思？
(A) 她必須為一場會議做準備。
(B) 她需要明確詳細的說明。
(C) 蕭爾小姐把文件櫃鎖起來了。
(D) 蕭爾小姐在另一間辦公室。

正解 (B)

PART 7

技巧 **94** 若試題內容中出現星號、斜體字或 Note，則該處即為出題重點。

■ tip!
強調或注意標示一般
都會出現在短文的結
尾處。

gas mileage 燃料消耗
率

try out 試用；試驗

Model: Wilmar Prasina-8
Price: $9,450

This model has air conditioning, heated seats, and a spacious trunk. It has passed
　　　　　　　　　　　4次　　　　　　　　　　　　　6次
all safety tests. Wilmar vehicles are known for getting excellent gas mileage.
　　20次　　　　　　　　　　　　　　　　　　　　18次

＊ If you would like to try out the Wilmar Prasina-8 yourself, please call Brent
星號　　　　　　　　試駕　　　　　　　　　　　　　打電話給 Brent Tinsley
Tinsley at 389-555-4661.

Q. According to the notice, why should people contact Mr. Tinsley?
　(A) To arrange an appointment for a test drive
　　　　　　　40次　　　　　　28次
　(B) To get an estimate for trading in a car
　　　　　　　　　20次

型號：Wilmar Prasina-8
價格：9,450 美元

此型號車款配有空調、加熱座椅和寬敞的後車廂，並且已通過所有安全測
試。Wilmar 汽車以其低油耗之特性聞名。

＊如欲試駕 Wilmar Prasina-8 車款，請致電 389-555-4661 聯繫布倫特‧汀
斯利。

Q. 根據這則公告，民眾為何要聯絡汀斯利先生？
　(A) 為了安排試駕預約
　(B) 為了取得車輛交易估價

---

1 短文中標示星號 (*)、斜體字或 Note 等欲強調或引起注意的地方，就
是出題點。

first-come, first-served
basis 先到先得準則

＊Seating is available on a first-come, first-served basis.
　　18次　　　　　　　　　　　　　2次　　　4次
座位是依照先到先入座的原則來提供。
NOTE: This service can only be used on purchases of thirty dollars or more.
注意：只有購物滿三十美元以上才能夠使用這項服務。

應用本技巧的題目

Volunteer Schedule for May 3 Children's Festival

Shift	Volunteers
9:00 A.M. – Noon	Veronica Garner, Ross Shelby
Noon – 2:30 P.M.	Luella Peralta, Gerard Boucet, Kiara Sarkis
2:30 P.M. – 5:30 P.M.	John Helms, Livia Spielman, Kazuya Ohira, Quinn Brady
5:30 P.M. – 8:00 P.M.	Helene Andris, Charlie Dayton, Tammy Keaton

＊ Please note that parking passes will be given to the morning shift workers only, as they will need to bring some supplies to the site.

Q. Why will only one group receive parking passes?
(A) They volunteered for the event early.
(B) They need to transport some items.
(C) They can receive a membership discount.
(D) They will drive all other group members.

volunteer 志願者；義工

parking pass 停車券
supplies 補給品；物資

5 月 3 日「兒童嘉年華會」志工安排表

班別	志工名單
上午 9:00—中午	Veronica Garner、Ross Shelby
中午—下午 2:30	Luella Peralta、Gerard Boucet、Kiara Sarkis
下午 2:30—下午 5:30	John Helms、Livia Spielman、Kazuya Ohira、Quinn Brady
下午 5:30—下午 8:00	Helene Andris、Charlie Dayton、Tammy Keaton

＊注意，停車券僅提供給上午班的工作者，因為他們需要帶一些補給物資到活動現場。

Q. 為什麼只有一組人員會拿到停車券？
(A) 他們很早就申請擔任志工。
(B) 他們需要載送一些物品。
(C) 他們可以獲得會員折扣。
(D) 他們會載送所有其他班別的成員。

正解 (B)

PART 7

技巧 **95** 若圖表或表格中的資訊出現在選項當中，十之八九為關聯題。

From: Keith Cho, Office Manager

The management team has hired Upton Co. to assist us with moving from
　　2次　　　　　　　　　　　　　　　　82次
Juniper Tower to the Foley Building next week. Employees will be responsible
　　　　　　　　　　　　　　　　　　　　　　　　　　　　8次
for preparing their own belongings. I will distribute the necessary boxes and
　　　　　　　　　　6次　　　　　　分發　　　　12次
packing supplies two days before the scheduled moving date for your floor,
　2次　　　　　　　　預定搬遷日的前兩天　　14次
箱子及打包用的包材
and everything should be ready to go by the time you leave work the day before
　　　　　　　　　　2次
your scheduled date.
　　2次

Upton Co. Schedule

Date	Area
July 10	2nd Floor: Sales, Administration 2次
July 11	3rd Floor: Finance, Information Technology 8次
July 12 7月12日	4th Floor: Human Resources 人力資源部

Q. When will Mr. Cho give supplies to members of the HR team?
　何時　　　　　　　　提供包材　　　　　　　　　人資部
(A) July 10　　(B) July 11

寄件者：行政主管卓凱斯

管理部已雇用厄普頓公司協助我們下週從珠尼柏塔大廈搬到弗立大樓。職員們要負責把自己的個人物品準備好，我會在你們樓層預定搬遷日的前兩天分發所需的箱子及打包用的包材。在預定輪到你的樓層搬遷的前一天下班時，一切皆應準備就緒。

日期	區域
7月10日	2樓：業務部、行政部
7月11日	3樓：財務部、資訊部
7月12日	4樓：人資部

Q. 卓先生什麼時候會提供包材給人資部的同仁？
　(A) 7月10日　　(B) 7月11日

應用本技巧的題目

Item	Stock Code	Price
Office Chair	OC48-974	15.00
Cushioned Chair	CC32-817	10.00
Marx Desktop Computer Set	MD88-315	500.00
Multi-line Telephone	MT64-582	30.00
		Total: 555.00

From: Tyrone Woods

We hired two new employees a few weeks ago. The thing is, since the new employees started, they haven't used their multi-line phones a single time. Since we're still within the return window, I want to see if we can send back the phones and get a refund.

Q. Which item does Mr. Woods want to return?
(A) OC48-974
(B) CC32-817
(C) MD88-315
(D) MT64-582

stock 庫存
cushioned 附有軟墊的
multi-line 多條線路的

return 退貨
window（有機會做某事的）期間
refund 退款

品項	庫存編號	價格
辦公椅	OC48-974	15.00
軟墊椅	CC32-817	10.00
Marx 桌上型電腦組	MD88-315	500.00
多線電話機	MT64-582	30.00
		總計：555.00

寄件者：泰倫・伍茲

我們在幾週前雇用了兩名新員工，問題是從新員工開始工作到現在，他們的多線電話機連一次都沒用過。既然還在退貨期限內，我想了解能否讓我們把電話機寄回去申請退款。

Q. 伍茲先生想要退貨的是哪一項商品？
(A) OC48-974
(B) CC32-817
(C) MD88-315
(D) MT64-582

正解 (D)

技巧**96** 如果是詢問廣告標的物的考題，請進攻短文的開頭。

▌tip!
很多時候都能夠從前
半段的提問或祈使句
型態的句子當中得知
廣告標的物為何。

electronic device 電子
裝置
electronics 電子產品
as good as new 完好如
新
cost 要價

E-Geeks

Are your computers, tablets, or other electronic devices not working as well as
如果需要維修電子產品就帶過來
they used to? Bring them to E-Geeks! We can repair and upgrade your electronics
20次　　　　　　　　6次
so that they are as good as new. Bring this flyer to get 20% off. Visit us at E-Geeks
12次
website to see a list of how much our services cost.
14次

Q. What kind of service is being advertised?
哪一種服務的廣告
(A) Software customization
(B) Electronics repair

E-Geeks

各位的桌上型電腦、平板電腦或其他電子裝置是否不像以往運作得那麼
順暢？把它們帶來 E-Geeks 吧！我們可以維修並且升級你們的電子產品，
讓它們像新的一樣狀態極佳。憑此廣告傳單可享 20% 的折扣。造訪我們
E-Geeks 的網站，查看各項服務價目表。

Q. 這是哪一種服務的廣告？
(A) 軟體客製化服務
(B) 電子產品維修服務

1 詢問廣告標的物的題型

What is being advertised?
這是在廣告什麼？
What kind of service does the business offer?
這家公司提供什麼樣的服務？

2 可從標題或短文開頭的內容掌握廣告標的物

Take your yoga to the next level!
讓你的瑜珈實力更上一層樓！
Don't miss the new washing machine.
46次
別錯過這台新款洗衣機。

應用本技巧的題目

deal 交易
rug 小地毯
combine（使）結合；
（使）合併
clearance 清倉拍賣

Pearson Décor Summer Sale
One day only!
Saturday, August 3

Get the best deals of the summer on home furnishings for every room!
Curtains 40% off
Rugs 50% off
Wall Mirrors 60% off

Sales prices cannot be combined with other offers. Items marked "Clearance" cannot be returned. Please note that our store will close two hours early the day before the sale in order to make preparations.

Q. What kind of business is being advertised?
(A) A home store
(B) A furniture store
(C) A photography studio
(D) A hardware store

Pearson Décor 夏季特賣
只有一天！
8 月 3 日星期六

把握今夏最超值的入手機會，
為每個房間添購居家用品吧！
窗簾下殺 **40%**
地毯下殺 **50%**
壁掛鏡下殺 **60%**

特賣價格不得與其他優惠並用。標示「清倉特賣」的商品不接受退貨。為進行事前準備，本門市將於特賣活動的前一天提早兩小時結束營業，敬請留意。

Q.這是在廣告哪一種類別的企業？
(A) 居家用品店
(B) 家具店
(C) 照相館
(D) 五金行

正解 (A)

技巧**97** 若是折扣、宣傳、補充資訊或申請方法等相關考題，請進攻短文後半段。

Consumers Advised to Check Their Kitchens
6次

April 26 — Presley Appliances, the nation's largest supplier of kitchen appliances,
3次

announced yesterday that it is voluntarily recalling its Cardona-K combi oven.
2次

Customers who own this device can return it to the place of purchase for a
replacement of equal value. The company made the decision based on numerous
14次   20次

complaints from customers saying that the temperature fluctuates greatly on
22次   2次   2次

the convection oven setting. For more information, call its customer service
                              如需進一步資訊   請致電客服中心

center.

Q. How people can get more information?
    如何獲得進一步資訊

(A) By calling the service center
(B) By visiting a store

建議消費者確認一下廚房

4 月 26 日——國內最大的廚房用具供應商普里斯立家電昨日宣布自主召回自家的 Cardona-K 多功能烤箱，家中有這台烤箱的顧客可至購買地點退貨並更換等值商品。為數眾多的顧客投訴這款烤箱在設定為旋風模式（對流式加熱）時溫度會大幅變動，該公司基於此因素做出了召回的決定。如需進一步資訊，請致電該公司的客服中心。

Q. 民眾要如何獲得進一步資訊？
   (A) 打電話到客服中心
   (B) 親洽門市

---

consumer 消費者
supplier 提供者；供應商
kitchen appliance 廚房用具
voluntarily 自願地；自發地
recall 召回
replacement 更換；替代品
equal 均等的；相當的
value 價格；價值
make a decision 做決定
numerous 很多的
complaint 抱怨；投訴
fluctuate 波動；起伏不定
convection 對流

應用本技巧的題目

Join the Southside Catering Team!

Southside Catering is now hiring part-time workers.

Available positions:
- Assistant chef: Help with food preparation prior to the event, working mainly in the kitchen at our headquarters. $10~15/hour. Minimum 1 year of experience working in a professional restaurant setting.
- Server: Serve food and beverages to guests, offering the highest standard of customer service. $9.50/hour. Minimum 2 years of server experience preferred.

If you would like to apply for any of the above positions, please attend our group interview session led by HR Director Anthony Parker on Saturday, May 21, at 10 A.M.

position 位置；職位
preparation 準備（工作）
headquarter 總部；總公司
setting 環境
standard 標準；水準
prefer 偏好

Q. How can interested parties apply for a job at Southside Catering?
(A) By calling a human resources employee
(B) By mailing a resume to the company
(C) By attending an interview event
(D) By completing an online application

interested party 有關的當事者；利害關係人
resume 履歷
complete 完成；填寫

加入 Southside 外燴團隊吧！

Southside 外燴工讀夥伴募集中。

職缺：
－廚房助理：協助活動餐點之事前準備，主要是在總部中央廚房工作，時薪 10 ～ 15 美元，至少要有在專業廚房環境工作一年以上的經歷。
－服務生：為顧客上餐點及飲料，提供最高水準的顧客服務，時薪 **9.50** 美元，具兩年以上服務生經驗者佳。

欲應徵上述任一職位，請參加 5 月 21 日星期六上午十點由我們人資部主管安東尼・帕克所主持的團體面試。

Q. 有興趣的人要如何應徵 Southside 外燴公司的工作？
(A) 致電人資部職員
(B) 寄送履歷至該公司
(C) 參加面試活動
(D) 上網填寫申請書

正解 (C)

PART 7

高出題率地圖

技巧 **98.** 徵才廣告絕對會出現業務內容及資格條件的相關考題。6次
技巧 **99.** 報導文當中絕對不能錯過引號 (" ----- ") 所標示的訪談內容。56次
技巧 **100.** 在電子郵件或信件類的文章中，要優先掌握收件者及寄件者。

技巧 **98** 徵才廣告絕對會出現業務內容及資格條件的相關考題。

Front Desk Staff Needed
徵才廣告

Callahan Hotel is <u>seeking</u> two part-time front desk receptionists to join our
14次
team. The <u>ideal</u> <u>candidate</u> will be outgoing and have <u>previous</u> experience
14次   36次
working in a reception area. <u>Responsibilities</u> include checking guests in using
業務 16次
our in-house system, <u>introducing the hotel's additional services to guests and</u>
介紹飯店的附加服務並鼓勵多加利用
<u>encouraging their use</u>, and processing payments upon check-out. We offer a
22次
competitive hourly wage and a <u>generous</u> <u>benefits package</u>. Email Valerie Meyer
10次   2次
at vmeyer@callahanhotel.com to apply.

Q. What is a <u>duty</u> of the front desk receptionist?
職責
(A) Promoting hotel services   (B) Inspecting guests' rooms

> 徵求前台接待員
>
> 卡拉漢飯店正在尋找兩名時薪制的前台接待員加入我們的工作團隊。我們的理想人選個性要外向，並且必須有接待方面的相關工作經歷。業務內容包括使用內部系統為旅客辦理入住手續、介紹飯店的附加服務並鼓勵他們多加利用，以及在旅客退房時處理結帳事宜。我們提供具競爭力的時薪和優渥的福利待遇。如欲應徵請寄電子郵件至 vmeyer@callahanhotel.com 聯繫 Valerie Meyer。
>
> Q. 下列何者為前台接待員的職責？
>   (A) 推廣飯店的服務   (B) 檢查旅客的客房

1 資格條件 **vs** 負責業務 必背★
  ① 資格條件：requirements / qualifications
                  14次   8次

candidate 應徵者；候選人
outgoing 外向的
previous 先前的；以前的
reception area 接待領域
in-house 內部的
encourage 鼓勵；促進
process 處理；辦理
upon 在～後立即
competitive 競爭的；具有競爭力的
hourly wage 時薪
generous 慷慨的；大方的
benefits package 福利待遇

② 負責業務：duties / responsibilities
<u>　　　　　　10次</u>

2 必要條件 **vs** 加分項目 必背★
　① 必要條件的用語：must、should、mandatory、required、necessary
　② 加分項目的用語：<u>preferred</u>、<u>a plus</u>、desirable
　　　　　　　　　　　　10次　　　　10次

應用本技巧的題目

Carbone Trucking Needs More Drivers

Carbone Trucking, originally based in Lexington, has been a reliable trucking company that supplied companies along the east coast for the past decade. Now, given its success and good reputation, it plans to start delivering across the entire nation.

In order to do so, more drivers will be needed. The qualifications are as below:
－ A valid Commercial Driver's License (CDL) holder
－ A two-year accident-free driving history
－ No criminal record related to driving
－ Qualified for a passport application

Q. What is NOT a requirement for a qualified candidate?
　(A) A certain kind of driver's license
　(B) No criminal records
　(C) A certain amount of work experience
　(D) An accident free driving history

base in 以～為基礎；
以～為根據地
reliable 可靠的；可信賴的
decade 十年
reputation 名聲；聲望
entire 全部的
nation 國家
qualification 資格證明；條件
commercial 商業的
holder 持有者
accident 意外；事故
criminal 犯罪的；犯法的
qualified 有資格的；合格的

卡波恩貨運公司需要更多駕駛員加入

Carbone Trucking 起初以萊辛頓為據點，在過去十年間為東岸沿海一帶的企業提供服務，是一家值得信賴的貨運公司。現在，基於營運有成及良好聲譽，本公司計畫展開橫跨全國的配送事業。

為此，我們需要更多的駕駛員，資格條件如下：
－持有有效職業駕駛執照者
－兩年內無交通事故肇事紀錄
－無行駛相關之犯罪紀錄
－具備申請護照的資格

Q. 下列何者「非」合格應徵者之必要條件？
　(A) 特定種類的駕駛執照
　(B) 無犯罪紀錄
　(C) 具有一定程度的工作經驗
　(D) 無交通事故肇事紀錄

正解 (C)

技巧**99** 報導文當中絕對不能錯過引號 ("------") 所標示的訪談內容。

(March 16) － Demetria Mazzi always dreamed of opening her own Italian restaurant so that she could <u>share</u> the delicious food that her grandmother
32次

taught her to make. The restaurant, Scelto, got off to a rocky start in its home in the <u>neighborhood</u> of Charleston Heights. <u>"With so many other restaurants
8次

in the neighborhood, it was difficult to find a way to stand out,"</u> Mazzi recalls.
「該地區的其他餐廳非常多」　　　　　　　　　2次

However, with help from her <u>skilled</u> chefs and <u>friendly</u> staff, her handmade
6次　　　　　　　12次

pasta soon began to gain recognition. Thanks to her success, Mazzi is already looking for a location for a second branch.

Q. What problem did Ms. Mazzi have with her business?
(A) There was a lot of <u>competition</u>.
4次
(B) There were not enough skilled employees.

get off to a rocky start
起頭非常不順利
neighborhood 鄰近地區
stand out 突出；醒目
recall 回想；記得
gain recognition 獲得認可
thanks to 由於～；感謝～；多虧～
competition 競爭；比賽

（3 月 16 日）──戴梅特莉雅・瑪琪一直以來都夢想著開一間屬於她自己的義大利餐廳，這樣一來她就可以將奶奶傳授給她的食譜做成美味餐點分享出去。這間位於查爾斯頓高地鄰近地區的 Scelto 餐廳的起頭非常不順利。「當時鄰近地區的其他餐廳非常多，很難去突顯自家餐廳。」瑪琪回憶道。然而，在技術純熟的廚師與親切員工的協助之下，她的手工義大利麵很快便開始獲得大家的認可。拜創始店的成功所賜，瑪琪已經在尋找第二間分店的地點了。

Q. 瑪琪女士的事業曾遇到什麼問題？
(A) 競爭十分激烈。
(B) 技術純熟的員工不足。

應用本技巧的題目

October 20 — Mulberry officials have approved plans for the construction of a shopping center in the northern section of town. Property developer McCabe Properties purchased the 19-acre plot of land for this project two years ago but had been waiting for planning permission. "We're pleased that this project can finally get underway," said Lisa Evans, a spokesperson for McCabe Properties. "Hundreds of people can get full- and part-time positions thanks to having a shopping center of this size in Mulberry," she added. The work is expected to be completed in four years.

Q. What benefit of the project is mentioned?
(A) It will create new job opportunities.
(B) It will attract visitors to Mulberry.
(C) It will solve the traffic congestion.
(D) It will help local children.

property 財產；房地產
developer 開發業者
plot of land 地塊
planning permission 建築許可
get underway 開始進行
spokesperson 發言人；代言人

create 創造；創作
job opportunity 工作機會
attract 吸引；引起（注意或興趣等）
solve 解決
traffic congestion 交通堵塞

10 月 20 日——馬爾伯里當地官方已核准座落於該城鎮北區的購物中心建設計畫。兩年前地產開發業者麥凱比地產開發公司就為此計畫購入一塊 **19** 英畝的土地，但是他們一直在等建築許可通過。「我們很開心這項計畫終於得以付諸實行。」麥凱比地產開發公司發言人麗莎·伊凡斯說道。「馬爾伯里地區有了這等規模的購物中心，未來將有數以百計的人能夠獲得<u>正職或工讀的工作機會</u>。」她補充說道。該建設工程預計將於四年後完工。

Q. 文中提及這項計畫有什麼好處？
(A) 它將創造新的就業機會。
(B) 它將吸引遊客到訪馬爾伯里。
(C) 它將解決塞車問題。
(D) 它將幫助到當地兒童。

正解 (A)

技巧**100** 在電子郵件或信件類的文章中，要優先掌握收件者及寄件者。

To: Southwest Water <billing@southwestwaterco.com> 收件者
From: Oscar Hicks <hicks_oscar@t-mail.com> 寄件者
Date: May 16
Subject: April bill

To Whom It May Concern:
I would like to inform you about a problem with my April bill, which shows a
late fee of $25. I have automated payments for this account, and the charge
    6次   19次

comes out every month on the 25th, a few days before the due date. I have
                                                              2次

attached a copy of my April bank statement to show that the payment was
            寄件者已附上月結單影本   2次

indeed made on time. Please remove the fee and issue a new bill.
   16次   18次

Oscar Hicks 寄件者

Q. What is true about Mr. Hicks?
(A) He sent proof of a financial transaction.
(B) He wants to set up automated payments.

收件者：Southwest Water <billing@southwestwaterco.com>
寄件者：Oscar Hicks <hicks_oscar@t-mail.com>
日　期：5 月 16 日
主　旨：四月份帳單

敬啓者：
來信向您反映一個問題，我四月份的帳單當中有顯示一筆 25 美元的滯納
金，但這個帳戶我已經設定自動扣繳，款項會在每個月的 25 日，也就是繳
款截止日的幾天前進行扣款。我已附上一份我四月份的銀行月結單影本，
以資證明款項已確實如期繳交。請移除該筆費用並核發一份新的帳單。

奧斯卡・希可思

Q. 關於希可思先生的敘述，下列何者為真？
(A) 他寄了一份金融交易證明。
(B) 他想設定自動扣繳。

1 出題類型
① 詢問電子郵件或信件的開頭、結尾處所顯示的收件者、寄件者之
身分或職稱的題型。
② 在考題中出現的關鍵字為收件者或寄件者等專有名詞的題型。
③ 在兩篇文章或三篇文章之題組當中，收件者或寄件者與考題間的
脈絡有關。

bill 帳單
late fee 滯納金
automate 使～自動化
payment 支付（的款
項）
charge 收取的費用
due date 到期日；期
限
statement 結算單；明
細表
indeed 確實（加強語
氣用）
on time 準時；及時
issue 發給

proof 證明；證據
financial 金融的
transaction 交易

應用本技巧的題目

To: customerservice@beltsvillecrafts.com
From: j.weaver@rmail.com
Subject: Billing Error

To whom it may concern,

I recently ordered a jewelry set of handmade earrings and a necklace from the Beltsville Crafts online store as a gift for my sister, but it seems that I was overcharged. The set was listed as $60, but I was charged $65 for it. I know that you normally charge shipping and handling, but I used a promotion code for free shipping for orders of over $50. If there is no reason for the extra charge, I would like to have it refunded to me. Thank you.

Judy Weaver

Q. How much will Ms. Weaver be most likely refunded?
　(A) $5　　(B) $50　　(C) $60　　(D) $65

recently 最近
handmade 手工的
overcharge 多收（款項）
charge 收費；索價
normally 通常；一般地
handling 包裝手續費

收件者：customerservice@beltsvillecrafts.com
寄件者：j.weaver@rmail.com
主　旨：計費有誤

敬啓者：

我最近上貝爾茨維爾手作坊的網路門市訂購了手工耳環搭配項鍊的珠寶套組，打算當作禮物送給姊姊，我好像被多扣款了。這個套組的標示價格為 60 美元，而我卻被收取了 65 美元。我知道你們通常都會收取運費及手續費，但是我當時有使用購物滿 50 美元免運的促銷優惠碼。如果沒有收取額外費用的理由，希望你們能把款項退還給我，謝謝。

茱蒂·韋佛

Q. 韋佛小姐最有可能拿到多少退款？
　(A) 5 美元　　(B) 50 美元　　(C) 60 美元　　(D) 65 美元

正解 (A)

PART 7

國家圖書館出版品預行編目（CIP）資料

New TOEIC 新制多益奇蹟筆記書／Engdangi Language
Institute, Jade Kim, Kwon, Oh Kyung 作；戴嘉緹譯. --
初版. -- 臺北市：波斯納出版有限公司, 2022.01
面；　公分
譯自：영단기 700+ 기적의 필기노트
ISBN 978-986-06892-3-5（平裝）

1. 多益測驗

805.1895　　　　　　　　　　　　　110019923

New TOEIC 新制多益奇蹟筆記書

作　　者／Engdangi Language Institute, Jade Kim, Kwon, Oh Kyung
譯　　者／戴嘉緹
執行編輯／游玉旻

出　　版／波斯納出版有限公司
地　　址／100 台北市館前路 26 號 6 樓
電　　話／(02) 2314-2525
傳　　真／(02) 2312-3535
客服專線／(02) 2314-3535
客服信箱／btservice@betamedia.com.tw
郵撥帳號／19493777
帳戶名稱／波斯納出版有限公司

總 經 銷／時報文化出版企業股份有限公司
地　　址／桃園市龜山區萬壽路二段 351 號
電　　話／(02) 2306-6842

出版日期／2022 年 1 月初版一刷
定　　價／320 元
Ｉ Ｓ Ｂ Ｎ／978-986-06892-3-5

〈영단기 700+ 기적의 필기노트〉
(700+ Miracle of Handwritten Note)
Copyright© ST Unitas
Author© Engdangi Language Institute, Jade Kim, Kwon, Oh Kyung
Authorized edition published under agreement with ST Unitas
Traditional Chinese character translation rights © 2022 Posner Publishing Co., Ltd.
Arranged through Imprima Korea Agency, Korea & Pelican Media Agency Ltd., Taiwan
ALL RIGHTS RESERVED

ß 貝塔網址：www.betamedia.com.tw

喚醒你的英文語感！

Get a Feel for English !